Loving in the wrong century

Tamara Demontis

Title book: **Loving in the wrong century**

Author book: Tamara Demontis

© 2023, Tamara Demontis

Publisher: BoD • Books on Demand GmbH, In de Tarpen 42, 22848 Norderstedt
Print: Libri Plureos GmbH, Friedensallee 273, 22763 Hamburg
ISBN: 978-3-7597-9416-1

FSC
www.fsc.org

MIX
Papier aus verantwortungsvollen Quellen
Paper from responsible sources
FSC® C105338

Who is this book for?

This book is for you, beautiful soul, and for all those who still believe in love in the 21st century, the kind of love that many people have only heard about without knowing its meaning. The kind of love that awakens a deep longing in the 21st century, because we live in a generation that talks about love but no longer knows how to love. Many say with nostalgia in their voices: I would like to fall in love like my grandparents or parents did. But how did people fall in love in the past, and could it come to the point where you have to ask yourself how you can learn to love, the most natural thing in the world?

What made the love of yesteryear so special? What was so different? The answer is simple: Everything.

First of all, the clear and defined roles of individuals, regardless of their sexual orientation, and then the perception of feelings. The way of getting to know each other and getting closer, the naturalness of the approach, and the magical journey to the first kiss—from the kiss to the gentle touch that creates the tingling sensation to the merging of the bodies in the act of love—everything had a different value then, and everything was somehow given a deeper meaning than today.

If you ask today's younger generation what a kiss between two lovers means, the most likely answer is: sticking their tongues down each other's throats. But if you ask someone from an older generation what a kiss means, you will probably get this answer: a kiss is undoubtedly the deepest and most intense ritual a couple can experience; it is the fuel for the fire of passion, an exchange of feelings, a silent and powerful message between two souls.

Not to mention the value that today's generation places on the sexual act. How many satisfy their natural instincts and needs without knowing what it feels like to make love to the person they love? How many confuse passion with love, and why do so many in this generation no longer know how to build a loving relationship? Perhaps it is because today there is an unbelievable range of offers and possibilities on the Internet portals, and it is no longer absolutely necessary to make an effort for person A or B or to make a commitment. Meeting in person, off-screen, can lead to confrontation and disappointment; online, behind the screen, you can put on a protective mask, block contact, or ignore the person through the classic and hated ghosting. Is this the created reality in which social media influences love relationships, the image of an intact family life, and interpersonal relationships? Or are many people suddenly giving up on relationships because people have become too complicated, because they lack trust in others, because for various reasons they have not been taught the importance of love, or simply because they come from a family where the teaching of certain values was not given too much importance?

There seems to be something that has changed the healthy perception of feelings and emotions, and while some seem to have resigned themselves to a life without love, even in the 21st century, many would like nothing more than to rediscover the magic of love, to have a protective and understanding partner, to experience the great "love story." Is love just a utopia, or is it all we need, and what does it mean in the 21st century to have a connection between two people who like each other, who understand each other emotionally, where the chemical reaction is explosive, and whose bodies and souls want nothing more than to love each other? How can such bonds be formed? Can relationships develop without the help of dating portals? And what is the difference between people who hide behind dating sites and those who find love the old-fashioned way? Where is the kind of person who looks at you and makes you feel hugged, who stares at you and makes you feel kissed, watched, and touched? How do you find people like that? How do you approach a person in the 21st century without seeming intrusive, without annoying them or embarrassing yourself?

How do you manage to bring deep emotions or feelings into the wrong century? Reading this story will give you some ideas.

Are you ready to feel the passion and share it with Eva and Valentin? Are you ready to deal with the behaviour of relationships in the 21st century?

Then I hope you will enjoy reading this modern story, set in a reality in which many of us will recognise ourselves.

Introduction

Eva, a girl from a middle-class family, marries her childhood sweetheart, David, in her beautiful hometown of Barcelona. The economic crisis that hit Spain in 2008 forced them to migrate to Canada.

No sooner has Eva arrived at her new job than she meets Valentin, the only son of her employer. There is an instant spark between them. The beginning of a dangerous game of love that touches all the senses, both emotional and physical. A passionate love is the fusion of two bodies leaning against each other, driven by something that is not limited to a sexual impulse but encompasses the essence of being together. Eva had never felt such desire before, not even with her sandpit lover David.

Kisses, words whispered in her ear: sensual gestures that fanned the flames of passion and imprinted themselves in her mind, and more than that, this man showed her a different approach to a partnership that she had never known before, and that was very different from the way her husband David did things.

Table of Contents

Prologue

————————◆————————

"Y ou're the new employee, aren't you?" asked Valentin
as Eva copied the latest texts into the computer.
"And who are you?"
"The company belongs to my parents; I've been
observing for a few days now," he replied.
"Are you responsible for observing new employees in the family
business? Is that your job?"
"No, I just watch you."
Eva, clearly taken by surprise by Valentin's behaviour just before the
end of the working day, stood up frantically to get her jacket and
accidentally knocked her papers off her desk.
Instinctively, they both kneel down to pick up the papers and bump
their heads. Their eyes met for a moment, and then they started to
laugh.
Valentin grabbed Eva's hand, pulled her towards him, looked deeper
into her eyes, touched her lips lightly with his finger, and kissed her
passionately.
Completely overwhelmed by the kiss, and without resisting it
She simply kissed him back.
"Where did you learn to kiss like that?" he asked as she remained
stunned and silent.
"I was wondering the same thing," she replied quietly, her face
flushed.

Within a moment she realised what had just happened, took two
steps back, put her hands in front of her face, and cried out in panic:
"What have we done? My husband will be here soon.
Passionate, he grabbed her hands again, pulled her towards him, and
kissed her again, but she pushed him away with an energetic
movement.

"I wanted to kiss you the first time I saw you. How hot are you? We haven't been introduced."

And she said, "Have you gone mad? First you kiss me twice, and then you ask my name?"

She quickly grabbed her bag, stormed out of the room, and ran straight to the staff toilet. She stood at the sink in front of the mirror for a while, washing her face several times with cold water, until she regained consciousness a few minutes later and made her way to the exit.

As she hurried towards the car park, she saw her husband David from a distance outside the gate, talking to someone and gesturing at her arrival until both men turned in her direction at almost the same time. At this sight, she suddenly stopped in her tracks as she realised who her husband was talking to.

"Madame, are you ill? You look as if you've seen a ghost," Valentin said. Then he looked deep into her eyes, and she felt that tingle again. It was that look again that said it all, that signalled to her: I want you.

Chapter 1 Transfer

Eva and David sit nervously in the conference room after an important announcement has been made. The internationally renowned pharmaceutical company where they have worked for years has been in decline for months and needs to be restructured.

"Three jobs in my department are going; I have a bad feeling," says Eva.

But before David can comment on the conversation with his line manager, there are two energetic knocks on the door.

"Good morning, everyone," Mr. Garcia says, beaming.

Eva and David looked at him nervously, then returned the greeting in a friendly manner.

"Let me give you a brief summary. As you have no doubt heard, the company is going through a period of restructuring that will affect not only our sales department but also 150 other jobs in various departments," said Mr. Garcia sadly.

"We were afraid of that," David replied in a worried tone.

"You and your wife needn't worry about your jobs. We have alternatives for good people."

"I'm glad to hear that. Then what do we have to worry about?" asked Eva, her voice trembling.

"Well, we have two vacancies for both of you in one of the head offices in Canada."

"In Canada?" they both asked at the same time.

"Yes, in Canada. You have two weeks to make a final decision."

"But what if we don't want to go to Canada? We're newlyweds, and we just bought our dream house six months ago," she asked excitedly.

"If you don't want to accept this offer, I would advise you to start looking for new opportunities now. We can't offer you any more jobs in this company."

Suddenly there was silence in the conference room. Mr. Garcia took the new permanent contracts out of the folder and placed them on the table in front of Eva and David.

"When do we have to start in Canada?" asked David.

"In three months. You are welcome to take the new contracts home with you to look over," Mr. Garcia replied.

Back home, Eva and David look for new job opportunities at several large companies in the country. In 2008, the economic crisis hit Spain like a hurricane. The job advertisements left a lot to be desired for the highly qualified, newly married couple.

David polished up his CV and picked out three jobs he wanted to apply for.

"Have you found anything suitable?" asked Eva.

"Well, there's nothing exciting, but I'm going to apply for three jobs; we have to try and stay here in the country."

Determined not to give up, they spent the rest of the evening diligently searching for new vacancies, sending their CVs to numerous companies, at least the few that were still looking for staff despite the economic crisis.

The next morning began with a series of disappointments, as they had already received several rejections by email, and although they didn't like the idea of having to leave their country, they had to reckon with the fact that they wouldn't be finding work any time soon.

"Honey, hurry up; my parents are waiting for us!" She called from the car.

Due to the tense situation, Eva and David had called their families for a crisis meeting even before they had made the final decision to move to Canada. The number of job advertisements was either very low or did not match their professional qualifications, so they were unable to find a new job quickly. It was time to return the contract that would open the door to new experiences in Canada.

"We're very excited, and we've already got something to talk about," says Eva's mother.

"Where did you get something to talk about? We haven't said anything about the reason for the presentation yet," David asked in surprise.

Eva's parents looked at each other and were silent, then David looked at Eva.

"We haven't, have we, darling?"

"Of course Eva hasn't told us the reason, but at our age we can already imagine what you have to tell us, can't we, Federico?" asked Eva's mother, waving her hand.

"Come on, bring the package now," she ordered.

"But Mum, what reason and what package? What do you mean?" she asked, becoming increasingly irritated.

Eva's father came rushing out of the kitchen with a parcel in his hand and put it on the coffee table. Eva and David looked annoyed. Eva's mother, Marion, picked up the package and put it on Eva's lap.

"We decided on a neutral colour; we hope you like it," Federico said in an excited voice.

"Mum, can someone tell me what's going on?"

Marion stood up euphorically and raised her hands in celebration.

"We're going to be grandparents!"

David looked at Eva with a tense expression and asked irritably:

"May I ask why your parents were allowed to know about the pregnancy before me? And above all, we wanted to take our time with the children first, remember?"

"What pregnancy? What's going on here?" Eva replied angrily.

"What do you mean, you're not pregnant?" asked Federico.

"Of course not! What makes you think that?"

Federico scratched his beard nervously, turned to his wife, and said firmly:

"Marion, this is all your fault."

Irritated, Marion sat down again, looked in Eva's direction, and asked, "If you're not pregnant, what is there to talk about?"

"We've been transferred to Canada!" Eva shouted.

Eva's parents looked at her wide-eyed and laughed hysterically.

"You're joking, right?" asks Federico.

Eva and David are silent.

"But what are you doing in Canada? You just bought a house a few months ago. What's the point?" asked Marion.

Calmly, Eva took the employment contract out of her bag and put it on the coffee table.

"We'll lose our jobs if we don't sign the new contracts," she explained.

The room suddenly fell silent. Eva's father picked up the contract and quickly read through the pages.

"How much time do you have to decide, and when do you have to be in Canada?" Marion asked, stunned.

"The employment contracts have to be returned on Monday. We have to be in Canada in three months," Eva replied with a hint of frustration in her voice.

On the way to meet David's parents, they both realised that immigration was not going to be a walk in the park. Eva's parents were the easiest part of the family to look after. The bigger challenge lay ahead.

David's parents were already standing happily in the front garden of their house, waving cheerfully as Eva and David arrived, not yet aware of what was to come.

"We couldn't arrange anything for dinner at such short notice," called David's mother, Leonor, from the other side of the garden.

"Mum, don't worry about the food; you'll have lost your appetite after our conversation."

"¡Por Dios! David, don't scare me. What's happened?" She asked, her blood pressure rising slightly.

"Please, let's go into the house first," David suggested.

Without further comment, all four of them went into the house. As soon as the front door was shut, David's mother jumped in. Her hysterical manner left no room for gentle explanations, so David ran straight into the living room, took the work contracts out of Eva's bag, and put them on the dining table.

"David, you still haven't told me what happened. What papers did you put on the table?" She She asked, her face flushed.

"Mum, we've only been here five minutes; we've already spent three minutes outside the door, and in the last two minutes you've gone hysterical before I can even say anything!"

With all four of them sitting around the table, David finally handed his parents the contract.

"You scared me; I thought something bad had happened, but you've just got a new job," said Leonor, relieved.

Cristiano looked at his wife and said firmly:

"Tell me, Leonor, can't you read? Isn't it bad enough that the job is in Canada?"

"Oh no... no! no! In Canada? David, you can't do this to me. You didn't take the job, did you?" She She asked in a panicked voice, suddenly standing up and pacing. She beat her hand on her chest and mumbled something no one could understand.

"David, why don't you answer? Cristiano, get the blood pressure cuff; I'm dying!" she cried.

"Mum, please calm down! There's nothing wrong; thousands of people work abroad these days.".

But David's explanation only made the situation worse. Eva was still sitting quietly at the table, watching what was happening, while Cristiano ran frantically into the living room with the blood pressure machine.

14

"Over here!" he thought, and as he ran in, the cable caught on the living room door, sending the sphygmomanometer flying through the air and crashing to the floor. Pieces of it were scattered all over the living room, and David threw up his hands at the sight. Suddenly Leonor stood up, took two deep breaths, and collapsed. The conversation about emigration ended for her in A&E.

"Honey, please say something; you haven't spoken for hours," David pleaded worriedly. worriedly."

"I didn't want to steal your mother's thunder. I know it's not an easy situation for any of us, but did it have to be so dramatic? Your poor father..."

"OK, that's fine. Let's change the subject."

At home, Eva and David avoided each other; it had been a difficult day; each had to deal with the events on their own. Determined, she took the employment contract and signed it, then switched on her laptop and did some research on her future employers and Canada. The company had provided her with a furnished apartment for the first six months, during which time she could have considered whether to continue her life in Canada or return to her home country. After careful research, Eva realised that Canada alone is almost the size of Europe, and she was already fascinated by the crystal clear waters and vast wilderness areas. At 27, Eva was the oldest of two siblings and the only one in the family who would be leaving Europe for the first time.

After a weekend full of turbulence, Mr. Garcia was waiting for David and Eva in the conference room on Monday morning, but they didn't have to wait any longer and came straight into the room.

After a quick and cordial greeting, Eva puts the contracts on the table. Mr. Garcia looks at David's contract sceptically and asks uncertainly, "You haven't signed your employment contract yet; will your wife be flying to Canada alone?"

15

"Well, my mother had a nervous breakdown at the announcement; you know, I'm an only child," he answers in a low voice.

"I see, and that's why they can't cut the umbilical cord, and will your wife emigrate alone? Do you know how lucky you are?? How many of your colleagues would like to have such an opportunity?"

David felt insulted by Mr. Garcia's words, and although he, like Eva, had decided to emigrate to Canada, he needed more time to think before signing the contract.

"We'll both take the job," Eva confirmed.

David took a pen from Eva's bag and signed his contract.

"Congratulations! This is going to be a great experience for you. My secretary, Mrs. Guzman, will be with you shortly to discuss all the details."

Eva and David said a friendly goodbye and left the boardroom.

In the information centre, Mrs. Guzman had set up a screen to show the structure of the company in Canada. The imposing building was set in park-like grounds, just two kilometres from the new home that Eva and David were to move into.

"So, what do you think?" asked Mrs. Guzman with a twinkle in her eye.

Eva looked at her David with excitement in her eyes.

"A dream!" he replied.

"Excellent! Then you can have the key to the apartment and this package. Here are all the contacts and emergency numbers for a good start in the new country."

"What's in the second package?" Eva asked curiously.

"We have put two mobile phones in the second package for them, so that they can contact their families directly when they arrive."

Everything was organised down to the last detail. Eva and David were impressed by so much professionalism and empathy. Grateful for their good fortune, they both left the room.

In the afternoon, Eva and David looked for solutions for their house, for which they had to pay a monthly installment.

"We can't leave the house empty; six months is a long time," she said regretfully.

"What do you suggest? Do you want someone else to sleep in your new bed?"

"Why not? A new mattress is cheaper than the monthly instalments, and if the house is empty, the cost can quickly become a burden."

"Yes, you're right. Let's try renting it out instead," he replied with conviction.

In the afternoon, Eva's parents and her younger sister Carmen spontaneously showed up at the door with dinner.

"You know, Eva, I think it's great that you're going to Canada; finally we have a reason for a holiday away from Europe," said Carmen, totally excited.

"After sleeping on it for a night, we think you've made a good decision, and we'll support you," Eva's father decided.

"I'm relieved to hear that. I thought you'd come here to get rid of your emotional baggage," David said carefully.

"Even if I had, no one here will be able to outdo your mother." Eva replied sarcastically.

The days passed peacefully, and they began to feel that the family members had accepted the transfer to Canada when one morning they were summoned to Mr. Garcia's office. An unexpected situation, which they had not anticipated, led to a change of plans.

"Good morning everyone; I hope you had a good breakfast," greeted Mr. Garcia.

"Actually we didn't get a chance to have breakfast; Mrs. Guzman practically dragged us out of bed," David replied.

"Well, there's a slight problem. The transfer to Canada has to be moved up a bit." Mr. Garcia burst out, his lips pressed together.

"That's no problem for us; we can be in Canada a bit earlier," Eva assured him.

"You have to be in Canada in four weeks, right after Christmas, which means eight weeks earlier for you!"

"In Canada in four weeks? That's impossible!" David replied regretfully.

"They'll be in their new jobs from 3 January!"

There was already a special leave of absence on the desk for the beginning of December. Faster than expected and with much more pressure, Eva and David would have to find a tenant for their house and deal with all the bureaucratic matters. A new crisis meeting with the family was organised at short notice, which this time resulted in David's mother being rushed to the hospital under lights.

"Blimey, that's all we need!" muttered David in exasperation.

David's father quickly packed a few things for his wife and followed the ambulance.

"I wonder what's going to happen next; I mean, if your mom collapses at the announcement, then we'll probably have to order a coffin before we even get on the plane to Canada, because I'm afraid she won't survive the separation," Eva said irritably.

In a bad mood, they decided to return home and look for a tenant. Eva placed an advertisement on the various property websites and waited hopefully. To her delight, the enquiries were not long in coming, because as soon as the ad was online, the phone rang.

"Unbelievable, isn't it? We have 7 potential tenants to choose from within 20 minutes. That's at least one reason to be happy today," she grinned enthusiastically.

"We have even more reason to be happy today; take a look at the bathroom," he said in an inviting tone.

Full of admiration, she looked in the direction of the bathroom that David had decorated with candles during her phone calls to potential tenants.

Thrilled by the pleasant surprise, she quickly undressed and jumped into the bathtub.

"I know why I love you so much!" she exclaimed to endear herself to her husband.

In the bathroom, lit only by soft candlelight, she lay relaxed in the steaming tub until he reached her and knelt before her. He gently massaged her neck down to her scalp. She closed her eyes, savouring the moment. He gently touched her lips and kissed her tenderly. With the aplomb of someone who knows what she wants, she took his hand and ran it lightly over her bare breasts, letting him feel her excited nipples as she let out a soft moan.

"I want you," she whispered as she pulled her still-clothed husband into the bath.

After a stressful week, Eva and David managed to rent out their house at short notice. Of all the interested parties, only one young couple was prepared to sign a six-month lease. This had to be celebrated, so David opened a bottle of cava and the two toasted their good fortune.

"This is an exciting moment," David said.

"We haven't heard from your parents all week; how come?" she asked in surprise.

"Let's enjoy the evening first. My mother has been sedated with medication."

"Do you have another tasty surprise for me tonight?" she asked.

"Mmhh, let me think... No, it's your turn tonight."

She leaves the living room with a seductive look on her face.

"I'll be right back!" she called from the hallway.

David waited patiently for a while, but she didn't come back. Tired of waiting, he called out to her several times, but she didn't answer. Irritated, he got up and searched the whole house for her but did not find her. On his way back to the living room, he suddenly saw her skirt outside the cellar door. A clue? Curious, he opened the cellar door and found her blouse on the floor. Then he walked briskly down the stairs and suddenly saw her pants and shoes on the last step.

"Darling, where are you?" he called, but there was no answer. All the clues led to the garage, so he opened the door cautiously, only to see her bra and pants on the floor, and the car horn honked before he realised she was naked in the car. Startled, he jumped aside, then she got out, laid down on the bonnet, spread her legs, and pulled him towards her, to which he reacted negatively.

Was the game too wild for him? Or had the stress of the last few weeks gotten the better of him?

"Aren't you going to kiss me?" she asked expectantly.

"Yes, but I'm not in the mood right now; it's been a very stressful week. Don't you think?"

Visibly disappointed, she packed her things, left the garage, and went to bed without saying a word.

The last week of work flew by. On their last day at work, Eva and David took time to say goodbye to their colleagues, but Mr. Garcia reached them just before the end of the working day.

"Where are you going in such a hurry? I forgot to give you something to take with you. Please follow me," he ordered.

Without asking any questions, they followed him until they were outside the conference room.

20

"Please lead the way," Mr. Garcia ordered.

David carefully opened the door to the pitch-black conference room.

"Are you sure we're in the right place?" asked Eva, a little apprehensive.

"Surprise!" shouted a crowd of people as the disco ball began to glow with coloured lights and the music started.

The countdown was on: only 14 days to go before they left for Canada. Although they had done a lot of research about the place where they were going to live, they were still unsure about what to expect, what kind of people they would meet, and what kind of clothes they would need to wear, as the climate in Canada was a particular challenge for them, as they were used to very different temperatures.

"How many more suitcases do I have to get from the attic?" he shouted.

"At least two for me and two for you!" she replied.

Sorting through her clothes, Eva suddenly realised that there were very few winter items in her wardrobe. In warm Barcelona, the winter temperatures were on a par with Canada's summer temperatures, and they were not prepared for such weather.

"Darling? I'm afraid there's a problem," she called out after a quick rummage through the wardrobes.

Not thrilled with what he had heard, he poked his head out of the attic and said firmly:

"We don't need any problems today, because we don't have enough suitcases, and that's already a big problem."

"Then it's all right, because we don't have enough winter clothes either."

"Excellent! So a change of plan after all," he said half-heartedly.

"Why don't we go shopping?" she suggested enthusiastically.

A shopping trip three days before Christmas Eve, with all the crowds in the city, wasn't exactly what they needed, but what the hell, at least one of them seemed excited to be on tour. The city was full of Christmas magic, people walking around happily with their bags full of presents, but none of it matched David's mood. What had happened to him in the last few days? Had the stress of the past few weeks and the excitement of the emigration taken such a toll on him that he could no longer pull the plug? He dragged himself through the city, taking time to do some last-minute shopping until they bumped into Eva's family and joined them for a meal at the Christmas market.

"I still can't believe it; in 14 days you'll be in another country," said Marion in a wistful voice.
Eva looks at her mother with melancholy eyes and says:
"Yes. It's like a dream for us; we're very excited.".
Eva's mother turns to David with a worried tone: "How are things with your parents?"
"Well, it's fine. My mom is on tranquillizers and has calmed down a bit; hopefully she will stay that way.".
"We would like your parents to join us on Christmas Eve. Why don't we all celebrate Christmas together this year?" suggested Marion.
"That's a great idea!" replied David.

Because of Leonor's boisterous nature, they were not used to the usual family celebrations, but this particular situation called for an exception; after all, Christmas is the celebration of love, the celebration of family, at least according to what Eva had experienced as a child.

Christmas was fast approaching, and while David was busy picking up his parents, Marion and Federico were preparing delicacies for the festive table. What was in store for them at this joint celebration? The last time they had celebrated together was at Eva and David's wedding, and they did not remember it fondly.

But this time it was different, because Leonor's mood was lifted considerably by the effects of the tranquillizers, and between Turrón, cream cheese with honey, and nuts, they managed to create a magical Christmas together.

At the departure terminal in Barcelona, David and Eva stood with their families and friends at the check-in desk, waiting for their turn to board their flight to Canada.

Visibly excited, David's mother clung to her husband.

"I can't believe we made it from the house to the terminal without incident; that's a great achievement," David whispered in relief.

But then his mother started pacing back and forth, suddenly clasping her hands to her chest, and ran off the line.

With a sense of foreboding, Eva looked at her David and said firmly, "I think you spoke too quickly; your mom is waving at the end of the line with an unhappy face. Can you see her?"

David turned quickly to see what was happening to his mother, but suddenly the loudspeakers announced boarding for flight CA335 to Canada, and people rushed to check in.

Desperately, David made eye contact with his father, who looked in his direction and shouted in panic, "The drops!"

In the rush to the airport, David's mother had forgotten to take the sedative drops and collapsed at the back of the queue.

"Check-in for flight CA335 is closing!" shouted Eva, pulling David's hand as the crowd pushed them further and further into the terminal.

Chapter 2 Eyes of Desire

"Welcome to your new workplace; we hope you will feel at home here," said the managing director of the pharmaceutical company Ritel.

Eva and David officially started their first day at work and were welcomed together, but not assigned to the same department. The introduction to the team was brief and warm, and David was assigned to the marketing department, just as he had been in Barcelona. Nothing about his job changed except the language. Everything changed for Eva, who was placed as an assistant to the management. As she waited to be collected after the welcome meeting, she tried to imagine what her job would be and in which office she would work. But suddenly a cheerful lady appeared in front of her and interrupted her thoughts.

"You must be the talented young woman from Barcelona. Mrs. Leblanc, the managing director, was deeply impressed by your professional profile. We will train you for your new job," said the unknown lady.

"May we introduce ourselves? I'm Eva Rodriguez."
"I'm Melanie Campbell, the former executive assistant."
"You're the former executive assistant?" Eva asked in surprise.
"Yes, that's right. I'm expecting my first child and have asked for a change of position. You're the only one qualified for the position after me," Melanie replied.

After a quick tour of the company's corridors, Eva is shown into her office, a beautiful, modern glass office adjoining the executive office, with a large desk, a leather chair, and a wonderful view of the park.

"You can sit down," Melanie orders.

"Can I sit in the boss's chair?"

"No, of course you can't sit in the boss's chair, but you can sit in your chair, so please sit down; this is your office," Melanie replied amusedly.

"This is my office?" asked Eva in complete astonishment.

"Yes, welcome to your office, Mrs. Rodriguez!"

After work, Eva and David met in the company car park.

"Hey, honey, I've been waiting for you for a while; I haven't heard from you all day," David said.

"You don't know what's happened. My duties have changed at short notice!" said Eva, still completely taken aback by what had happened.

"In what way?"

"I'm now an executive assistant and have my own office next to the manager's."

"Wow, that should be celebrated!"

"That's a great idea!"

David drove out of the complex at high speed and parked on a forest track.

"Where are we going? What are you up to? It looks a bit spooky here at dusk," she said, a little frightened, as he pushed the seat back and began to kiss her fiercely.

"Hey, we're in a hurry today," she whispered, unbuttoning the first two buttons of his shirt and then biting his neck gently.

Caught up in the urge, he put his hands on her waist and pulled up her skirt, running it gently over her thighs, pausing on her mound until she moaned softly.

"I want you!" he said in a voice full of desire.

Captivated by passion, Eva sat down on David and let the game lead her. He gently caressed her breasts under her blouse. Moaning, she moved over his excited body, giving free rein to her passion.

"Oh sh*t, all the windows are steamed up; have you got any tissues??" asked David after realising that he could no longer see outside.
"Unfortunately not. I didn't expect it to be this late at night."
"It's already dark; how are we going to clean the windows quickly?"
"Here, take my pants and just clean the windscreen; we live just around the corner."

They cleaned the windscreen with Eva's pants and drove home. Eva wasn't really prepared for a shot of passion in the car, given the situation at home in Barcelona when she wanted to surprise David naked in the car.

Clothes are everywhere in the modern apartment. On their first day in Canada, the two had to prioritise and were in no hurry to tidy up their luggage.

"It looks like your suitcase exploded in the living room, doesn't it?"
"Yes, we have the same problem in the bedroom with your two suitcases," he replied in a somewhat ironic tone.

But then they realised that it was urgent to put an end to the chaos, and they started to put their things away until the doorbell rang.
Who could visit them in Canada when they'd only been there a day and didn't know anyone?
The concierge had received a report that their car was in the wrong parking space.

"Is the car with the steamed-up windows yours?" The man asked kindly.

Perplexed, Eva and David looked at each other.

"Which car do you mean exactly?" asked David.

"I mean the white car with the steamed-up windows. The car park is almost empty; a vehicle with steamed-up windows will quickly attract attention. By the way, the parking spaces are numbered."

Assuming that he didn't understand what he was talking about, David followed the caretaker downstairs, where the real owner of the car park was.

"Your car park is right next door, see? That's number five! But from the look of your windows, I imagine you missed number five. What on earth happened to your car?" The caretaker asked helplessly.

Embarrassed and without further comment, David apologised to his neighbour, shook his hand, and parked his car in the right place. Cleaning the windows with Eva's knickers proved less successful.

The next day, Eva and David met in the company car park during their lunch break.

"Hustle and bustle and at the same time an oasis of calm, an incredible place," he said admiringly as he looked around.
"Yes, that's it. What are your colleagues like?"
"I don't know all their names yet, but it's a very close-knit team. I like that. What about you?"

"I can't say much about my team; my only colleague is Mrs. Campbell when she's here. I think I'll be completely settled by the end of the week. It's like I already know how everything works. It's strange."
"We're lucky," David said gratefully.

The first week passed quickly, and Eva and David made their first trip to Ottawa. Hand in hand, like newlyweds, they stood on the frozen Rideau Canal in the middle of the city centre at the world's largest skating rink.

"Kiss me!" she commanded, pulling him towards her.
David took Eva's face in his hands and kissed her gently on the lips as she wrapped herself tightly around him.
They seemed to have discovered the secret of a good marriage; with all their years together, they knew each other inside out; a quick glance was enough to understand each other.

"You get jealous just looking at her," a voice said behind David's back. What a great surprise! David's work colleague Steven and his wife Martha were also standing by the canal watching their children skate.

"So you lovebirds, are your kids there too?" asked Steven.
Eva and David laughed.
"We don't have any children yet," David replied.
"That's what I thought when you kissed," Martha added enviously.
"What are you trying to say?" Steven grumbled back, immediately asking more questions to get off the subject of kissing:
"Have you eaten yet?"
"Actually, we were just about to. Do you want to go?" David asked politely.
"There's a nice chicken wing place around the corner. Shall we eat there?" suggested Martha.
"Sure, it's perfect; let's eat there," David confirmed.

Fascinated by the twins, Alexa and Moira, Eva asks Martha a lot of questions, and Martha is delighted with her interest, explaining the peculiarities of raising two children at the same time and giving up her job as a secretary to devote herself entirely to her children.

"Have you already planned to have children?" Marta asked curiously.

"Yes, yes, but we still have time; we're newlyweds," Eva replied.

"You can tell that the relationship is still very fresh," Martha said with a touch of nostalgia.

"Well, it's not that fresh; we've been together for over twenty years. Since the sandpit," David pointed out.

"What, more than twenty years? You're still so young!" Steven exclaimed, completely surprised.

"Does that mean you've never been intimate with anyone else?" Martha asked indiscreetly.

"Why, is that a bad thing?" asked Eva.

The questions were starting to get too personal, but the four of them didn't seem to have a problem with that; they looked at each other a little confused and laughed.

"Well, that's a rare constellation at your age," Martha noted with amusement.

The second working week was hectic and stressful right from the start. The managing director, Mrs. Leblanc, had been in hospital after a horse-riding accident over the weekend, and her former assistant had only been able to cover part of the time due to her pregnancy problems. There was no specific candidate to replace Mrs. Leblanc.

Eva tried to keep her head and work through the list of priorities without panicking. Not only did she have a lot of paperwork to do, but she also had to take Mrs. Leblanc's calls and coordinate appointments. It was much more than she had been taught to do.

Just before closing time, she was so absorbed in her work that she didn't even notice someone knocking on the glass door.

"You're the new employee, aren't you?" asked Valentin as Eva copied the latest texts into the computer.

"And who are you?"

"The company belongs to my parents; I've been observing them for a few days now," he replied.

"Are you in charge of observing new employees in the family business? Is that your job?"

"No, I just watch you."

Eva, clearly taken aback by Valentin's behaviour just before closing time, frantically gets up to get her jacket and accidentally knocks her papers off the desk.

Instinctively, they both kneel down to pick up the papers and bump their heads. Their eyes met for a moment, and then they started to laugh.

Valentin grabbed Eva's hand, pulled her towards him, looked deeper into her eyes, touched her lips lightly with his finger, and kissed her passionately.

Completely overwhelmed by the kiss, and without resisting it

She simply kissed him back.

"Where did you learn to kiss like that?" he asked as she remained stunned and silent in front of him.

"I was wondering the same thing," she replied quietly, her face flushed.

Within a moment she realised what had just happened and took two steps back, putting her hands in front of her face and shouting in panic, "What have we done? My husband will be here soon."

Passionate, he grabbed her hands again, pulled her close, and kissed her again, but she pushed him away with an energetic movement.

"I wanted to kiss you the first time I saw you. How hot are you? We haven't been introduced."

And she said,"Have you gone mad? First you kiss me twice, and then you ask me my name?"

She quickly grabbed her bag, stormed out of the room, and ran straight to the staff toilet. She stood at the sink in front of the mirror for a while, washing her face several times with cold water, until she regained consciousness a few minutes later and made her way to the exit.

As she hurried towards the car park, she saw her husband David in the distance outside the company gate, talking to someone and gesturing to her to come in, until both men turned in her direction almost simultaneously. At this sight, she suddenly stopped in her tracks as she realised who her husband was talking to.

"Madam, are you unwell? You look as if you've seen a ghost," Valentin managed to get out. Then he looked deep into her eyes, and she felt that tingle again. It was that look again that said it all, that signalled to her: I want you.

Still reeling from what had happened at the office and not knowing what they had been talking about in her absence, she sat in the car without comment, waiting for David to get into the driver's seat.

"What's going on? Do you know who that guy is?" David asked, irritated at her behaviour.

"No, of course not. You tell me!" she replied, annoyed.

"You've had a bad day, haven't you? That guy is the only son of our bosses!"

"How should I know who this arrogant guy is? My boss is ill, and I had to cover for her in all sorts of things today!"

"Things will be different tomorrow."

"Well, thank God Mrs. Leblanc will be back tomorrow!" she cheered.

"No, she won't. Her son Valentin Leblanc will probably take her place for the next two weeks."

With the car ready and the engine running, Eva opened the door and threw up several times.

"I told you, you've had too much stress today. Let's go home."

Even at home, Eva couldn't relax and took a hot bath.

Thinking he could use the opportunity to his advantage, David got undressed and lay down in the bath in front of Eva.

"Would you massage my feet?" she asked.

"Actually, I had something else in mind," he replied, leaning in to kiss Eva on the lips.

"I'm not in the mood today. The day has been too stressful, and I can't switch off.".

Realising that the evening was not going to end as he had hoped, David took her right foot in his hands and massaged it lovingly.

"Oh yes, that feels really good. You're the best husband anyone could ask for," she said, leaning her head back and closing her eyes.

The next morning, Eva is on her way to the office when a colleague calls her into the meeting room. Valentin and five other people were sitting around the round table.

After a quick glance around, she notices that a seat has been reserved for her next to Valentin.

A little taken aback by the unexpected meeting, she stood motionless in the middle of the room.

"Mrs. Rodriguez, right? Please sit down next to me," Valentin ordered.

With a forced grin on her face, she nodded and sat down next to Valentin. The two-week substitution plan had been discussed at the crisis meeting. She sat nervously next to Valentin, her handbag on her lap, her hands under the table, pressed together over the handbag, listening intently to what her counterparts had to say.

By the end of the meeting, it was clear that she and Valentin would be working together intensively for the next two weeks, which made her nervous. A team of five, Eva as assistant and Valentin at the helm, would be replacing Mrs. Leblanc for two long weeks.

"Are the tasks for the next two weeks clear?" asked Valentin in general terms.
Those present looked at each other and nodded in agreement.
After the meeting, Eva hurried to her office, turning back to see if Valentin had followed her. Because of his presence and cooperation, she had to accept the fact that her everyday life would become even more stressful. From ordinary employee to executive secretary, fate had already put her to the test when she started working in Canada, and Mrs. Leblanc's horse-riding accident made things even worse. What other surprises did fate have in store?
The phone in the office was already ringing when she arrived, the fax machine was spitting out sheet after sheet, and now what? Eva had already dismissed the idea of going out for lunch when David suddenly appeared from behind the glass door, bringing food with him!
"Surprise!" he exclaimed, lunch in hand.
"I thought you were already in the canteen."
"And I thought your lunch was cancelled today, so I brought you some food."
It was only a few minutes after they had eaten that the phone rang.
"Please don't answer it!"
"I can't; I have to answer it."
During the brief conversation, she is asked to put some documents in a folder and go to the exit. She has to accompany Valentin to an

outside meeting, but when she arrives at the meeting point, she can't believe her eyes.

A car is waiting for her at the main entrance. The driver: Valentin.

"Where do we have to go at such short notice? There was no appointment for noon today, and where is the company driver?" She asked excitedly.

"I'm the driver today," he replied, opening the passenger door.

Eva gets into the car, and Valentin drives off.

"Which customer are we going to?"

"Have you had lunch yet?"

"Since when do we call you Mr. Leblanc?"

"Valentin. My name is Valentin."

"Please tell me immediately where we're going."

"Only if you tell me if you've had lunch."

"I was just about to when I got the call."

"Perfect, then let's have lunch first. I'm hungry too."

"I hope they're not serious; I've got a lot of work on my desk, and they're just driving me around unnecessarily."

Without another word, Valentin drove for a few minutes to the south bank of the Ottawa River, stopped, got out, and opened the passenger door.

"We're here," he says, holding out his hand to help her out of the car.

"Does the meeting with the client have to take place here, in the middle of nowhere?" she said, irritated. But

He took her hand and helped her out of the car.

"Turn around; what do you see over there?" He pointed into the distance.

She followed Valentin's finger with her eyes, lingering on the breathtaking view.

On the hill, right before her eyes, the majesty of Parliament Hill.

"What a beautiful sight... Yet I don't see any clients here who want to attend a meeting with us."

"Yes, a truly beautiful sight," he said, referring to her beauty.

Looking deep into her eyes, he reached out to touch her hand.

"No, not again! Haven't you been taught how to behave?" She asked with excitement in her voice.

As if she hadn't said anything, he went on, looking deeper into her eyes, slowly pulling her towards him, burying his face in her hair and moaning softly as if her ghosts had already undressed and touched her body with their hands.

She stood motionless as if she had been mummified.

After a few seconds of trance, he took a step back and gazed tenderly at her flushed face.

"I've been saying all along, you're just crazy!"

"And now let's have dinner at the Riviera Ottawa restaurant," he suggested, as if nothing had happened.

"Dinner? What about the date outside?"

"We already had it."

"When we're done with the outing, I want to go straight to the office, not to a restaurant. There's a lot of work waiting for me on my desk!"

"After lunch, we'll go straight to the office, I promise. We don't want anyone to wonder why we're back so early."

She quickly realised that there was no point in arguing with Valentin. Without warning, he just went ahead with his plan; it was clear that she was dealing with a spoilt mama's boy.

At the Riviera Ottawa restaurant, they were both greeted in a friendly manner, and Valentin was immediately addressed by name. The waiter seemed to know not only his name but also what he liked to eat and drink. There was an elegant table in a quiet corner, already set with appetisers and drinks. The waiter took their coats and invited them to sit down, but Valentin moved his chair closer so that Eva could sit down.

He seemed to know all the rules of the dress code when dealing with women.

"Do you always behave like a gentleman when you bring women here for dinner?" she asked curiously.
But he laughed amusedly.
"What's so funny?" she asked, irritated.
"This is the first time I've brought a woman to this restaurant."
She looked at him and fell silent.

"You can look at the menu," he suggests.

She looked nervously at the menu and then decided on salad.

"Why do women look at the whole menu and then choose a salad?" he asked.
"Wait a minute, you said it was the first time you came to this restaurant with a woman. It was clear I wasn't serious."
"Of course I was serious. I'll only eat in this restaurant with my family."
"But I'm not part of your family, so what are we doing here?"
He looked at her again with his deep gaze and whispered,
"We're complete strangers, and yet I feel like I've known you since the first day I saw you in the company car park on my first day at work. And I'm not talking about the usual physical attraction; I feel a rare

36

spiritual connection between us. I feel that I have always been looking for you, not for someone who looks like you. Because your soul and mine must have met somewhere in this universe. There were so many people and cars in the car park in the mornings after the Christmas holidays, in the first days of January, but I only saw you, your long brown hair, and your beautiful radiant face. Since that day, I've stopped in the car park in the mornings and watched you get out of the car."

She looked at him with a sense of confusion but had to admit that this man had stirred something in her that she had never felt before, and yet she had a husband at home.

"I'm happily married," she tried to clarify.
"Then why are you sitting here with me?"
"Well, how could I resist you? Apart from the fact that you're my boss at the moment, you almost kidnapped me."
Without responding to Eva's comments, Valentin orders the check.

Back in her office, Eva didn't know what to do first. The desk was full, the answering machine was blinking, and the fax machine was overflowing with messages. In her mind, Valentin's gaze wandered and the whispered words on the south bank of the river. In her imagination, his hands touched her whole body. His gaze caressed her soul; his kisses warmed her heart. His scent made her burn with passion. What the hell was happening to her?
But the knock on the glass door interrupted her chaotic thoughts. David was standing there, ready to go home.

"Hey honey, we're off work. How was your day?" he asked.
"End of the day? I've only just started!"
"How come you've only just started? How long were you at the off-site appointment?"

"Until 15 minutes ago? There's no way I can go with you; I have to work for at least another two hours; it's all over here!"
David looked around the office and said, "I wouldn't want to swap places with you right now!"

"You go shopping; I'll walk home later."
"Walk home alone? That's out of the question; it's already dark outside. I'll be in the car park at 7 p.m. There must be other colleagues who have to work late. There's good lighting in and around the building.

As David left the office, she looked out the window; the parking lot was already half empty. Focused, she did one task after another. The first hour flew by. It was quiet around her, and she kept looking through her glass office. The corridor was slowly darkening, and all but two of the offices on her floor were empty. A few sheets of paper were still stuck in the fax machine, some of them belonging to an urgent order. Annoyed, she turned the machine on and off, opened the paper tray, and tried to solve the problem of the paper jam, but the fax machine was uncooperative and wouldn't let go of the paper.

"It's already out of order. I mean the fax machine," said a voice behind her.
Sure that she had heard this voice before, she turned to see Valentin standing unexpectedly in her office. Instinctively, she looked down the corridor, but the whole floor was now dark.

"I'm sure you're just getting off work too, aren't you?" She asked nervously.

"Why are you still here? I saw your husband leave," he asked, making eye contact as she looked at her watch.

"I'm being picked up in 20 minutes. If you'll excuse me, I have urgent matters to attend to; this afternoon's trip has taken up many hours of my time at work," she said hurriedly, running back to the fax machine.

But Valentin was standing behind her, their bodies gently touching, then he buried his face in her hair, his lips brushing her neck.

"I want to drown in your lips, to whisper in silent words the desire I feel. I've been searching for these feelings all my life; everything in me yearns for you. You are this desire that I can't hold back," he whispered.

She turned abruptly to say something, but he covered her mouth with a kiss before she could get a word out. Without resisting, she allowed herself to be drawn into the state that had become reality in her mind only moments before. Only now could she feel his hands and the warmth of his body. Both burning with a passion she had never felt before. He reached out and took her in his arms. Slowly he brushed the tip of his tongue over her lips; she wrapped her arms around his neck and let herself be drawn into a passionate kiss. Within seconds, they were both out of control. The game was interrupted by the sound of a car horn.

Startled, Eva pulled away from Valentin and looked out of the window. Her husband David was waiting for her downstairs in the car park. Still shaken by the passion she felt, Eva tried to calm herself.

"My God, how could it happen again?" she said, frantically reaching for her handbag.

"I don't know about you, but I can't control this desire."

"It will never happen again!" she shouted hysterically and quickly left the office.

Good David waited patiently in the car park as she hurried in his direction.

"You look pretty exhausted today; did you at least manage to catch up with your work at the office?"

"Almost everything."

Relieved, David leaned down and kissed her tenderly on the lips. She returned it with a quick kiss.

"I've cooked something delicious for us," he said enthusiastically.

After dinner, Eva was enjoying a hot shower when David stood naked in front of her.

"Oh no, darling, please not now, after such a day," she said with a tired voice.

"Oh yes, darling, right here and now. After a day like this is just the thing," he replied with an amused look, then placed his hands on her buttocks and lifted her up. She let herself be infected by her husband's passion.

The next morning, the fax machine in Eva's office was fixed, and the missing pages from the big job were on the desk next to the keyboard. On the keyboard was a paper flower made of printer paper. How could this impossible man do origami and also shock her senses?

Her emotions were already on a rollercoaster in the early morning.

She kept picking up the paper flower, smelling it, and putting it in the bin. With so much work behind her, she certainly couldn't afford any more risky fantasies.

The only good thing about this morning was that there was still no sign of Valentin. At noon, she was picked up by David for her lunch break. As soon as she stepped through the canteen door, she met Valentin's fiery gaze. There he was, standing in front of the cash register with his tray in his hand, looking in her direction. She looked at him, fighting a tingle that went from her heart to her crotch. She quickly turned her face away to avoid his gaze and looked for a seat far away from him.

"Look, darling, your work colleagues are over there; let's go to them,"
Eva said, pointing to the last table at the end of the canteen.
"This table is already so full, are you sure?"
"Yes, look, there are exactly two seats left. I'll go ahead and sit down;
just bring me a salad, please."

With the aplomb of a man who knows what his wife likes to eat,
David chose a salad and walked towards the group, still unaware of
the surprise that awaited him.

"Before the break, Robin and I received a letter. We have to go to
Montreal from Friday to Saturday for a seminar. In return, we're free
on Monday," Steven said.

"Oh boys, I don't envy you," David replied amusedly.
"If I were you, I wouldn't cry victory just yet, because there's a letter
for you on your desk," Robin replied, also amused.

"Oh shit! My wife can't spend a night alone in a foreign country,"
David said regretfully.

"Relax, mate, she's a big girl, plus she can spend time with our ladies;
we'll be back on Saturday night," Steven said.
"I'll survive," Eva added.

After her lunch break, Eva quickly completed the previous day's
tasks with full concentration. After a phone call from a client, she
noticed that her diary had a new entry for Friday afternoon. An
unannounced meeting with the management was on the agenda, and
that was enough to give her new fantasies. For a moment she
brushed her fingertips across her lips and lightly bit her lower lip, but
a few seconds later, back in her right mind, she shook her head and
returned to her work.

On the way home, David and Eva discussed the schedule for the days in David's absence. For the first time in a long time, they would not be sleeping under the same roof.

"Don't worry about me; I'll work all day on Friday, and you'll be back on Saturday evening," she said calmly.

"What are you going to do all day on Saturday? You're not used to being alone."

"I'm going to have brunch with Martha and Sila. A girls' day out! I haven't done that in a long time."

"Sounds like a good plan. Let's go shopping together today, and then we can have a nice evening tomorrow," he suggested.

"That's a good idea."

When they arrived at the supermarket, they realised that they weren't the only ones who had come up with the idea; Steven and Robin were also there with their wives.

"Look who's here; did you do this on purpose or did you just happen to be here?" Martha asked in surprise.

"We just decided on the spur of the moment. Where are the children?" asked Eva.

"The children are with their grandparents, so we can go shopping in peace. Shall we have a bite to eat here in the mall afterwards?" asked Steven.

"That's a very good idea," the group replied.

At the table in the pizzeria on the first floor, the group marvelled at the contents of their plates. Slices of pizza served in every imaginable variation—this was the successful concept developed by two Italian expats. Eva and David had never seen anything like it. But the conversation quickly turned to the seminar that had been announced at the last minute for the weekend. In all the years they had worked for the company, they had never been sent on an overnight seminar before. The men thought it was because of the company's international reorganisation.

"Shall we go shopping together on Saturday after brunch?" asked Sila.
"That's a great idea!" replied Eva enthusiastically.
The next working day began in the meeting room. The team of five and Valentin are already talking at the round table. The only free seat for Eva is again next to Valentin.
"Am I late?" asks Eva, surprised to see everyone there.
"No, don't worry, we're the ones who are early. We started talking an hour ago," replied Valentin.

Relieved, Eva took her folder out of her briefcase and put a pencil next to her notebook. Then she put her hands back in her lap and tried to concentrate fully on what everyone was saying. But during the meeting, Valentin gently touched her hands under the table. Frightened by the thought that someone might notice what was going on under the table, she remained motionless and watched the people talking. But the temptation was too great. She casually took Valentin's hand between hers and began to stroke his palm.
"Mrs Rodriguez? Aren't you going to write down those last notes?" Mrs. Jones asked with a critical eye.
"Of course," she replied, quickly putting her hands back on the table.

Back in her office, Eva was under the spell of feelings she had never felt before—a longing and desire she had never felt before. Her fantasies became desires. She longed to feel Valentin's mouth on hers, to hear his whisper, to feel his breath between her ears and over her shoulders, to smell him.
Luckily, the demanding tasks in the office always brought her back to reality, for that was the real reason why she had taken a job in this company. Now her phone rang at exactly twelve o'clock, and David

and his colleagues were waiting for her in the canteen. She had completely lost track of time with all the work and hot dreams. Where was everything going? She had been preparing for all sorts of situations for days.

She quickly left the office and went to the lift, but as she stood in front of it, she quickly looked in her bag to see if she had her mobile phone with her. Distracted, she didn't notice that the lift door had opened and someone had stepped out. Unconcerned, she got in and pressed the button to go down to the ground floor, just as Valentin quickly slipped in and pressed the button to stop the lift.

"What are you doing? My husband is waiting for me in the canteen!" she asked excitedly as Velantin hugged her and pulled her into a kiss. She arrived at the canteen panting, but for no reason, as David had already fetched the salad she wanted and placed it on the table for her.

"Sorry, the phone rang again as I was leaving the office," Eva excused herself before her husband could ask any questions.

After work, Eva and David went straight home. Over dinner, David spoke openly with Eva about how her behavior had changed since she had taken on this stressful job as an executive assistant.

"You come home in the evening, and you're just exhausted."

"This will certainly change when Mrs. Leblanc comes back to work. I miss her presence! I've had a lot more work to do since she left," she explained.

David could never have imagined the real reasons for Eva's change, and they had nothing to do with the extra work caused by Mrs. Leblanc's absence. He could never have imagined that his wife was burning with passion for another man.

Friday morning dawned. After a healthy breakfast, David accompanied his wife to work and then picked up his colleagues to drive to Montreal. For David, too, it was one of the rare occasions when he did something without his wife. A man's weekend, although in his case it was about work.

After a busy morning, Eva checked her diary again just before lunch because she still had no information about where the out-of-office meeting would take place and, more importantly, which client it would be with.

How could someone change the day's plans without discussing it with her? How could she organise the necessary documents for the meeting?

Now the company car with chauffeur was at the door at 4 p.m. on the dot. Exactly as planned.

Valentin got out and opened the door for her. She looked at him in silence with a puzzled expression on her face and sat down in the car.

"You can go," Valentin ordered.

After a short drive, the chauffeur pulled up in front of a building near the Ottawa River.

Valentin got out, opened the door, and waited for Eva to get out. Without comment, the chauffeur drove straight on.

"Where are we? I don't see any offices here," Eva asked, confused.

Valentin held out his arm and pointed to the building opposite.

"See that penthouse up there? That's my apartment."

Chapter 3 Fiery Days

"**M**rs Rodriguez? Hello?" called Mrs. Leblanc. On her first day back at work after the weekend, Eva, lost in thought, was taken completely by surprise.

"I'm sorry, I was so focused on my work that I didn't hear you come in."

"Yes, I saw that. And what is the smell of that piece of printer paper you were sniffing so intensely?" asked Mrs. Leblanc, amused.

Ashamed to have been caught at the wrong moment, Eva quickly put the paper down on the desk and felt the warmth on her now flushed cheeks.

"You know, I've been back in the office for two weeks now, but I have to admit that I'm still not really up to speed. I have to meet a very important client in Toronto next Tuesday, but I can't go due to the slow healing of my broken vertebra. You will have to cover for me; I have full confidence in your work," said Mrs. Leblanc.

"Thank you for your confidence, but I'm your assistant, and I'm not familiar with all the arguments for negotiating with a client of this rank."

"I understand your uncertainty, but don't worry, my son Valentin will handle the negotiations. You will accompany him on this trip. You will leave next Monday and be back on Wednesday," Mrs. Leblanc said, placing the itinerary on the desk.

Honoured and nervous at the same time, she accepted the task set before her, knowing how it would turn out, for the mere thought of being with Valentin again gave her an immediate tingling sensation.

They hadn't spoken in two weeks, but she couldn't stop thinking about him. Was he feeling the same?

The memories of the night she had spent with him while David was at the seminar with his colleagues in Montreal were still vivid; all she had to do was close her eyes to smell the scent of his bare skin and touch his body. The thought of touching his skin made her want him even more. This desire to kiss him, just to taste his lips, to feel his passion.

Just before she left her office at the end of the day, she saw Valentin standing through the glass door in his mother's office. Excited and with her heart pounding, she hurries to the lift so as not to keep David waiting in the car park.

"Darling, you're on time today. My colleagues have invited us to watch the carnival parade and are waiting for us in town. Are you excited?" he asked.

"But we're not even masked."

"May I present Mr. and Mrs. Penguin! Here you can open the zip, slip into the costume, and close it again. Keeps you warm, and no one will recognise you. Let's go now."

As she left the car park, Eva instinctively glanced up at the window of the manager's office and saw Valentin watching her from the top floor.

"Brilliant, let's go quickly!" she asked.

When they arrived at the meeting place, they saw that Robin and Steven were already there. In a party mood and dressed as a turtle and a crocodile, they were both waiting for their loved ones. Eva and David had never seen such a large crowd of masked people and floats before. Loud music, happy people dancing in the open air — everything was perfect. Only Sila and Martha were missing, but suddenly they saw two figures waving their hands and heard familiar voices from the crowd.

"We are here! Come and dance with us!" they both shouted, trying to stand out from the crowd.

A crowd that was swept up in the music and the fun. Costumes of all shapes and colours everywhere. It was impossible not to be infected.

They blended into the crowd with enthusiasm and ease, until the group was pushed left and right by David's colleagues and suddenly separated. Squeezed from all sides, Eva lost her bearings in a matter of seconds and desperately searched for David until a drunk trying to get through the crowd pushed her and knocked her to the ground. The fun turned into a very threatening situation for her as people began to trample her as she danced. She desperately tried to shield her face with her arms as a person dressed as a clown leaned over her, lifted her up and led her out of the crowd to safety beside her car.

"You'll be safe here," the masked person said as he ran off.

"Valentin?" she shouted as loud as she could.

Without hesitation, the clown disappeared back into the crowd, returning a few minutes later with David. With a wave of his hand, he showed him where Eva was standing, then turned and walked away.

"I've been looking all over for you. What happened? Who was the person dressed as a clown who brought me to you?" David asked, still panicking.

"I want to go home," she replied quietly.

Exhausted, and in the middle of the night, Eva and David arrived home. They will remember this carnival for a long time, but not only because of the incredible parade.

"Honey, with all the carnival, I forgot to tell you that I have to go to Toronto next week to represent Mrs. Leblanc at a meeting with an important client."

"Let's talk about it tomorrow; I'm so tired," he replied, yawning.

The time for Eva's departure was fast approaching, and the thoughts of what clothes and underwear she would take with her and wear during her stay in Toronto were almost as intrusive as the thoughts of what she would do with Valentin during that time. But much worse were the reactions these thoughts caused in her body. A flood of desire and tingling in the most sensitive parts of her body overwhelmed her.

Choosing her underwear for the trip was now causing her far more stress than meeting the important client, and as the time to leave drew nearer, the moments in Valentin's apartment became more intense. The moments when they kissed on the lips, when she let her dress fall while he looked into her eyes and his hands caressed her feminine curves, crossing the border of lust. In that moment, it was not her mind that begged to be touched, but her soul that demanded it.

Then a knock on the door interrupted all her thoughts, and Mrs. Leblanc suddenly stood before her with a file in her hand. On that Friday afternoon, when Eva had been thinking more about her meeting with Valentin than about the meeting with the client, Mrs. Leblanc had made sure that everything was in place and had prepared an agenda with all the key points for the entire duration of the meeting with the client because the negotiation had to go perfectly.

"This folder contains the detailed program for the meeting in Toronto, which will make the process easier and error-free. I know you are up to the task," said Mrs. Leblanc confidently.

"I am proud to be involved in this important meeting," Eva emphasised.

Back home after work, Eva waited impatiently for David to slip into the shower so she could hurry up and pack her suitcase so she could put her hot laundry plan into action. But David had other plans and expected her to keep him company.

"Darling, what is taking you so long? Come and have a shower with me!" he called from the bathroom.

"Not today; I have to finish packing."

"Darling, it's Friday; you're not leaving until Monday, and you have all the time in the world to pack. Come and have a shower with me. Shall I come and pick you up?"

To avoid arousing suspicion, she hurriedly closed her suitcase, undressed, and jumped into the shower. But when he began to caress her naked, damp skin, she quickly realised what her husband's intentions were.

"Every inch of your body drives me crazy; I already know I'm going to miss you terribly when you travel," he whispered.

Dutifully, because of her old-fashioned upbringing, and without giving it much thought, Eva allowed herself to be infected by her husband's passion. Pleasure and pain became one under the soothing water of the shower. But her husband didn't seem to have had enough and thought about going into the kitchen while she was at the stove. He walked quickly behind her.

put his hands on her hips and whispered in her ear:

"There are only two things a man and a woman can do on a boring Friday night. And I don't like to watch TV."

"Come on, we just finished a few minutes ago; you don't want to go on like this all weekend, do you?"

"Of course I do!" he replied amusedly.

She quickly gave him a gentle tug to push him back and brought the food to the table.

"I just want to eat and relax. Besides, I like to watch TV, especially with a big plate of chips and a glass of Coke in front of me. Shall we watch a funny comedy?" she asked.

After a weekend that seemed to last forever, Eva arrived at the station with David on Monday morning. Her eyes searched eagerly for Valentin, but he was nowhere to be seen. After a few minutes, a voice announced the arrival of their train at the station, while David still held her close. She quickly realised that she would have to make the train journey alone.

During the ride, she tried to understand why she was travelling alone, since Mrs. Leblanc had said she was to accompany Valentin on this business trip. The thought of being alone in Toronto and having to introduce herself to the client was beginning to get to her. Had the plans changed at the last minute and no one had told her? But when she arrived at Toronto station, she saw a smartly dressed man on the platform holding a sign with her name on it. It gave her hope that someone was waiting for her.

"I'm the person you're looking for," she said shyly.
Silently, the chauffeur took the suitcase from her and led her to the limousine.
"Wow, you picked me up in such a big car; didn't you know I was alone?" she asked curiously.
"Well, my job was to pick you up in this car and take you to the Shangri-La Hotel," he replied, and they set off.

When they arrived at the hotel, Eva went straight to check in and had to swallow twice when, after traveling alone, she was faced with a second problem. What was going on? How could such a prestigious company organize business trips so badly?

"I think there's been a mistake; I'm here on a business trip; I wasn't told that a suite had been reserved for me," Eva explained, a little tense.

"We have been instructed to reserve a suite for you. Lunch has already been delivered to your room," the lady pointed out.

"My employer will not be happy about this. I don't think an employee is given such a budget for a client meeting. Are you sure? I don't want to get into trouble," Eva insisted.

"You are Mrs. Rodriguez, aren't you?" the lady asked.

"Yes, that's right."

"Then please follow me."

Resigned, Eva followed the hotel clerk, got into the lift, and rode to the top floor. A small, luxurious corridor and only one door were in front of them when they reached the top. She turned to the clerk with an uncertain face.

"There is only one suite on the top floor. I hope you enjoy your stay," the lady said simply.

She carefully opened the door, put down her suitcase, and looked around, then approached the table and saw that it was set for two.

Looking again, she noticed there were two more doors, and then she realised she wasn't alone.

"Hello, is anyone there?" She called out as the door to the right of the table opened. Valentin was standing in front of her.

A brief but intense look was all it took for them to fall into each other's arms in a long, silent embrace.

"Everything about me longs for you," he whispered.

"I long for you too. I long to feel your lips on mine, your skin against mine, the touch of your breath in my hair. These past few weeks without you, I felt like I was going crazy with longing," she whispered, her voice cracking.

With all the passion they had, they lost themselves in an endless kiss. Ardent looks and lustful touches alternate. He caressed her neck with his tongue.

and kissed her from the nape of her neck to the zip of her dress.

With expert hands and full of desire, he gently removed her dress and threw it to the floor. In a frenzy of lust, she unbuttoned his shirt and kissed him on his manly torso, then he placed his hand on the back of her neck and brought his face close to her earlobe.

"Your kisses are not a foretaste of other tenderness; they are simply the highest point," he whispered in her ear.

"My skin trembles at your every touch. I'm so excited; my heart is about to explode. We're together at last.

Kisses, touches, the scent of desire, and skin glowing with passion made them lose themselves in a world that was theirs alone.

Like two lovers, they walked hand in hand through Kensington Market in the afternoon.

"Wow, look at all the interesting stuff here. Let me look for funky souvenirs for my family while we're at it," she said enthusiastically.

"OK, but only if you promise we'll check out the hippie district behind Chinatown afterwards," he said, taking her in his arms, spinning her around, and kissing her on the lips.

"If you keep kissing me like that, I can't guarantee anything."

Then he set her down, and they walked on until they came to a playground. They played on the swings like two children, laughing out loud. A fantastic, carefree afternoon, as if they alone existed in this new dimension, as if there had never been another life, as if it had always been like this, with a unique familiarity and feeling of timeless connection.

"I don't know about you, but I'm on cloud nine, head over heels in love. I don't think I've ever been so happy," he said, his voice moving. "I feel at home in your arms, and yes, I too am hopelessly in love," she replied, and they continued their walk towards the market, which was only a few meters away.

In the middle of the market, Valentin picked her up and kissed her again for a long time, as if she were the only one there. But suddenly there was applause from the crowd, which interrupted the long, passionate kiss. Then Valentin set Eva down, and the two of them stood in the crowd, their faces flushed.

"Come on, let's walk quickly to the hippie district; at least no one knows us there yet, and I can kiss you again," he said, taking her hand.
"You've never told me about your father. I've never seen him at work. Don't your parents work together?" She asked thoughtfully.
With a veil of sadness in his eyes, Valentin looked at her and said:
"My father has been in a wheelchair for several years. He can't come to the office."
"I'm very sorry. I can understand if you don't want to talk about it."
"It happened on a hunting trip with Elsch. He was just waiting for the right moment to shoot the moose when a wolf attacked him, and during the attack he dropped his rifle on the ground and was unable to grab it in time to defend himself. My uncle Bruno rushed to his aid, but the wolf had begun to tear at his legs. My father ordered him to shoot the wolf, but my uncle first fired a shot in the air to make the wolf let go. As if in a frenzy, the wolf was undeterred and continued to tear at my father's legs until he ordered my uncle to shoot it again. He was able to kill the wolf with a single shot, but some of the stray bullets also hit my father, causing him to lose the use of his legs.".

Moved to tears by the sad story, she took his hand and brought it to her heart, then they embraced in silence.

"But from now on there will be no more sad memories. Would you like some Mexican food?" he asked, trying to change the subject.

"I'm so hungry that I would eat anything, no matter what nation."

At the restaurant table, Valentin took Eva's hands in his and stroked them lovingly. Still incredulous at what they were feeling, they looked into each other's eyes and touched.

"I would like to stop time and hold this moment forever. Returning home already scares me—me alone with the longing for you and you in your husband's arms. I'm going mad at the thought. Let's escape together, to a faraway place where no one knows us, just you and me."

"I can't," she replied sadly.

"It's not fair. I'm meeting the person of my life, and she's tied to someone else. How can you be so unlucky?" He asked bitterly.

"At least you're alone. It's much worse for me; I have to think of you and fulfil my duties as a wife at the same time. Tell me which is worse!"

"We really have a damn big problem," he said.

"That's what it looks like," she replied.

After an unforgettable afternoon together, Eva and Valentin headed back to the hotel. The next day's meeting with a client such as Algata Pharma required Eva's preparation, so Valentin left her alone to go through the documents for the meeting and went swimming in the meantime.

An hour and a half later, the receptionist called Eva to her room and invited her to the pool.

Once in the spa area, Eva was ushered into the cubicle, and her swimsuit, bathrobe, and slippers were placed on a chair for her.

"As soon as you step out of this door, you'll be in the swimming pool," the nice lady pointed out.

Eva quickly slipped into her swimsuit and left the cabin, where she was surprised to find that there were no other people there except Valentin. However, a closer look revealed other juicy details: Valentin was sitting in the pool, his swimming costume lying on the floor at the edge of the pool next to a bucket of ice and cold drinks. The late evening light was atmospheric, and music was playing softly from the ceiling. What kind of evening program had he come up with? Well, the clues pointed to something very tasty.

"Why are you standing there watching? Jump in. I can't wait to kiss you underwater," he shouted.

"Can I keep my bikini on?"

"For now, yes, but I'll rip it off with my teeth in a minute," he said with a look of fire in his eyes.

"Are you sure we're alone and no one will come in?"

"No one will bother us!"

Without thinking, she leapt into his arms.

"The seductive scent of your skin is driving me crazy," he whispered, kissing her lightly on the neck. He slowly pulled down the strap of her bathing suit, kissing her bare shoulder and caressing her breasts.

"My God, how is it possible to feel such emotions?" she whispered, her voice cracking. "With you, I realize that sensuality can be expressed in every gesture, in a kiss, in tenderness, in the simple touch of skin with wet lips."

He looked deep into her eyes, glowing with desire, and slowly untied the knots that bound the briefs of the bathing costume that had them both completely out of control until the music and the hot atmosphere were interrupted by the announcement of the time.

"How could this happen? We've been in the water for over an hour; we still have to eat dinner and go to bed early; tomorrow's the big day!" she said, having completely lost track of time.

They hurried out of the pool and into their room, where a romantic dinner awaited them.

"Wow, why is the food already in the room?" she asked in surprise.

"I had it all arranged before you arrived at the hotel."

"You're amazing; it's a madness to love you, a lack of sanity that only two people who feel these tremendous emotions can have."

Flattered by the compliment, he cupped his hands over his ears and grinned.

"Don't say those things, please, or I'll pick up where we left off in the pool!"

Well prepared for the important client meeting and optimistic about the outcome of the negotiations, Eva and Valentin went to the conference room early in the morning. Everything seems perfect for the occasion, but before the special customer from the large pharmaceutical company Ritel arrives, they take a last look at the glasses, drinks, and snacks on the table. Even these little things are important when dealing with a client of this size. And then, behind the frosted glass door, the silhouettes of two people could be seen.

A very elegant man and his companion entered the room.

"You must be Monsieur Leblanc Junior, right? Your mother spoke very highly of you," the gentleman asked.

"That's right. And you must be Mr. Wilson. My mother spoke very highly of you too."

The women stood silently in the room, waiting to be introduced, then Mr. Wilson looked in Eva's direction.

"Who is your lovely companion? Aren't you going to introduce her to me?" He asked, addressing Valentin.

"It is my pleasure to introduce you to my mother's right-hand woman and confidante, Mrs. Eva Rodriguez. And who is your lovely companion?"

"My lovely companion is Mrs. Mayer, my secretary and partner of many years," Mr. Wilson replied, uninhibited and full of pride.

Happy to be introduced, they took their seats, then Valentin pointed to the drinks on the table, took a bottle of champagne from the ice bucket, and poured some into the crystal glasses.

"To us, good luck today and good business in the future," Valentin said, raising his glass.

As Valentin and Mr. Wilson focused on the requirements for future collaboration, the ladies studied the spreadsheets full of figures and exchanged ideas as if they had known each other forever.
After three hours of discussion, Valentin and Mr. Wilson managed to reach an agreement that was even better than Valentin's mother had suggested.
Proud of the outcome of the negotiations, they decided to have lunch together to celebrate the success of the meeting.
In the restaurant, Mr. Wilson watched in silence as Valentin and Eva enjoyed their delicious meal.

"I don't want to be indiscrete, but you two would make a really beautiful couple," he suddenly said to Eva and Valentin, causing Eva's cheeks to blush.
"I'm serious," he added.
"I'm married," Eva replied in a low tone.
"We were too, before we fell in love," Mrs. Mayer replied with a beaming smile.

Eva and Valentin had not expected such an intimate statement.

"Ladies and gentlemen, here are our desserts of the day," the waiter joked as he approached with a trolley full of delicacies, prompting the group to greet him with a round of applause.

After a delicious lunch and an exchange of professional and personal experiences, it was time to say goodbye, and Mr. Wilson suggested that they meet again in six months' time to analyse the results of the collaboration.

"Where are we going in such a hurry?" asked Eva as Valentin walked briskly to the reception desk with the documents.
"I just want to put the documents back in the safe and pick up where we left off yesterday by the pool. This is our last night here; I don't want to waste a single second of this precious time with you," he replied with the look of a man who knows what he wants.
"But wouldn't it be better if we went to the room and changed first? I haven't even got my swimming costume on yet."
"That's no good. You make me burn; not even the chastity belt could stop me."

Once in the cabin, he quickly slipped his hands under her blouse and unhooked her bra. He gently brushed his lips over the nipples visible through her blouse until she moaned and whispered, "All my senses are working together to love you. The sense of sight... admiring your beauty. The sense of touch touches your warm skin. The sense of taste tastes your every kiss, and the sense of hearing hears you moan."
Another moan escaped Eva's mouth as Valentin touched her breasts again. Driven by her stormy passion, Eva began to undo the buttons of Valentin's shirt. "I want to feel you inside me," she whispered in a broken voice, pulling him towards her with force.

"Shh... let's go to the pool first," he whispered, continuing to undress her very slowly.

"Take my body at last. I want you now!" she begged again in a longing voice and jumped on top of him. Unable to contain his passion, he grabbed her thighs and gently pressed her back against the wall, making her feel his desire and causing her passion to explode.

When they reached the pool, they cuddled up in the deckchairs and held each other in silence until tears suddenly welled up in Eva's eyes. Moved, Valentin took her hand and placed it on his heart, then brought it to his face. He too had tears in his eyes.

"From tomorrow on, my life will be empty again without you. Every moment together gives me unique feelings. There are many ways to be happy, but for me, it is enough to be near you to feel happiness," he whispered with emotion in his voice.

"I feel at home with you," she replied with a sad voice.

After spending their last night together, the next morning Valentin accompanied his beloved Eva to the station. After their wonderful days together, the separation was heartbreaking for both of them. On the platform, they cuddled in silence as they waited for the train.

"Please come with me on the train; don't let me go home alone," she begged with tears in her eyes.

"I can't. Please forgive me. I think I might die if I saw your husband waiting for you on the platform with a bouquet of flowers, holding you in his arms," he replied in a dejected voice.

"Please don't say that; it hurts me to hear it," she replied with tears in her eyes.

"Your attention, please. The express train to Ottava station is now arriving at platform 4," said an electronic voice.

It's time for them to say goodbye. Eva and Valentin look into each other's eyes again and burst into tears, then he takes her hand and leads her onto the train. "Promise me we'll find a way to see each other again," she whispers, her voice choked with tears, clutching his hand.

"I promise," he replied, getting off the train.

On the platform at Ottawa station, David stood with a beaming smile and a bouquet of flowers in his hand. He was visibly happy to see his wife again. A picture of perfect love, but she sees him through the window and starts to cry.

He runs happily towards her to fetch her suitcase.

"Darling, why are you crying? You've only been away for three days. Come on, don't cry; I've missed you too," he said, giving his wife a tender kiss on the lips as she remained motionless in her husband's embrace.

"Come on, let's go to the car, then you can tell me how the deal went and what your impression of Toronto was," he said in a relaxed tone.
Once in the car, Eva slowly regained control of her emotions.
"The meeting with Algata Pharma went better than expected. The next meeting is scheduled for six months," she said.
"The boss will be very proud of you. We had no doubts about your professional skills," he said with a proud voice.

When they got home, the first thing Eva saw was that David had prepared dinner for them.

"Damn, you've gone to so much trouble to make a nice dinner, and I'm not even in a good mood. What a terrible wife I am," she said, touching, and then they looked at each other and burst out laughing.
"I'm sure you'll make it up to me later," he said, slapping her bottom.

This unique way in which they had communicated and clarified things over the years reassured Eva. They had grown up together and always found a way to crack a smile, but Eva was occasionally distracted at dinner while David peppered her with questions and told her what he had been up to over the past few days. And there was big news to report, as David and his colleague Steven had now joined a golf club. Steven had been looking for an outlet for his marital problems with Martha and found that golf was just the thing.

"How long have Steven and Martha had relationship problems?" she asked curiously.

"A long time, obviously. The birth of the twins put a damper on the couple's intimacy."

"Are you serious? Children don't ruin a couple's love life. Do you really believe that?"

"Well, seeing how they are, I'd say yes. Then two kids at once... But we don't care; we haven't planned any children yet."

"I'm not hungry anymore. If you don't mind, I'm going to take a shower. I have to be at work early tomorrow; Mrs. Leblanc is expecting me in the conference room at 7.45," she added, heading for the bathroom.

"Of course, darling, I'll come straight to you."

Eva had no intention of showering with David, so she went into the bathroom and locked the door for the first time in the history of their relationship. She looked in the mirror several times in a panic, discovering several hickeys on her shoulders and buttocks, and gasped for breath. Then the predictable happened: David tried to open the bathroom door, and she hurriedly slipped into the shower.

"Honey, since when do you lock the bathroom door?" he asked loudly from behind the door.

"Sorry, after two nights in the hotel, it must have become an automatic action without thinking," she replied in a loud tone.

"I'll unpack my bags quickly if you want to take a shower in the meantime," she said as she came out of the bathroom in her pyjamas.

But he seemed to have other intentions and stood behind her, wrapping an arm around her waist and touching her wet hair with his hand.

"I've missed you a lot, you know?" he whispered.

"I've missed you too, but now I have to unpack. Work before pleasure," she replied, releasing her grip.

"All right, go ahead. Can I tell you something? I'm going to go golfing with Steven and some of the other guys two or three times a week. Is that all right with you?"

"Sure! I think it's a great idea. Normally you never want to do sports, but I think it's really nice that you want to do something for yourself.

Before going to bed, Eva makes the room pitch black so that David won't notice the hickeys. The fact that you could barely see anything in the room didn't seem to bother David. His goal for the evening was to rip off his wife's pyjamas, so he started foreplay right away.

He kissed her softly on the lips and slipped his hand under her pyjama shirt, then slowly moved down to her neck and fondled her breasts. Without moving or offering any resistance, she lay still and let him do his thing. Giving in to the urge, he pulled up her pyjama shirt, gently kissed her stomach near her navel, then knelt on the bed and pulled her towards him. "I've missed you so much," he whispered.

In the dark and with tears in her eyes, she crossed her legs around his waist and kissed him as he pulled down her pyjama bottoms. Then he took her hips in his hands and pulled her even closer until they were lost in the gentle rocking of their bodies.

The next morning, Mrs. Leblanc and Valentin were waiting for Eva in the conference room. She entered the room on time and greeted everyone with a formal handshake.

Visibly pleased to see them, Mrs. Leblanc sat down next to Valentin and motioned for Eva to sit opposite her, then looked at them both with a satisfied expression and invited them to help themselves to drinks.

"I am convinced that about half of what separates successful entrepreneurs from unsuccessful ones is sheer perseverance. I've done things in the past that I wasn't ready to do. I believe that is the only way to grow. Managers are people who do things the right way. Leaders are people who do the right thing. And as a leader, I did the right thing by relying on both of you. A big compliment to both of you. To Valentin, our junior manager, and to her, our trusted and irreplaceable right-hand woman," says Mrs. Leblanc, delighted with the results.

Valentin looks at Eva with a subdued expression and winks at her. Her face turned red.

"Mrs. Rodriguez, there's no need to blush; I just wanted to pay you a compliment; you deserve it. Do you know what an incredible job you've done?" asked Mrs. Leblanc with a beaming smile.

"Of course, thank you. I apologise for the excitement," Eva replied humbly.

"Oh, don't worry, you'll have to get used to it; in two weeks we're off to Montreal to Rartis Pharmaceuticals; I'm sure they'll do a good job there too."

Astonished, Eva looked at Mrs. Leblanc and asked firmly, "Seriously?"

"Absolutely!" she replied with conviction.

At lunchtime, Eva and David met in the canteen. David's colleagues were already at the table.

"I'm being sent to Montreal in a fortnight; Mrs. Leblanc doesn't seem to be in good physical shape since her last riding accident," Eva told them.

"But how, again? You're her secretary, not her postman," David said in an irritated tone.

"Please, let's talk about this at home; I'm sure I can explain the situation better."

"Let her go, my friend, then we'll have more time to spend on the golf course," Steven said in an amused tone.

"Word around the company is that Mrs. Leblanc is preparing her son Valentin to take over as director," Robin told him.

The men look at each other and begin to laugh.
"What's so funny?" she asked.

"Who, this spoilt mummy's boy, is going to run a company like this?" asked Steven, laughing even louder.

"The best he can do is look after the security checks on the lace pants of all the company's employees," Robin replied.

Astonished, Eva looked at David's colleagues, who suddenly fell silent.

"What now? Have you finally run out of laughs?" she asked sarcastically.

"No, they noticed that the lace pants they were wearing were sticking out of their trousers," a voice behind her replied.

After recognising Valentin's voice, Eva turned to him and covered her face with her hands in embarrassment.

"Oh my goodness. Mr. Leblanc, are you here too?" she asked, her cheeks turning red.

Chapter 4 Passionately yours

"Please don't stop; my skin trembles every time you touch me. Don't go!" pleaded Valentin as Eva zipped up her dress.

"I can't stay any longer; David will be back from his golf game soon. It's a miracle he decided to go and play," she replied in a hurry, but after she'd dressed, she leaned over and kissed him gently on the lips and stroked his manly torso with her hand.

"If you go on like this, I won't let you go tonight," he said with his fiery gaze.

Knowing that he would do as he promised, she stood up quickly, grabbed her shoes and walked briskly to the exit.

"¡Te amo!" he shouted as she closed the door behind her.

When they got home, Eva found that David had already cooked and set the table.

"Oh my goodness! You're already home, and you've already cooked. Did the tournament end early?" She asked in surprise.

"Our car was seen a couple of times in an upscale neighbourhood near the Ottawa River."

"Shall we say hello first? We haven't seen each other all day." She asked, trying to change the subject.

Obviously in a bad mood, he approached her and gave her a quick kiss on the lips. But she, who was not used to that kind of reaction from her husband, felt queasy.

"Who saw our car near the Ottawa River?"

"It doesn't matter who saw it; someone saw it. May I ask what you were doing in that area?"

"Excuse me, but what do you think I was doing in that area?" She asked in an offended voice.

"If I knew what you were doing there, I wouldn't have asked you, would I? So just tell me what you were doing there."

"What's this game of questions?" she asked, increasingly worried that someone might have seen her with Valentin.

"In eight weeks it will be exactly six months that we've been in Canada, and this apartment has been given to us on a six-month trial basis. Our house in Barcelona has been rented to strangers for six months, and we have to decide together whether we want to continue our lives here or go back to Barcelona. We only have eight weeks. I have reason to believe that you are doing something behind my back," he accused her in a suspicious tone.

"But darling, what do you think I'm doing behind your back?"

"You're probably looking for a nicer flat in a more expensive area because we're earning better now and you've probably already decided to stay here longer, but I'm not prepared to pay more for a flat. We're in a foreign country, far away from home, and I want to save what I earn, not spend it on rent!"

Relieved to hear that David only suspected that she was looking for a new flat, she exhaled sharply.

"You're right, darling, and I apologise for coming up with the idea of looking at properties in this area. It won't happen again."

Happy to have cleared the air, Eva approached David, took his hand, and led him to the table.

When Eva entered her office the next morning, she found Valentin already sitting at her desk with a document for her to sign. Happy to see him, she approached him, and he took her hand, pulled her towards him, and kissed her.

"What are you doing here? Where's your mother? Someone might see us. And what's that document you left on my desk?"

"Hey, hey, hey, so many questions at once... Come here, sit on my lap, and relax. Why are you so upset so early in the morning?"

"My car was seen twice near your apartment. Isn't that something to be upset about?"

"I understand. You seem to have had problems at home and a fight with your husband. Have you separated? Is that why he sent an email to my mother asking for a lease extension? The document only has his name on it," he asked, handing her the document.

She looked at him in astonishment, as if she were in the wrong film.

"Have you broken up or not?" he asked with a glimmer of hope in his eyes.

"No, we haven't split up. David thought I was looking for an expensive flat in the neighborhood. That's all he was thinking about."

Disappointed, Valentin puts the document on the desk and leaves the office in silence. Left alone, she began to cry.

Mrs. Leblanc, who had just entered the company, opened the door to her office and saw Valentin coming out of Eva's office.

"Valentin Leblanc, what are you looking at? I know that look."

"Mum, please, not now. I need some fresh air."

"You're in love with Mrs. Rodriguez, aren't you?"

"Could you please keep your voice down? I'm going to get some air. I'll see you later at the Algata Pharma meeting."

"Damn it, Valentin, there are so many women who would do anything to marry you. Why her? Why a married woman?"

"Mother, please speak quietly now and calm down! I'll see you later."

Annoyed, he turned and walked to the lift without further comment. Valentin wasn't the only one in the car park who needed some fresh air. David was also pacing and talking on the phone in an annoyed tone, not even noticing that he wasn't alone. Valentin instinctively looked up at Eva's window and met her gaze. Who was David arguing with?

Meanwhile, Valentin's mobile phone was ringing. His mother was calling him into the office, and it was then that David realised he was not alone out there. He abruptly ended the call and hurried back to the company.

In his mother's office, Valentin asked for an explanation of the urgency of the call.

"Valentin, please listen carefully and don't interrupt me."

"Mum, there's nothing to talk about; I'm in a hurry and have to prepare for our meeting. Please. I don't understand all this unnecessary worry."

"For some weeks now, since your last trip to Montreal, I've noticed a certain closeness between you and Mrs. Rodriguez. Are you trying to deny the facts to your mother, who knows you better than anyone?"

"Mum, you're exaggerating. I'll see you at the meeting later," he replied irritably and started for the door.

But she walked up to him, grabbed his arm, and asked him to turn around.

"Stop, Valentin, look at me! Did you sleep together on your last trip to Montreal?"

"Mum, have you completely lost your mind?" shouted Valentin angrily.

"All right, I'll see you at the meeting later. There will be another meeting with Algata Pharma in Toronto in six weeks, and I will go with you. We will then find a secretary, a man who will accompany you to business partners in the future until you have learnt to keep your testosterone under control," she said caustically.

"Are you planning to fire Eva?"

"Ah ha, so you and Mrs. Rodriguez are already on a first name basis? She's staying on; she's my secretary, not yours. We'll find someone else for you."

He left the office in a huff and without another word.

As planned, Mrs. Leblanc, Valentin, and Eva met in the conference room to discuss the agenda for the upcoming meeting with Algata Pharma. With Eva's help, Mrs. Leblanc had prepared a presentation that could be projected on the screen, and now, to Eva's great surprise, all the tasks that had previously been assigned to her were being replaced. Without batting an eyelid, Mrs. Leblanc began to explain the reasons for the changes before Eva could ask any questions.

"Mrs. Rodriguez, when the meeting with Algata Pharma takes place, you and your husband will have completed your sixth month in Canada. A few days ago, your husband asked me to extend the lease on the apartment provided by the company. I assume that they feel comfortable with us and have decided to stay in Canada for the long term. I'm very happy about that. They will probably need a few days to do the paperwork for their extended stay here in Canada and to get settled. At the moment my health is taking a positive turn, so I will be able to travel with Valentin to Toronto for the meeting with Rittel," Mrs. Leblanc said in one breath.

"As you wish. Will I support them from here while they are in Toronto?"

Smiling, she pushed a large envelope on the table in Eva's direction.

"During this time, you and your husband will be in Barcelona to deal with bureaucratic matters and to see your families again. I have already organised their flights and will give them two weeks' leave. We will cover for you during that time and take care of the work.".

Without understanding what was going on, Eva looked at the envelope in silence.

"Aren't you happy about the two weeks' holiday?" Mrs. Leblanc asked curiously.

"Of course, yes. I don't know what to say. It's really very generous of you; I thank you from the bottom of my heart," she replied quietly.

"Excellent! Now you can get back to work. I'll see you later."

Valentin stared in front of him without saying a word, waiting for Eva to leave the conference room so that he could speak clearly to his mother.

"Why are you doing this? Tell me why you're doing this!" he asked angrily.

"In a few months, you'll thank me for doing this. I just don't want you to suffer unnecessarily," she replied.

Without answering, he got up and left the conference room in silence.

At a walking pace, Eva entered a country lane that led to the Leblanc family's country house. Valentin's sports car was already parked in the courtyard. A cloud of smoke rose from the chimney. The silence was broken only by the chirping of birds. She knocked excitedly on the massive wooden door until Valentin was standing in front of her. Silently, they threw themselves into each other's arms.

"Why are we here?" she asked worriedly.

"Let's go inside; I'll explain everything."

The Leblanc family mansion was impressively large and luxuriously furnished. Numerous hunting trophies hung on the walls. The floor-to-ceiling windows were draped with pastel-coloured curtains that matched the upholstery of the armchairs and sofas. Impressive chandeliers and a mix of antique and modern furniture gave the room a timeless and fascinating feel. Eva had never seen anything like it. But she wasn't there to admire the rooms. It was during the

last three-way conference that she realised something strange was going on.
Valentin silently took her hand and brought it to his heart.

"Eva, darling, listen to me. I don't know how some things will turn out in the next few weeks or months, but I want you to know that my heart belongs only to you."
"You scare me. Why do you say that? Has something happened?"

"My mother suspects that I've fallen in love with you, and believe me, that's a lot worse than your husband claiming to have seen your car near my flat."
"Does your mom think we're in love?" She asked in surprise.
"She thinks I've fallen in love with you, and she's trying to keep me as far away from you as possible. That's why she's going to Toronto now, and that's why she got you tickets to Barcelona."
"Will I lose my job?"
"Not if I stay away from you. My mother doesn't want any scandals in the family; she's been pushing me to get married and have children for a few years now. I think she's going to put more pressure on me now. You're a married woman; she really likes you as a person and as a worker, but she's afraid I'll ruin   your   marriage.".
Eva looked at him in horror and burst into tears.
"These are the consequences of forbidden love," she sighed.
"Please calm down; it breaks my heart to see you like this," he said.

But Eva is plagued by strong feelings of guilt. Valentin takes her in his arms to calm her down.

"Anyone who thinks they can plan love is mistaken and knows nothing about love. Love just happens without warning. None of us did it on purpose; we were overwhelmed by these feelings without being able to do anything about it, without being able to defend ourselves against them," he whispered.

"Everything is against us, first my husband because of the car that was seen near your apartment, and now your mother, who is also booking plane tickets to keep us apart. Maybe it would be better to take some time to think. Wouldn't it? I think we need to be very careful about what we do now," she continued, sighing in a heartbreaking tone.

"No! I can no longer imagine a life without you. I don't want to belong to any other woman in this life," he said.

and held her even tighter in his arms.

"Do you want to see the whole house? One day it will be ours and our children's," he continued, trying to distract her from the conversation.

"Our children?"

"Yes, our children. My heart tells me we will have a future together."

She looked at him with a loving gaze and kissed him gently on the lips.

When Eva came home in the late afternoon, she found that David was still out. A little surprised and happy to be home alone, she started to put the shopping away until her mobile phone suddenly rang. David seemed to be enjoying himself at the golf club and decided to stay a little longer. For Eva, a full-blooded Spaniard and a jealous wife who until recently would not have accepted her husband being away from home so often and for so long, the whole thing was no longer a problem because now Valentin had won a place in her heart. Without a care in the world, she prepared a delicious dinner and uncorked a bottle of wine. After a few glasses, she felt nostalgic and decided to call her family to tell them about her upcoming trip.

"Eva cariño! You sound a bit strange, are you all right? We miss you so much; it feels like we haven't seen each other for ages. And how are you?"

"Strange? I haven't felt this good in a long time. I'm going to have a nice evening alone."

"Alone? Where's your husband? Since when do you spend your evenings at home alone?"

"Come on, Mum, this is the first time I've spent an evening alone. David's playing golf with friends. You know, it's good to be alone for a change."

"Your husband plays sports? That's a good joke... In our country, husbands take their wives with them when they go out."

"Mum, please. Maybe couples your age... Forget it; the conversation will just turn negative... Don't you want to know the real reason for my call?"

"Are you drunk? Is that what you want to tell me?"

"Oh, Mum! We'll be in Barcelona in a fortnight."

"Ah, I see, you had a good reason for the toast. Are you staying here for good?"

"Mmhh ... I'm not going to tell you just yet. You'll find out more when we meet again... Good night, Mamacita, my eyes are closing!"

"Eva, wait, I want to know what you've decided right away!"

"Good night, Mum. ¡Te quiero!"

The few glasses of wine took effect sooner than planned, and Eva fell asleep on the sofa, unaware that David had returned home shortly afterwards.

But the next morning she found herself on the sofa, still dressed and with a blanket over her.

"Darling, won't you get up? It's time to get ready for work," David called from the bathroom.

"Damn, how did I miss the alarm?"

"By not turning it on?"

"Are you serious? That's never happened to me before."
"The wine must have been good; you were snoring like an old locomotive when I got home."
"My God, how embarrassing."
"And that wasn't the only sound coming from your body..." he winked amusedly.

She jumped into the shower without asking David how the evening had gone.
When she arrived at the office, she spotted Valentin behind the glass wall in his mother's office. Looking closer, she also seemed to see a third person with them. Without stopping, she entered her office and closed the door. The work of the last ten days before the departure had to be done; there was no time to be distracted by other things. But a few minutes later the telephone rang: Mrs. Leblanc was asking her to come into her office.
Stunned, she blinked when she saw Valentin sitting next to a stunning beauty who looked at her with obvious discomfort.

"Mrs. Rodriguez, please sit down. May I introduce you to our new Mrs. Oliveira, the junior manager's secretary?" asked Mrs. Leblanc with a perfidious look.
She must have gone to a lot of trouble to find such a secretary when she had originally wanted a man to be Valentin's secretary.

Obviously unhappy with the situation, Valentin avoided looking at Eva, and she did the same. Not wanting to show emotion at an inappropriate time, Eva took the initiative and shook Mrs. Oliveira's hand, then politely asked her to return to her work.
Back in the office, on the verge of a heart attack, she tore open the window and tried to recover from the shock. This was what Valentin had tried to tell her at the country house. No one knew his mother as well as he did. A thousand thoughts ran through her mind, but she

had to control herself. The most dangerous thing that could happen now would be to fall for Mrs. Leblanc's provocation.

As punctual as ever, David turned up at her office to pick her up for lunch.
Ironically, Valentin and his new secretary were also in the lift.
"Are you going to the canteen too?" asked Valentin, addressing David and Eva.
"Yes, but our table is full. If you'll excuse us..." Eva replied quickly, before David could say anything.

Visibly disappointed, Valentin lowered his eyes in silence.
When they arrived at the table, David's colleagues were already waiting for them, chatting about the only subject they seemed to find interesting that day.

"Did you see that hot chick that came into the canteen with the manager's son?" Steven muttered excitedly.
"Come on guys, stop drooling; you look like you've never seen a woman before," Eva said in a sour tone.
"This is not just any woman; everyone has turned to look at her. She's a grenade!" Steven repeated.
"I'm not in the mood to have lunch with a group of teenagers in a hormonal state of emergency. I'll take my lunch to the office. You can keep drooling."

Eva promptly got up and headed for the exit with her lunch.
"Honey, come on, you can't be serious," David shouted.
But she walked on without turning around, stopped in front of the lift, and pressed the button. On the verge of a nervous breakdown, she went down two floors and locked herself in the ladies' room. Nervously, she rinsed her face several times with cold water as she fought back tears, but in her excitement she didn't notice that

Valentin had followed her and was in the ladies' room. Without saying a word, he took her hand, gently pulled her away from the sink, and led her to the toilet, where he locked the door and took her in his arms as she burst into tears.

"Look at me, darling; my heart belongs only to you. Can you feel that?" He whispered softly, holding her hand over his heart.
With tear-filled eyes, she nodded without answering.

The ringing of the mobile phone in Eva's bag interrupted them both. David also seemed to be disturbed by Eva's reaction in the canteen. He hurriedly grabbed a piece of toilet paper, dried his tears, and ran to the lift to go to the office. The fear that David might realise that she and Valentin were not in the canteen reactivated her brain function on the spot.

"What the hell got into you in the canteen today?" David scolded.
Now she blamed her mild irritability on the night on the couch, the wine, and her tiredness.

The day of departure for Barcelona was fast approaching... and while David was now playing golf with his friends several times a week, Eva was often alone at home in the evenings. Day by day, Valentin was taking over more and more of his mother's duties; his schedule became more and more demanding, and they had no chance to spend time together. The fear of losing him filled her empty evenings as she reminisced about the good times at home.

Three days before his departure, David and Eva met in the city after work to buy some things for the family. After stopping at a restaurant for a bite to eat, Eva noticed a change in David's character and said to him with admiration:

"Since you've been playing golf, I can see that you're very relaxed and at peace with yourself. That's what golf does to you, and that's a great thing. Maybe you just spent too much time at home before.".
"Yes, maybe. I must say I've never felt so good."

"Everyone says exercise is good for your health, so it will be," she said.
Somehow the two of them didn't have much to say to each other, even though they spent less time together than usual, so after dinner they got the last things and went home.

At home, Eva filled the bathtub, lit some candles, and created a romantic atmosphere. The intimate moments between her and David had lost their intensity; now neither of them seemed to be missing anything, and while David seemed to have found fulfilment in sport, she felt lonely and missed the passionate moments with Valentin.

"Darling, I'm naked in the bath; do you want to join me?" She called from the bathroom.
"I'll fly to you," he replied and jumped into the bath.
Without much foreplay, Eva sat on David and began to bite his lips tenderly.
"Mhhm, are we still hungry today?" He whispered, overwhelmed by his wife's passion.
Driven by the desire to satisfy her needs, she led the game of pleasure.
Still in ecstasy, David looked at his wife and said,
"I don't remember you being so wild before."
"I'm sure it's because we haven't seen each other much in the last few weeks. It seems to have done our sexuality some good," she replied simply.
"Well then, let's leave it at that," he replied flattered.

"As you wish. But tell me, your colleague Steven, how are things between him and his wife Martha? You told me they were having a marital crisis."

"Actually, it was like that before we started playing golf. Maybe they were getting on each other's nerves because they were spending so much time together."

"Blessed be the day you came up with the idea of going golfing," she said amusedly.

The next morning in the office, Eva found a folded letter under the computer keyboard. Curious, she immediately began to read it.

"My beloved Eva,

I am losing my mind without being able to touch you. My nights sink into your absence. I search for you, your breath, your smell, and your body next to mine. It is incomprehensible that you are not here with me. My mind wanders, my thoughts come, go, and crowd together; my body can't understand your absence, but it wants you; it wants to lose itself in your warmth for a moment. My nights are suffocated by your absence. In a few days you will leave for Barcelona, and the thought of knowing you on the other side of the world is already driving me mad. Tomorrow my mother will be busy for a while with some clients from Arizona; it would be the right opportunity to meet. I'll be at the country house at five, waiting for you.

Yours sincerely.

Valentin".

With tears in her eyes, she clutched the letter to her heart when suddenly there was a knock at the door.

"Good morning, Mrs. Rodriguez, I need you to prepare some documents for tomorrow that I need for my meeting with the client from Arizona. This may mean that you have to work late today, but tomorrow you'll have the day off. Tomorrow is the day before you leave for Barcelona, right?" Mrs. Leblanc asked politely.

"Yes, that's right. I'll get straight to work."

Eva had barely started preparing the documents when the phone rang.

"Darling, would you mind if I played a round of golf with Steven and Robin tomorrow afternoon before we leave? The boys have already booked me in. I can't say no," David asked with conviction in his voice.

"Of course I wouldn't mind. Today seems to be starting off really well."

"What do you mean by that?"

"Nothing; it's all good, darling."

In order to complete the tasks set by Mrs. Leblanc, Eva gave up her lunch break, which turned out to be extremely positive because a call from Valentin was not long in coming.

"Darling, it's me; please speak quietly. I'm in the conference room on the third floor, and I need to know if you found my letter and if you'll be at our meeting place tomorrow."

But before she could answer, Mrs. Leblanc opened the office door and put more papers on the desk.

"If you talk to your husband, tell him to bring you some food because it's going to be late tonight," Mrs. Leblanc recommended as she left the office.

"Did my mother enter your office without knocking?"

"Well, that's what it looks like."

"Unbelievable, she's getting more and more pushy. But let's forget it. I can hardly wait to see you again. So, see you tomorrow?"

"See you tomorrow," she replied in an amorous voice.

The next morning David packed his gym bag and headed off to work.

The suitcases for the forthcoming trip were already packed in the hallway, so Eva decided to start her day in a relaxed manner.

But the insistent ringing at the door abruptly interrupted her attempt to relax. Valentin's private chauffeur, Mr. Bonelli, was downstairs. Irritated, she ran downstairs to see why he was standing there.

"Mr. Leblanc has sent me to collect you. Please dress in practical clothes suitable for the weather."

"But where is he? I thought he was working today."

"Theoretically, he's working, but practically, he has other plans for today. I'll wait for you here," he replied kindly.

Overwhelmed by her feelings, she ran into the flat, quickly changed into something comfortable, and packed some spare clothes into a bag.

After 20 minutes of uninterrupted driving, Eva became impatient and wanted to know where he was taking her.

"Mr. Bonelli, right? Where are you taking me?"

"Mr. Leblanc has rented a farm outside the city for today. Myself and a few trusted people will be there to give you a nice day out."

"Has he done all this for me?"

"Yes, he did."

"How can we be sure that none of them will talk to Mrs. Leblanc about this meeting?"

"If Mr. Leblanc is sure, you can be sure."

When they arrived at the farm, Eva saw Valentin waiting with two saddled horses.

Happily, she jumped out of the car without waiting for the driver to apply the handbrake and ran into Valentin's arms, whereupon he buried his face in her soft, fragrant hair.

"Who needs words when you can kiss?" he whispered, covering her mouth with a long, passionate kiss.
"I've missed you so much," she whispered, kissing him again.
"Have you ever ridden a horse?" he asked.
"Of course there are horses in Barcelona," she grinned.
"Then let's go for a nice ride around the lake."
On a warm early summer's day, they rode through the scent of blooming meadows and a breathtaking panorama. A light breeze caressed their faces. All around them was the sound of unspoilt nature.

When they reached the lake, Valentin dismounted, took the reins of Eva's horse, and helped her down. In front of them were lush green trees and crystal blue water. It was the most beautiful sight she had ever seen.
"I think I'm dreaming," she said.
"Then let me see if I can kiss you awake," he said, kissing her deeply.
"Are you awake now?" he asked.
"Mmhh, no... I don't think so yet," she replied in a dreamy voice, her lips glued to his.
"Do you trust me blindly?" he asked.
"Sure, why do you ask?"
Without answering, he lifts her up, takes a few steps forward, and, with her nuzzling his neck, jumps into the water without warning...
After a brief moment of shock, they looked at each other, laughed loudly and then kissed each other passionately.
She quickly pulled off his shirt, touched his naked, damp torso with her lips, and then swam away.

"Where are you going? The intoxicating smell of your skin has already driven me mad," he cried.

"Then catch me if you can!" she said amusedly, throwing the hot thong at him.

Without thinking, he swam after her to the jetty.

She turned to him with a longing look, took off her top, and threw it to him.

With skilful hands, he fished her top out of the water, held it to his nose, and smelt it.

"I hope you brought some spare clothes, because I'm going to keep this until you get back from Barcelona," he said, stepping onto the jetty.

Caught up in their passion, they tore off his wet trousers and made passionate love on the jetty under the warm rays of the sun.

But suddenly the sound of a car horn interrupts the magic moment. Valentin and Eva quickly covered their naked bodies. The boss, Mr. Bonelli, beckons Valentin over.

This does not bode well for them.

Eva watches the scene from a distance. The driver is talking to Valentin when he suddenly puts his hands over his head. Something serious seemed to have happened. Eva quickly got dressed and walked towards them. From a distance, it looked as if Valentin was crying.

"My father fell down the stairs in his wheelchair.

He was taken to Saint-Vincent hospital in a critical condition," he sighed.

"Oh no! How is this possible?"

"I don't know; I've got to see him right away."

They drove back to the farm in a hurry, splitting into two cars. On the way, Valentin took Eva's hand and put it over his heart.

"I don't want to leave until your father is stabilised; I don't want to leave you alone at this difficult time," Eva whispered tearfully.
"I know, but what explanation would you give your husband if you didn't go to Barcelona? My mother would be the first to throw you out of the company. I can't let that happen. God knows what I would do to have you with me forever," he sighed.
"Please let's find a solution; I don't want to leave you alone," she replied, but there was no time to argue.

When they arrived at the farm, a second car was waiting, and from now on they had to travel separately. Eva sat sadly in the car, trying to see Valentin through the dark windshield. Tears streamed down her face. Valentin signalled to the chauffeur to start the car.

Eva was standing next to David in the baggage claim queue at Macdonald-Cartier International Airport in Ottawa when the news of the day was broadcast.
"Maurice Lablanc, director of the pharmaceutical company RITEL, died in the early hours of the morning after a fall at his home yesterday," reported the journalist, who was recording below the Saint-Vincent hospital.

Eyes wide open, Eva turned to David, looked at him, and fell unconscious.

Chapter 5 Canada forever?

"You're finally here!" shouted Eva's parents at Barcelona airport.

"To be honest, it's a miracle that we got on the plane after Eva fainted half an hour before takeoff," said David, still visibly worried.

With a look of shock on her face, Eva's mother walked over and hugged her as Eva burst into tears.

"¿Qué pasa mi chica?" Eva's mother asked worriedly.

"It's too complicated. Mum, please let's go home; I need to rest."

"We'll be under the same roof for a fortnight; you'll have a chance to tell me all about it," Marion said.

"Since we've known each other, we've never spent so many days in such close quarters. It will certainly be exciting," David added with a little self-mockery in his voice.

The next morning, everyone sat down to breakfast.

"You still haven't told us what you're up to. Does this visit mean you'll be working in Barcelona again soon?" Eva's mother asked curiously.

"We'll stay in Canada forever, at least as long as we can work there," David replied.

"Excuse me? When did you make that decision? And without even asking my opinion?" asked Eva in a voice that was both surprised and irritated.

"Did you make this decision on your own, without asking your wife?" asked Eva's father.

"Exactly, did you make this decision without asking me first?" asked Eva in an uncertain tone.

"Why did you make this decision without asking your wife?" Eva's mother replied in a penetrating tone.

With some tension caused by the situation that had arisen, David turned to his wife and asked firmly, "Darling, don't you want to stay in Canada while we still have work there?"

"Of course I do. But I just want to ask you one thing: 'Tell your mother about this decision alone. I can't take any more stress today."
Eva's family accepted her decision with a heavy heart. What alternative did they have? They both had to work, and with the economic crisis in Spain, they had no choice. Determined and ready, David drove to his mother's house after breakfast, while Eva looked for an excuse to leave the house.
Arriving at the first payphone, she began to dial Valentin's mobile number. After five unsuccessful attempts, she was about to hang up when he answered before the last ring. Deeply moved, Eva couldn't say a word.
"Hello? Eva, darling, is that you?" he asked.
"I'm so sorry," she sighed. "I'm so sorry I can't be with you."
"I know. It's a terrible situation. An indescribable pain, but it's not your fault you can't be here."
"How is your mom coping? It must be terrible for her too."
"My mom is a strong woman. You know, my parents have been in a difficult situation since my father's accident."
"I would give anything to be close to you now. I was at the airport when the news came on. It was the worst thing that ever happened to me; there was nothing I could do."

"The funeral will take place in four days, on his 65th birthday. I don't think the fall was an accident; it was a decision he made. He had no quality of life and was very lonely and restricted in his last years. He had withdrawn from everything," he sighed.

"It's so terribly sad that I can't find the words to comfort you for this terrible loss."

"The fact that you called me is already a great comfort to me. It does me good to hear your voice. I wish I could have you with me forever."

"You will," she confirmed in a confident voice.

"You seem sure of what you're saying right now."

"Yes, I am. David announced today that he wants to stay in Canada forever."

"How did this decision come about?"

"There's hardly any work here now because of the economic crisis, so he wants to stay in Canada."

"What I'm about to say isn't nice, but bless this crisis that brought you to me."

"How about I call you every two or three days?"

"Yes, please, that would make me very happy," he asked.

Eva had to interrupt her conversation with Valentin as her mobile phone rang insistently.

"Darling, you don't have to wait for me today. After the news about our stay in Canada, my mother collapsed and ended up in the hospital again." David said resignedly.

"Well, I didn't expect anything else from her. That's why I didn't come."

"I'm going to stay at my parents' house tonight to keep my father company. If that's OK with you, I'll see you tomorrow for breakfast."

When she got home, Eva's parents showed her the itinerary for their planned stay in Canada.

"Look, this will be our first Christmas in Canada," Eva's mother pointed out.

"Mum, are you serious?"

"Yes, we're sure. Aren't we, Federico?"

"Absolutely!"

"And what does Carmen say?"

"Well, to be honest, she kind of made us do it," Federico replied with a twinkle in his eye.

In the middle of the conversation with her parents, Eva remembered that they still had to sort out the matter of the house because the tenants still didn't know what was coming; they hadn't been informed of the decision to "live in Canada for the rest of their lives." After all, she and her family had only known about it for a few hours.

"Surprise!" exclaimed David as he handed Eva a bag of fresh churros.

"I'm sorry, I was so engrossed in my favourite book that I didn't hear you come in. How come you're back so early?"

"You know my mom by now, don't you? Well, the doctors at the hospital... have already done that, so she was discharged early."

"And you brought me churros to celebrate?"

"Well, to sweeten the rest of the evening," he replied, taking the book from her hand.

"At other times you've sweetened my days in other ways, or do I have the wrong memory?" she asked in a seductive tone for him.

"The churros are just to fortify you before the performance," he pointed out in a joking tone.

"Do I need to worry? Remember, we're not alone in the house."

"I thought of that too; in fact, I brought tape to cover your mouth."

"Come on, really? Let me see..." she asked sceptically.

He promptly opened the bag, took out a cloth eye mask, a scarf, and a roll of tape, and laid them on the bed.

"If you analyse the contents of the bag, it's not hard to see what you're getting at. But you're not really going to tape my mouth shut, are you?" She asked in a slightly worried tone.

But David grabbed the second bag and pulled out the contents. A cardboard box. Then he took the tape and put it on the desk with the package. Amused, they looked at each other and laughed in the unique harmony of a couple who have known each other for years.

Ready for action, he put the mask on her, and while she sat on the bed, he tied her hands with the scarf.

"Remember that my mother has the hearing of a cat; she can also hear the vibrations of the neurones in the brain when she needs to.".

But David didn't care at that moment; he kissed his wife gently on the neck and unbuttoned her dress. Now she couldn't let go completely; she couldn't even use her hands because he had tied them up, so her husband was in control of the game.

He hastily slipped his hands into the half-opened dress and gently stroked the naked skin.

"Mmhh, you're not wearing a bra," he whispered in an excited tone.

After a few minutes, Eva gave in to a little lovemaking and kissed him on the mouth while he ran his hands all over her. Passionately grabbing her, he kneeled down, pulled up her dress, and kissed her gently on her pubic mound.

A soft moan escaped her mouth.

"Boys, dinner's ready!" called Eva's mother just inches from the door.

"Did you lock the door?" whispered Eva in panic, but David shook his head no.

"We're coming!" Eva replied.

How long had Marion been behind the door? Because

When they left the room, she was standing right in front of them, looking at them with a question mark on her face. Unconcerned, they looked at each other and laughed out loud.

"Why are you laughing?" Eva's mother asked, irritated.

"Nothing," Eva replied and made her way to the kitchen.

As the surprise of the day, one that would spoil more than one person's appetite, David decided to make an important announcement, so he tapped the glass with his knife to get attention and cleared his throat before making the important announcement. But Eva was already looking at him with concern.

"My mother had another nervous breakdown after I told her about the decision to stay in Canada. This time, when she arrived at the hospital, a psychologist was waiting for her, which was very positive for all of us. After she was discharged, she decided to join us in Canada for Christmas. Apparently, the psychologist advised her to enjoy life and say goodbye to the drama forever.".

"¡Santa María del Camí!" shouted Marion, making the sign of the cross.

"Wow, incredibly exciting; yes, I mean incredible; do you think so too?" asked Eva with a mischievous giggle.

"Come on, it's not that wild; I was expecting something worse," said Eva's father.

"Federico, what are you talking about? It's enough to ruin Christmas!"

"Mum!" Eva scolded.

Now dinner had turned into a gossip session, and Eva and David could hardly wait to get back to their room and enjoy some peace and quiet. But Marion had her next question ready: "When are you going to make us grandparents?"

"Mum, what do you say we tidy up the kitchen first and then go to our room? We don't want to shoot all our bullets in one day." Eva suggested, trying to change the subject.

"Alright, you can go to your room; I'll take care of the kitchen."

Once in the room, Eva remembered the appointment with the tenants for the next day and tried to talk to David about it, but he had picked up the mask and scarf again and was heading for the door to lock it.

"Let's pick up where we left off with your mother," he whispered, pulling the mask back over her eyes.

The next day, before talking to the tenants, the two decided to drop in on David's parents. David's mother was in an unusually good mood and invited them in for some fresh lemonade.

"Dear Eva, I think you're a bit thin; isn't the air in Canada good for you?" asked Leonor in a semi-sarcastic tone.

"The air in Canada? Actually it is; that's why your son decided to stay there," she replied ruthlessly.

"Darling, have you checked your watch? We have a meeting in a minute. I think we should get going," David said, deliberately interrupting the conversation between his mother and Eva.

"But how? You've only just arrived!"

"Yes, Mum, and we have to go; our tenants are waiting for us."

"What do you think about having lunch together tomorrow?" David's father asked politely.

"We'd love to," Eva replied, and they headed for the door.

In the car, on the way to talk to the tenant, Eva noticed a certain nervousness in David.

"Is something wrong, darling? I saw you abruptly stop talking to your mother."

"What choice did I have? You could see how it would end. I know my mother."

"Well, mothers-in-law all seem the same."

"What do you know about mothers-in-law after having the same one for decades?"

"Female intuition just..."

When Eva arrived at the house, she was overcome with emotion. The tenants are also quite nervous because this is the big day when they will find out if they will be allowed to live in this beautiful house for the long term. Everyone seemed nervous except David, who seemed to have gotten used to the idea of not having to live there anymore and remained quite calm.

"Your house seems to have brought us luck; I'm pregnant," Mrs. Martinez reveals before Eva and David can say anything.

"Really? What wonderful news!" says Eva enthusiastically.

"Then you'll probably want to stay longer, won't you?" asked David.

"If you don't mind... Yes, we would," Mrs. Martinez replied in a shy voice.

"And how long would you like to stay?"

"As long as possible!" the tenants replied simultaneously.

"Well, we were expecting a different kind of conversation today, as you originally only gave us a six-month lease. If I'm not being too indiscreet, I'd like to ask them why they're giving us the opportunity to stay longer," added Mr. Martinez.

"Simply because we are going to be in Canada indefinitely for professional reasons, and we are very happy to know that our home is in good hands," David pointed out.

After talking to the tenants, David and Eva decided to go into town to get something to eat. The idea of going straight back to Eva's parents' house didn't appeal to David at all, and he'd been wanting to get a haircut for days. Among the many restaurants in the centre of Barcelona, the new sushi place was very popular with young people, so the two decided to eat there.

"How does it feel for you to be back here, at home in our home country?" asked Eva, curious to know the answer, as they waited for their food.

"To be honest, I didn't think it would affect me so much."

"Are you serious?"

"Absolutely."

"Wow, your answer shocked me a bit. What about your parents? You're an only child; they're not going to live forever; have you thought about that?"

"Of course I've thought about it. Is that a reason to feel guilty and cling to your parents?"

"I didn't mean you should cling to your parents, but I didn't think you were capable of feeling so disconnected."

"The way we feel changes with age, don't you think?"

"No. I think the way we feel is part of our basic make-up and therefore part of our character. What changes, in my opinion, is who we feel what for.

"It gets complicated. I'd rather go to the hairdresser, and as I don't have an appointment, it might be late.".

"No problem, I'll go shopping then; I'm looking forward to it."

David's superficiality in some of their conversations had come to the fore recently. Or did Eva perhaps attach more importance to the way he expressed himself?

The time alone in David's absence was an opportunity to hear her beloved Valentin, so she pushed aside all thoughts of David's character and ran to the first free payphone, inserted the coins, and dialled Valentin's number. After only three rings, a woman's voice answered.

"Hello? Who is this?" said the voice on the other end of the phone.

Uncertain about the woman's voice and whether she had dialled the right number, she interrupted the call.

But after checking that the number was correct, she repeated the call.

"Eva, darling, is that you?" Valentin asked overjoyed.

"Who was the woman who answered the phone earlier?" She asked without hesitation.

"Just my secretary."

"You mean the secretary everyone's talking about?" She asked with a hint of jealousy in her voice.

"Well, I only have one secretary; luckily, my mother hasn't had time to deal with any other attacks on me."

"Yes, and that one is enough to cause enough trouble."

"My heart belongs only to you; you know that," he pleaded in an affectionate tone.

Now the affectionate tone was not convincing enough to appease the jealousy of a young woman with southern fire.

"What's she doing with you when you're busy with the funeral arrangements?" She returned in an uncertain voice.
"The answer is simple; you're not here. And someone has to take care of the organization. There was an important meeting with Algata Pharma in Toronto in a few days, and it had to be postponed. There were also other clients to attend to. What happened to my father has shaken us all.".
"I'm so sorry; I didn't mean to make you feel bad at such a difficult time. Please forgive me."

"Please remember: if anyone is capable of feeling jealous, it's me. You are there with your husband, while I have to bear my pain here alone," he replied bitterly.

As expected, Eva began to cry. Her emotions were on a rollercoaster, and the distance made it harder for her to control herself.

"It's not fair," she sighed.
"The whole thing isn't fair; you meet the love of your life, and she's married to someone else."
Suddenly the conversation was interrupted by a knock on the phone box. Carmen, Eva's sister, stood there waving. Eva hurriedly said goodbye to Valentin, wiped away her tears, and left the phone booth.
"What are you doing in a phone box? Don't you have your mobile phone with you? And why are you crying?" Carmen asked insistently.

But before Eva could answer her sister's question, the mobile phone in her pocket began to ring. With a sense of foreboding, she looked at the display and saw Valentin's number. After a moment's hesitation, she quickly put the phone back in her pocket without answering the call.

"Eva Maria Fernanda Rodriguez, will you tell me what's going on? Why were you crying, and where is your husband?" asked Carmen, irritated.

"The mobile phone had no reception, so I used the old-fashioned phone booth."

"Yes, I saw the old-fashioned phone box, but I also saw your tears. Who was at the other end of the phone?"

"What is this interrogation about? I'm your big sister, and I don't owe you any explanations."

"Are you serious? Your answer makes me even more aware that I do owe you an explanation."

"Bitch alert!" a voice shouted from behind them.

Deep in conversation, Eva and Carmen didn't notice David standing behind them.

"What are you doing here already?" asked Eva, surprised to see her husband again so soon.

"The hairdressers weren't busy, maybe because it's lunchtime; lucky me. By the way, I've been trying to reach you; why don't you answer?"

"I've been having problems with my mobile. That's exactly what I was trying to tell my sister when you interrupted us. Didn't you, Carmen?"

Annoyed, Carmen looks at her sister and shrugs as if to say, If you say so....

When she arrived at her parents' house, Eva locked herself in the bathroom to check the missed calls on her mobile. She was surprised to find that Valentin had sent her a message for the first time since they had met. It was he who had advised her not to put herself in danger by writing messages that could be forgotten and discovered. Out of this fear, she even saved Valentin's phone number under the name Dolores.

"My heart belongs to you. I love you," were the only words in the text message that broke the rules.
"And mine is yours. I love you," she wrote back, then deleted all the messages.

The next morning, Eva got up early to bake a cake for David's parents' lunch and bumped into Carmen in the kitchen packing her bag for university. A quick glance out the window revealed her parents working peacefully in the garden.
"Tell me, Eva, does David treat you well? I mean, is he a good husband?"
"Are you starting again? I thought you wanted to be a foreign language teacher, not a detective. What's with all the questions?"
"I don't know; I don't see you as happy. Your husband has always been strange, the typical only child."
"David is a good husband; now hurry up and go to university before it is too late."

Carmen's curiosity began to worry Eva. But her mother-in-law's lunch was far worse than her sister's curiosity. She couldn't afford to go empty-handed, so she turned on the radio, found a Latin station, and started mixing the cake. But while she was preparing the dough, she was interrupted by a text message.
"You don't know how much I want to kiss you."
Her heart started beating fast at the mere sight of the message, and she replied immediately:
"We touch each other with thoughts and words. But to feel it with your skin is a completely different feeling. I miss you."
"Great, now I want you even more," came back.

But the romance is suddenly interrupted by the oven alarm: The temperature for baking the cake has been reached. As if that weren't enough, David came into the kitchen and showed her the clock on the wall. She was horrified to see that there was only an hour until lunchtime, so she rushed to finish the dough and put it in the oven while David jumped in the shower. Then she picked up her phone again and rushed to text:

"I want you too; you can't imagine how much. I'll text you later. Love you."

Were they getting more and more careless?

The table at her parents' house was already festively laid when Eva placed the still-warm cake on the table and waited for her mother-in-law's reaction, which was not long in coming.

"The still warm cake might ruin my table.".

Of course, this was not the reaction Eva had hoped for.

"Come on, Mum, Eva held it on her lap on the way over, and it didn't burn her. Look, it's only lukewarm. Please take it easy; we just want to have a nice day together."

David's father, who was in charge of the drinks, waved from the kitchen to announce that drinks could be served, but when his wife turned her back on him, and he poured a few drops of cordial into her glass from the small bottle he was holding.

"Let's have a toast; here are the glasses. ¡Salud!"

"¡Salud!" and they all raised their glasses.

"Why is there only fruit juice in my glass?" asked Leonor, irritated.

"You know, Leonor, I think the doctors in A&E are very nice, and since they know us pretty well by now, I don't want them to get a bad impression of us, and that could happen if our visits there became the order of the day. Alcohol is known to exacerbate certain problems... don't you think?"

Leonor looked at her husband with little enthusiasm, walked into the kitchen without further ado, and began to carry the food into the dining room.

"Unbelievable, Mum, so many delicacies; you've really outdone yourself this time. Why did you go to all this trouble? There are only four of us; you could have made something simple without trying too hard," David praised.
"No problem; I was happy to do it. Besides, you can make it up to me at Christmas when we come over for ten days.
"You mean when you come to Canada to a nice hotel and we invite you to stay with us, don't you?" asked David, perplexed.

"Would you be able to let your beloved mother sleep in a hotel for ten days in a foreign country?" she asked in a slightly raised tone.

Everyone looked at each other as Leonor suddenly left the table and walked nervously into the kitchen.
"Laonor, why don't you come to the table? What the hell are you doing in the kitchen?"
"I forgot to take my blood pressure pill today; I've got a tingling sensation in my head; I feel like I'm going to faint," she replied, falling to the floor.

Right on time, and with every conflict, Leonor fainted as soon as she didn't like something and ended up in the hospital.

With a resigned look on his face, David's father waved from the hospital parking lot. His sadness was visible from a distance.

"Your mother has already reacted like this to what you told her to put pressure on us. She's a mean woman. I feel so sorry for your father; he's living a life without any good moments, just full of stress and worry. Poor man. Don't even think about bringing your mom here for ten days at Christmas, or I'll file for divorce,' Eva said irritably.

"You talk as if your mom is better off."

"Don't compare my mother with your dysfunctional mother."

Wow, what had happened to Eva? She had never dared to talk to her husband like that before, especially not about his mother. Well, it seems that two scary mothers-in-law, one in Canada and one in Barcelona, had managed to open the valve, so the evening ended with some distance between David and Eva.

The next morning, Eva noticed that David had left the house early, which probably meant that his mother was still in the hospital. And that was good for her, mean as it may sound, because it was the day of Valentin's father's funeral, and she wanted nothing more than to be close to him, no matter what. But after sending him several messages that went unanswered, she decided to go to the phone box. When she arrived, this time she made sure her sister Carmen wasn't there before putting in the coins. Desperate, she tried and tried to reach him. To no avail.

The day passed with no news from Valentin. A thousand thoughts ran through her mind, but the most plausible was that he was torn apart by grief at his father's departure. The thought of knowing him in mourning filled her heart with pain.

David, meanwhile, decided to spend the night at his parents' house to keep his father company. Strangely, the doctors had decided to keep Leonor an extra day to carry out neurological tests. The stay in Barcelona turned into a nightmare for Eva and David.

During the night, Eva kept checking to see if Valentin had replied to her messages. To no avail. Fearing that Valentin was in emotional distress, she spent a sleepless night. But at dawn, still half asleep, she heard her phone vibrate. At last!

It was a message from David:
"During the night, my father was taken to the emergency room by ambulance. I didn't want to wake you. Unfortunately, he had a small heart attack. I think he's suffering from all the stress my mother has caused him. You're right, my mom is a difficult woman. I'm sorry I reacted inappropriately yesterday when you tried to make me understand."

In the chaos of emotions, Eva immediately called her husband back, realising that she had to support him in this difficult situation.

"How is your father? It breaks my heart to know that he couldn't take the stress in the end."
"Me too. He always took care of all of us; it's not fair that it turned out like this."
"And how is it going with your mom?" Is she leaving the hospital today?"
"Fortunately not. I know it's selfish of me to say this, but my father needs to rest now. She'll be moved to a therapy and rehabilitation unit for people with mental health problems. She will be able to visit my father once a day, but only when accompanied by a nurse."
"I think this is very positive news, and I'm sure the doctors have made the right decision in her case. I'll get changed and come straight to you."

Another day passed with no news from Valentin.
On top of that, David's parents were hospitalised, adding to the emotional strain. The days in Barcelona were no walk in the park;

Eva's family was also caught up in the stress; the word holiday became just a verb, just theory, because there was no time for practice.

Five days before leaving for Canada, David's father was finally released. One of his father's cousins came from Portugal to support him, as Leonor had to stay in the psychiatric ward for another 10 days. It was a dramatic situation for David. It seemed as if the whole system was collapsing around them and they could do nothing about it.

Since Valentin hadn't called back, Eva decided to call him and took the opportunity to find a phone box while David was with his father. When she got to the phone box, she tried to call him, but quickly realised that his phone was switched off and there was no connection.

Why had Valentin turned off his mobile? Had something happened to him? Or had he met another woman who would always be by his side?

Desperate, Eva fought back tears and left the phone box to head for her parents' house.

Lost in thought on her way home, she suddenly heard a car honking. Her father pulled up beside her and opened the car door.

"Do you want to get in?" he asked, then looked at her again: "Darling, what happened? You look so sad."

She was finally allowed to let her tears flow freely. No one could give her more security than her father, the stable and loving pillar of her family.

"The holiday is coming to an end; we're leaving in a few days, and I'm more exhausted than when I arrived. These days have been incredibly stressful for all of us," she sighed.

In view of Eva's emotional state, Federico stopped on the hard shoulder and took his daughter in his arms.

"I know that, darling, and I can see it, even if you don't say anything. I understand you even in silence. You can tell me everything if you want, but I already know how you feel."

"There are so many things that add up to an indescribable amount. I will miss you so much. Promise me you'll come and see me before Christmas."

"I promise."

The last two days before her departure flew by. Between visits to the hospital and helping out at David's parents' house, Eva had very little time to spend with her family. The only thing she found time and space for were the thoughts that had plagued her for days. What had happened to Valentin? Why had he turned off his mobile?

With an emptiness in their hearts, Eva and David stood with their family at Barcelona airport; only David's mother was missing, a blessing for all present. Carmen, who had made sure there was enough food and reading material for the journey, had started to leaf through an international edition of a magazine.

"Stop! Turn back two pages, please!" David ordered as Carmen continued to leaf through the newspaper.

But David noticed the name of his Canadian employer, RITEL Pharmaceutica, and insisted that Carmen turn the page back. After some tugging and pulling, the newspaper fell to the floor, right on the page David was interested in, revealing the revealing picture.

Visibly amused, he picked up the paper and turned to Eva:

"Darling, look, isn't that our junior boss, Mr. 'I know all our employees pants', in an intimate pose with his new dynamite secretary?"

Chapter 6 Stranger kissed?

"Pssttt, hey Eva, over here... Come here," a soft voice called from behind the lift.

Attracted by the familiar voice, she craned her neck to get a better look at who was hiding around the corner. But her heart suddenly stopped.

"You bastard!" she whispered, slapping his chest hard as he pulled her close and sealed her mouth with a kiss.

"Please come with me and let me explain everything," Valentin pleaded.

Silently, he led her behind the lift, where there was a special door that led to an area of the company that Eva didn't know about, a kind of secret passageway. From there, they stood in front of a staircase that led to another metal door in the lower part of the building.

"Where are you taking me? Your mom will be the first to give me trouble if I don't get to the office on time."

"My mom will be out of town for a fortnight to mourn her loss; now I'm your boss, and I'm ordering you to follow me."

"What if I don't want to?"

Without further discussion, Valentin opened the metal door that led to an underground housing complex.

"Is this a bunker?"

He nodded silently and looked at her with a fiery gaze before pulling her close and kissing her again. Still angry at the events of the past few days, she tried to push him away, but he lifted her up and pressed her back gently against the wall.

With their bodies touching, Eva lost control and surrendered to the magic and alchemy that only he could make her feel. Full of longing, she looked up at him and wrapped her arms around his neck. Lips to lips, breath to breath, they touched, looked at each other, and kissed with fervour and passion. With a little impetus, he pushed her against the wall, held her thighs with his hands, and made her feel all his desire. A moan escaped Eva's mouth.

Strong hands touching every inch of her skin, warm breath, and a voice whispering loving words. Every inch of her skin trembled at his touch. Sensuality shone in her eyes, her mouth seductive, her gaze full of passion. They both moaned with pleasure, letting themselves be drawn into a magical game, the game of two bodies melting together in love.

"Do you have any questions for me?" He asked after gently kissing her eyelids.

"You bet I have questions for you! Apart from the fact that you've had your mobile phone switched off for days, which has caused me a lot of worry, there's also the fact that you're having an affair with your secretary, and it's all over the papers!" She shouted angrily.

He silently placed his hand on the back of her neck and gently pulled her towards him until their lips touched and melted together.

"Anything else?" he asked.

"Are you kidding me? I expect an answer to my questions.".

"Would you believe me if I told you that my mobile phone had broken down and that I hadn't been able to buy a new one in my grief? Look at this mobile phone. It's not the one I had before and that you knew about. I only found the time to buy it yesterday.".

Sceptical, she picked up the phone and searched for her name in the contact list until a grin lit up her face when she realised that her contact was stored under "Eva, my amor." Satisfied, she looked at him and handed the phone back to him.

"What about the photo of you and your secretary, taken from behind, while she put her hand on your shoulder and kissed you on the cheek? That was at your father's funeral, wasn't it?"

"Yes, that's right. But there was no kiss, although it looked like there was from the position the photo was taken. As she couldn't shout at me during the funeral, she just tapped me on the shoulder and whispered in my ear to tell me that more wreaths had arrived, that it wasn't clear who they were from, and that she didn't know whether to accept them or not. The journalists immediately made it the story of the year. My heart belongs only to you; you are the woman of my life, and I will wait for the moment when we can finally be together.".

Overjoyed at what he had told her, she held him close and whispered, "I've missed you so much; I can't imagine life without you.

After a great start to the day, the accumulated workload in the office seemed easy to manage, even though Eva's desk was full of papers and documents of all kinds. While Valentin managed his appointments, she had to sort and prioritise them.

However, the request from the client, Algata Pharma, for a meeting at short notice made her curious, especially as the appointment required the presence of Mrs. Leblanc or Valentin with the person who had accompanied him to the last meeting, i.e., Eva. This requirement left no room for any other option. But how could that work? Mrs. Leblanc had already prepared everything for this important meeting a few weeks before and had decided to leave Eva out, so she decided to contact Valentin in his office.

"Hello, this is the Ritel pharmaceutical company; Mrs. Oliveira is on the line; what can I do for you?"

After a few seconds of silence, Eva answered confidently:

"Good morning, Mrs. Oliveira, Nice to have you on the phone. I'm Mrs. Rodriguez, Mrs. Leblanc's secretary, remember?"

"Of course, what can I do for you?"

"I'd like to speak to Mr. Leblanc; the client, Algata Pharma, has sent us a very specific request, and I need to clarify the terms with him."

"I have explicit instructions from Mrs. Leblanc to personally look after the foreign customers together with Mr. Leblanc."

"Yes, I can imagine that, but in this case it is different, and if we are not able to fulfil the request, Algata Pharma will not conduct any further negotiations with the pharmaceutical company Ritel. I can't believe that Mrs. Leblanc's motives go beyond her desire to work with a client of this calibre," Eva said, remaining silent as she heard Valentin's voice in the background, intrigued by this unusual conversation and wanting to know what it was all about.

"Mrs. Rodriguez is asking for you; it's about the client, Algata Pharma; what should I do?" Mrs. Oliveira asked Valentin.

"Have the client's request sent to my email address immediately and thank Mrs. Rodriguez; I'll take care of the rest," he replied.

Half an hour after Valentin had received the email, Mrs. Oliveira got back to Eva:

"Mrs. Rodriguez, you had prepared all the documents for the meeting with Algata Pharma in Toronto before you left for Barcelona. We know for a fact that Mrs. Leblanc will not be able to attend the meeting in Toronto as requested by the client. This client had full confidence in your recent representation in Mrs. Leblanc's absence, so please be prepared to travel to Toronto on Sunday evening and return on Tuesday.".

"But does Mrs. Leblanc agree to this?"

"We have no choice; those are the terms."

When she arrived at the canteen, Eva looked for the table where David and his colleagues were having lunch.

But when she found the table, she noticed that the three of them were having a lively conversation instead of enjoying their meal.

After looking around a bit, she had no trouble understanding what they were talking about, because a few tables away were Valentin with his secretary and Valentin's driver, Mr. Bonelli.

"So, boys, how are you today? How's the food?"

"Hey Eva, we haven't started eating yet; we wanted to wait for you," Steven replied.

"Did you really wait for me? To what do I owe this honor?" she asked ironically.

"Actually, the boys were wondering how our junior boss's new secretary had managed to get him through the days of mourning because she never left him alone for a moment," David whispered.

"Aha, I see, boys-only topics. I'll probably have to eat my salad in the office. I don't want to get caught at a chat table. You know what I mean, don't you? My work is very important to me. I hope you have a good time."

"But... Come on, darling, wait, we were just having fun."

"See you later..." she waved and left the canteen.

But this time David picked up his plate and followed his wife.

"What are you doing there? Come on, go eat with your colleagues," she said calmly.

"What will my colleagues think of me if I let you go alone?"

"I don't know; you know them better than I do. They're your friends, aren't they?"

"Yes, they are. But I don't always agree with what they do or say. Today, for example, they went too far again with those newspaper articles in the office."

"What do you mean?"

David instructed Eva to get into the lift. When they arrived at Eva's office, they both sat down and unpacked their lunches.

"Aren't you going to tell me what your colleagues have done with the magazines?"
"Robin brought magazines summarising the events of the Leblanc family over the past two weeks."
"Well, Mr. Leblanc's death came as a surprise; it's normal for such news to cause a stir," she said.
"But it wasn't the only news that caused a stir."
"And what else?"
"The junior boss and his secretary in a familiar pose. They've been seen and photographed together several times; they're in practically every regional newspaper, and not just"
As if by remote control, Eva continued to chew on her lunch, swallowing bite by bite with a speed that was unusual for her.

What had Valentin been doing during the two weeks she had been away? Had he told her the whole truth about his secretary's role in the funeral arrangements? Was there more to it than he had told her? But David interrupted her thoughts.

"Darling, are you all right? You're eating so greedily, it seems like you haven't eaten for a week."
"Of course everything is fine. But do you see this mountain of work on my desk? This is serious business, not newspaper gossip. Don't get caught gossiping about such things in the company. I think the consequences would be bitter."
"Yes, I can imagine," he replies, packing up the leftovers.

During the afternoon, Eva dealt with one request after another. But then Valentin sent her a text message.

"I want you!"

Not thrilled with what she had been told today, she decided not to reply and continued working.

After half an hour of silence, another text arrived: "And you? Do you want me too?"

With a slight change of heart, she looked at the message, took a deep breath, and simply put the phone down.

If a Canadian thought he could ingratiate himself with an angry Latina with a few nice words, then he had no understanding of other cultures, Eva thought to herself, then looked at the message again, put the phone down, and went back to work.

Regardless of the fact that Valentin had Mexican roots on his father's side, with genetic links going back to the fifth generation, Eva decided to teach him a lesson by ignoring the message. Still, the whole thing made his blood boil enough that he showed up at her office.

"Why don't you answer my texts? I saw you leaving the canteen in a hurry at lunchtime." What's going on?"

"You tell me, I'm sure there's more to tell than what you told me this morning. That kiss with your secretary wasn't a kiss. And all those other pictures in the regional magazines? Were they also fake kisses, caresses, or other things you're hiding from me?"

"Have you gone completely mad? I've never kissed Mrs. Oliveira or done anything else that has nothing to do with my work or organising my father's funeral. And you must believe me, I only love you!"

"Then how is it possible that there are all these pictures of you?"

"I don't know yet, but my faithful chauffeur, Mr. Bonelli, is helping me to find out. That's why we were all sitting together in the canteen earlier."

Valentin took Eva's hands lovingly, brought them to his lips, and kissed them. "Please believe me," he said afterwards.
"Tell me about the bunker, why it was built, and who knows about it?"
"You know, some companies here in Canada have a high-security bunker. It was built before my parents joined the company. Only my parents, Mr. Bonelli, and you know about it."
"How can you blindly trust a chauffeur?"
"Mr. Bonelli is more than just a boss; he's like a father to me. He has been with me since before I could tie my shoes. I've known him all my life; he's always been my personal chauffeur. When I came home from school, he was waiting for me when my parents didn't have time to pick me up. He is faithful and loyal, as a father should be to his children."
The ringing of the phone interrupted their conversation, and a quick glance was enough to see that the call was from Valentin's office.

"Mrs Rodriguez, I'm sorry to disturb you, but I can't find Mr. Leblanc. I assume he went to see you because I found the Algata Pharma papers on his desk. The meeting on the second floor starts in 10 minutes; I was told the client had already arrived.".
"Yes, he was here briefly, but he's already left, probably for the boardroom."
Valentin gave her a quick kiss on the forehead and disappeared towards the lift.
This man was capable of making her feel the deepest form of love she had ever felt.

Their first kiss was the birth of a love she had never felt before—a form of trust she thought she could only feel towards her father, the only man who would never hurt her.

The empty childhood Valentin grew up in touched Eva deeply. She was sure that she would give her children all the love her heart could feel.

On the way home, Eva told her husband David that she had to leave for Toronto on Sunday afternoon. Surprised, David reacted calmly to the news.

"I'll be back on Tuesday afternoon, depending on the train schedule."

"Uii, storm-free days... Don't worry about me; the boys and I will find a way to pass the time."

"If you make sure the apartment doesn't get trashed, I'll give you the green light for a party," she said cheerfully.

"By the way, why is the junior boss content to take you with him and leave the grenade here in the office?" he asked.

"You're forgetting one small but important detail: the grenade is his secretary, but I am Mrs. Leblanc's right hand, the CEO of this company, and I know the needs of these clients, so I've prepared the documents for the meeting accordingly. The client has specifically written in the invitation that Mrs. Leblanc's presence, or mine, is desired. You'll probably have to deal with the grenade in the next few days.

"Uii, that will certainly make the boys happy," he said with a grin.

"How about you go and buy a few things for dinner, and I'll start sorting out the things we brought back from Barcelona? Some of our luggage still needs to be sorted."

I say, "Yes, that's perfect; it's still early, and we have time to do everything in peace. I'll drop you off and go to the shop."

Eva would never have thought it possible to appreciate the time she was allowed to spend alone at home without David. The time in

Canada brought them both to maturity. Even David, who all those years had wanted nothing more than a house and a job, found a passion in golf.

The next day there was so much work to do that Eva decided not to go to the canteen.

While looking through the files, she found a sealed letter addressed to the boss's secretary with no return address. Unsure whether it was addressed to her or to Mrs. Oliveira, she decided to leave the letter for Valentin, who had already sent a text message.

"What's more sensual than a kiss?"

"Two kisses," she replied.

"See you in the bunker in 20 minutes? I'm burning for you."

"Your share of Mexican chromosomes shows up at the most unexpected times. And what do I do with my work?"

"You're excused for an hour; put the meeting sign on the door."

Flattered by the invitation, Eva hurried into the lift and got off at the landing that led to the bunker. As she was about to knock on the door, she noticed Valentin standing behind it, waiting for her. But instead of greeting him, she immediately pressed the letter into his hand.

"What's this?" he asked.

"You'll find out," she replied, pulling his tie and planting her lips on his.

"How would you describe that kiss?" she asked.

"It's a kiss with a form of intensity I've never experienced with another woman, without doubt for me the most profound and intense ritual I've ever experienced."

"Wow. And this?" she asked, undoing his tie to kiss his neck.

He gently slid his hands under her skirt and said, "That makes me really hot."

Without wasting much time, they undressed each other and threw themselves into their passion.

When Eva returned to the office, she found a note on her desk from David saying that they had to leave the office on time today as they were meeting David's colleagues and their wives for dinner in the city.

Having sent the agenda for Monday's meeting to Algata Pharma, Eva was starting to work when her mobile phone rang.

"Where are your colleagues waiting for us again?"

"At the Tosca restaurant on the Ottawa River."

"The name makes it sound Italian."

"Yes, it is. Robin and Sila have something to celebrate; they're expecting their first child. Unexpected happiness for them; after seven years of marriage, they didn't think they'd ever have a child."

"Oh, there seems to be a pregnancy epidemic at the moment," she commented amusedly.

Arriving at the restaurant, they saw that the others were already seated at a table overlooking the river. A beautiful spot, even at dusk. But this harmonious picture was disturbed by the Hello magazine on the table.

"Well supplied with the latest gossip, eh?" asked Eva, pointing to the newspaper.

"Please take a seat so we can talk about the latest events," Sila asked as the waiter brought two more glasses of wine to the table.

"Have you heard about the latest events?" Sila asked curiously.

"That depends on what you're referring to," Eva replied.

"We're going to be parents," Sila said excitedly.

"To love and lots of children!" exclaimed Steven.

"How wonderful, you two! Finally some news that has nothing to do with the tabloids," Eva replied with some relief.

"Actually, there is some gossip to be had. See those two over there in the corner?" asked Steven as Robin slid the open newspaper under David and Eva's eyes and pointed to a particular page: "That woman is a journalist from Hello Magazine." The paper that's been publishing the Leblancs' entire lives for the past two weeks."

"Interesting. She's probably having dinner with her husband, like the rest of us," David commented.

"Take a good look at that man without him noticing. Don't you recognise him?" asked Steven.

"No," David replied.

"That's understandable; you're still very new to the company, and it's not easy to recognise him without his uniform. He's the driver for Mrs. Leblanc, the CEO of Ritel Pharma, our employer!" explained Steven, who has been with the team for 15 years.

"That could explain a lot... but never mind, let's enjoy the evening with this wonderful news about Robin and Sila," said Eva.

By the end of the evening, David had drunk so much that he was unfit to drive. Just like the other men at the table, who would have no chance of getting home without their wives.
On the unusually dark evening, Eva parked the car under the house. But when they arrived at the entrance to the building, David was so unsteady on his feet that Eva almost had to push him into the lift. In a

drunken stupor, he pressed all the buttons in the lift and began to laugh wildly as the lift came to a halt between floors.

"Have you gone completely mad? Can you believe we're stuck here?" She scolded, trying to press the right button to get the lift moving again.

"Stop it; I'm in the mood for sex right now," he said, pulling up her skirt.

"I'm telling you, you have gone completely mad. You smell of alcohol, and you can't stand it. How are you going to convince your friend to perform here in the lift? Let's get out of here as soon as possible; I'm about to lose it," she scolded angrily, pressing the button to go up.

As the weekend approached, Eva avoided distractions and picked up the pace in the office as the trip to Toronto loomed. The train tickets were already on her desk, and once again the trip had been booked for just one person. Her emotions did somersault at the mere thought of spending two nights alone with Valentin.

Would everything be as indescribably perfect as it had been six months ago? Sleeping in Valentin's arms for two whole nights and feeling his warmth and the scent of his skin already made her feel like she was in heaven on earth. Shaking her head vigorously, she tried to banish the thoughts that caused an immediate reaction in her body and continued with her work.

At home in the evening, David sought physical contact with his wife. She had avoided it completely since the incident in the lift.

"Can I know why you're avoiding me? Can we talk about it?" David asked, not beating around the bush.

"Well, your drunken behaviour in the lift disgusted me; I'm not used to seeing you like that."

"You could have laughed about it, don't you think?"

"Maybe, but I couldn't. Still, there's no need to be offended."
"Maybe you're right, and it's the stress of work right after the holidays that's making me overreact. Shall we go and have a bath?"

"Yes, but only if you give me a good foot massage."

He hugged her tenderly and kissed her on the lips. In spite of her husband's gentle nature, Eva was beginning to have problems sharing intimate moments with him; her love for Valentin was taking up more and more space in her heart, in her soul, and in her life. This man had become an indispensable necessity that could no longer be repressed. The idea of having to belong to two men aroused unpleasant feelings in her, but she was aware that she had to fulfil her duty as a wife, at least until she could find a way to devote herself solely to the man who had taken her heart, Valentin.

At midday on Sunday, David and Eva waited on the platform of Ottawa station for the train to Toronto. Around them was a chaotic crowd in the midst of summer holiday fever.
"I hope your boss has reserved a seat for you, because it's going to be impossible to find a free seat with this crowd," David said, perplexed.
"Yes, of course, in first class."
"Why couldn't you have travelled with the junior boss? They say in the company that he only travels by helicopter."
"You're forgetting one little detail: I'm just a secretary. Besides, I'm not interested in being the next one to get involved in a scandal and end up on the front page of the newspapers."
"You're right, let's leave the exclusives to the grenade; maybe one day the two of them will really get together," David pointed out amusedly.
"I've noticed that you and your colleagues seem to enjoy making fun of them, so much so that you haven't noticed that my train has already arrived. Would you like to help me get on?"

During the train ride, Eva thought back to the last time she had been in Toronto, all their shared experiences still fresh in her mind, as if there had been no interruption between then and now. But suddenly a message on her mobile phone interrupted her reverie.

"I can hardly wait to explore your body... to unlock its deepest secrets and drive it mad... the intoxicating smell of your skin, the sound of your voice, everything makes my desire for you vibrate."

This man had always known how to twist her mind.
He was the only one who could touch her and make her feel it without being there.

"I feel like this ride will last forever. It's impossible to resist when this passion invades your heart and mind."

"My chauffeur, Mr. Bonelli, will be waiting for you at Toronto station. From now on, you will only travel with him."
"Why did you take your chauffeur? Something tells me it's not good."
"We'll talk about it when you get here. Mr. Wilson will call me in ten minutes. I love you."

Accompanying Mr. Bonelli on this business trip to Toronto meant that Valentin could no longer trust anyone. Eva knew him so well by now that she realised there could only be one serious reason for him to take this step.

When Eva arrived at the station, she immediately recognised Mr. Bonelli in the crowd and approached him. He kindly took her suitcase and politely asked her to follow him.

"May I ask what's going on? What are you doing in Toronto?" Eva asked anxiously.

"Mr. Leblanc will explain everything to you calmly."

"May I ask where your name comes from? Looking at you, I would say you have Mexican roots; could that be it?" She asked, trying to change the subject.

"Yes, that's right. I'm a full-blooded Mexican!"

"Fine. Let's just talk in Spanish," she asked.

"We can always talk in Spanish; that would make me very happy."

"Do you have a family, I mean a wife and children?"

"Well, it's complicated to explain... Can you see the hotel? We'll be right there; Mr. Le Blanc is waiting for you," he replied, quickly ending the conversation.

This time, all we had to do was show our ID at the reception, and we were escorted straight to our suite. Soft lighting, a beautifully laid table, and candlelight awaited them in the dining room. Valentin was waiting for her in the dim light, and when she arrived, he approached her, kissed her hand, and charmingly led her to the table.

"Please sit down; the hours of waiting have been unbearable."

"Aren't you going to kiss me first?" she asked, pursing her lips.

"No. I mean, yes, but you'd better not; otherwise, we won't eat anything tonight, or rather, I'll just eat you."

"Those delicacies on the table are calling me; can you hear them? The kiss and everything else can wait," she said with a grin.

After leading her to the table, Valentin went to his seat opposite and uncovered the trolley next to the table. What was on the table was only part of what was planned for dinner. She watched in amazement; never before had she been served so many delicacies all at once.

"Are we expecting anyone else?" she asked at the sight of all this goodness.

"No, that's all for us; the evening has only just begun."

"Would you like to tell me why Mr. Bonelli is here? Did you know he's Mexican and speaks fluent Spanish?"

"Do you remember the letter you gave me a few days ago? I have reason to believe that someone in the company is selling information to journalists."

"Do you think there's a mole? What did the letter say, and to which of the two secretaries was it addressed? To me or to Mrs. Oliveira?"

"To the person who would be willing to sell information about my family. The letter came from a well-known press house, HelloMagazine.".

Suddenly Eva became pensive. Was it a coincidence that the head of Ritel Pharma and a journalist from Hellomagazin were sitting together in the Tosca restaurant?

"Darling, is something wrong?" he asked.

"I don't know if it's a coincidence, but a few days ago, when we were having dinner with David's colleagues, we saw one of your drivers sitting confidentially with a journalist in the same restaurant. Now I understand it's your mother's driver. David's colleagues, who have worked for you for more than ten years, recognised him.".

Valentin is stunned by this information. Is there really a mole in the company who has been spying on the Le Blanc family for years? An inconspicuous person waiting for the right moment to reveal who knows what news? Or are several people conspiring against a family that has managed to remain scandal-free for years?

"Let's not talk about it tonight; I'll deal with it as soon as I get back to the office. Let's drink to our love. To the crazy feelings you make me have. To you, the love of my life," he said.

Deeply moved by his words, she looked deeply into his eyes in silence, then got up, ran to him, took his face in her hands, and whispered, "I love you.".

United in an intimate embrace, they looked into each other's eyes in silence. They were both in a deep emotional phase that was growing stronger by the day. With the look of someone who knows what is about to happen, Valentin took his plate and cutlery from the table, sat Eva down on the table, spread her legs, and ran his exploring hands over her thighs, gently and seductively up to her garter belt. Then he gently bit her lower lip.

"The food is getting cold," she whispered with a soft moan.

But he put his hands on her hips and pulled her towards him until their passionate points made contact.

"What else do you want?" he whispered, biting her earlobe.

"Everything," she replied, pulling him even closer.

The next morning, Eva and Valentin were in the conference room very early, waiting for Mr. Wilson. Everything was perfectly prepared for the next successful milestone. They had barely put the last of the documents on the table when there was a knock at the door.

"It's a pleasure to see you again. Firstly, I would like to express my deepest condolences on the sudden loss of your beloved father."

"Thank you, and please excuse my mother for not being here in person," Valentin said.

"It's understandable that your mother can't be here, but don't worry; I have every confidence in you. I don't want to be indiscreet again, but you really are a lovely couple," said Mr. Wilson, addressing Valentin and Eva.

"Thank you; you and your wife are also," replied Valentin, referring to himself and his wife Mayer.

"Wait, are you really a couple now?" Mrs. Mayer asked curiously.

"We're just an efficient team. Aren't we, Mrs. Rodriguez?" asked Valentin.
"Absolutely!" agreed Eva.

But before they sat down at the table, Mrs. Mayer handed Eva an envelope that looked like an invitation or something and said, "We would be delighted to have you as our guests at our company party tonight. We have organised games, a barbecue, and a bonfire for our staff party. Dress casually, and you will mingle with the participants.".
"Will there be any journalists present?" asked Valentin.
"I understand your concern about that, but don't worry, the only journalist present won't be interested in you; he has a very specific schedule to follow and won't have time to pay attention to anything else. No one will know they are on our guest list. We look forward to welcoming them at 6 p.m.," said Mr. Wilson with a wink.

Back to the reason for the meeting, Mr. Wilson showed several graphs of the business performance over the last six months. In all the years that Ritel Pharmaceutical and Algata Pharma had worked together, they had never seen results like this. This was due to Valentin's embracing of other opportunities, as opposed to the old-fashioned way of negotiating that had remained true to his mother. As a young mind, he had opened up new horizons in this market and brought a breath of fresh air to the business with this customer. Sales had effectively doubled in the last six months.

"I was expecting good results, but these are excellent!" said a delighted Valentin.

"They really are! And thanks to your modern proposals. You have a flair for business like no one else in your family. I mean, your parents did a very good job in their time, but your ideas and drive are unique.".

"Does that mean you will remain loyal to us?" asked Valentin.

"If you promise me that I will only deal with them in the future, yes. Definitely yes."

The four of them looked at each other and clapped with joy. Who would have thought that the scion of the Leblanc family, who everyone thought was a mummy's boy, would be doing millions of dollars worth of business with one of the biggest pharmaceutical companies in the world?

"This event needs to be celebrated with a good bottle of champagne, so I hope you have a driver to take them back to the company." Valentin added.

"Of course, uncork the bottle at last!"

After an afternoon by the pool, Eva and Valentin drive to Algata-Pharma. Dressed to the nines and accompanied by their trusty chauffeur, Mr. Bonelli, they enter the company premises. What awaited them was something they had never seen before at a company event, at least not at a staff party. The company garden was divided into several areas and set up with group games of all kinds. From jumping rope, sack races, and boccia to piñatas and apples hanging in trees for blindfolded players to bite into. Fire bowls filled with wood were ready to be lit in the dark. There were barbecue stands with buffets and bar tables in many locations, a healthy way of showing gratitude to their staff and their families. Mr. Wilson and Mrs. Mayer, also dressed in jeans and T-shirts, mingled with the visitors.

"Welcome, let's have a drink and start the game!" called Mr. Wilson, patting Valentin on the back.
"Good idea, where shall we start?" asked Valentin.

"Let the ladies decide," he replied.

Excited by the choice, Eva and Mrs. Mayer had a quick look around and decided to start at the less crowded play areas, pointing to the sack race.

"That and skipping rope are the first games we need to start before our drink kicks in," Mrs. Mayer suggested amusedly.

"Absolutely, mon chéri," Mr. Wilson replied with a languorous look.

"I could imagine being your age and looking as much in love as you do. You make a wonderful couple," Eva said with a dreamy look.

"Let's start the game before we're overrun by alcohol," Valentin also suggested, to take our minds off the subject of love.

Between games and drinks, Mr. Wilson and his beloved Mrs. Mayer proved that they weren't just a well-rehearsed couple at work. Valentin seemed to be the only one who didn't know how to jump rope and sack race. An inexplicable fact for a young man like him.
"Valentin, you seem a bit clumsy. How do you explain that you forgot how to play at such a young age?" asked Mr. Wilson amusedly.

"Well, if I'm honest, it's the first time I've played; I didn't know all that."

Eva knew very well what Valentin was alluding to because he grew up alone, with little time with his parents and no opportunity to socialise with other children after school. Several times a week, his parents sent him from one class to another to keep him occupied. Education was more important than being a child. At his age, he spoke four languages perfectly, played the piano, and could do many other things that   most men his age could not.
His parents had literally invested in him. With a certain irony and having grasped the circumstances, Mr. Wilson suggested we move on to the next game.

"Now that the alcohol has taken effect, I suggest we play the game of hanging apples; what do you think?" Mr. Wilson countered.

"What's the game about?" asked Valentin.

"In this game, you face each other with your hands tied behind your back and blindfolded, and you try to bite into the hanging apple. They start first while we finish our drink," explains Mrs. Mayer.

In a row of 6 hanging apples and as many couples waiting to start the game, Eva and Valentin were placed opposite each other in row 3. One person blindfolded them, tied their hands, then stood next to them and held the apple until their lips touched it. At the whistle, the apple was released, and the pairs had to try to bite into it. The fight began blindfolded, but after several bites, the apple slipped to the side and Valentin's lips touched Eva's lips. They immediately forgot the point of the task, and instead of continuing to try to bite into the apple, the two lingered with their lips together until Valentin finally bit Eva's bottom lip, and the two began to kiss as if there was nothing else around them.

"To the two lovebirds in row 3: the game is over and you have been eliminated for failing to comply with the rules of the game, which state that players must bite into the apple and not the lips of their playing partners and make out uncontrollably. Hello, can you hear me?" said a loud voice over the microphone.

Still blindfolded and with their hands tied, Eva and Valentin paused for a moment, still half engrossed in their captivating kiss, just because someone had tapped Valentin on the shoulder.

"Well done, my boy, for not knowing how to play the game... Carry on!" said Mr. Wilson.

Chapter 7 Secrets

"Y ou can't lose him, do you understand?
"Do everything you can to save him!" shouted
Valentin as his chauffeur, Mr. Bonelli, was
resuscitated in a pool of blood.

"He's losing too much blood and has almost no pulse; his condition is extremely critical. We've called a helicopter to take him to the nearest hospital; he'll die if we don't give him a blood transfusion," replied the emergency doctor.

"Here, take my arm and connect it to my circulation immediately," Valentin ordered.

Desperate, Valentin sat down on the floor next to Mr. Bonelli and held his hand as he lay unconscious. With dexterity, the paramedic did exactly as Valentin had asked and prepared the necessary materials for the person-to-person blood transfusion when the helicopter arrived a few minutes later to take them both to Saint-Vincent Hospital.

"Ritel Pharmaceutical, this is Mrs. Rodriguez; what can I do for you?"
"Eva, darling, it's me; please sit down; I need to tell you something before the news spreads throughout the company," Valentin said exhaustedly on the other end of the phone.
"What's happened? You sound so different," she asked worriedly.
"Mr. Bonelli and I were on our way back from a meeting when there was a serious accident at the last motorway exit before entering the city. A truck rammed into us out of control. Mr. Bonelli reacted in a split second and managed to turn the car into the position in which

he was sitting, which saved my life. Now we don't know if he can be saved.".

"Is that why your mother left the office in such a hurry half an hour ago?"

"I didn't know that's why my mom left the office; I didn't see her here."

"I want to come to you right away!" she said in a voice choked with tears.

"You can't come here; it's crawling with journalists. I'm fine; don't worry, I'll be discharged soon.".

But the conversation is interrupted by a doctor who wants to speak to him urgently.

"Mr. Bonelli is in surgery; we need more blood; would you be willing to donate?"

"Yes, of course, but this is a hospital; don't you have any blood?"

"Yes, we have more than enough; it's a bit complicated to sort out, but Mr. Bonelli has quite a rare blood type; it's actually not very often that we have AB-negative patients. There is the possibility of having blood units brought to us, but that would take too long," the doctor said with a downcast look.

"I see, but why is my blood compatible with his?" (Valentin)

"I can't tell you that. We don't have much time; if we don't give him a transfusion, he won't survive the operation," the doctor replied, asking him to sit down.

"I am ready. Please start," Valentin said, stretching out his arm.

While the blood was being taken, the doctor cleared his throat several times and said to him, "Your mother has been here since you arrived. She's outside the operating theater in a protected area."

"My mother is waiting outside the theatre. Why wasn't she told I was here?"

"Your mother knows that you're here and that I'm with you. I'll leave as soon as we've taken the blood sample."

Valentin is a little confused now. Why did his mother go to see Mr. Bonelli first and not him? And why does his blood match Mr. Bonelli's? These are strange coincidences that leave room for many different scenarios.
"Excuse me, but have you contacted Mr. Bonelli's family and informed them that he is in a critical condition?" asked Valentin with interest.

"His family is already here. We'll be ready in a few minutes, and they can help their mother," the doctor replied, bowing his head.

Valentin was slowly approaching the operating theatre when he saw his mother crying from a distance.
When he reached her, he realised that she was crying from the bottom of her heart. He had never seen his mother like that, not even at his father's funeral. After the visit, the doctor left her alone and took the blood to the operating theatre.

"Mum, what's going on, and where is Mr. Bonelli's family?"

With despair written all over her face, she wiped away her tears, took Valentin's hand between hers, and whispered, "Well, we are his family. Please forgive me."

Valentin stood transfixed, unable to say a word, until a few minutes later when the doctor came out of the operating room with a satisfied smile and shook his hand.

"Miraculously, no vital organs were damaged in this terrible accident, and our colleagues managed to stop the bleeding. He also suffered numerous broken bones and had to be stitched up in several places; he lost a lot of blood, but we are optimistic that he will make it. We need to keep him in intensive care for the next 24 hours, but you can visit him later. Without your quick intervention at the scene of the accident, your father would not have survived."

"My father?" asked Valentin, surprised and confused at the same time.
"Yes, Valentin, Ricardo is your biological father," his mother replied with tears in her eyes.

Silently and in a state of emotional chaos, Valentin left his mother outside the operating theatre and walked away, but a crowd of journalists was waiting outside the hospital for the exclusive. Not knowing where all the journalists were stationed, he decided to borrow some clothes from the hospital to make himself unrecognisable and have Eva pick him up.

"I almost didn't recognise you. Hurry up and get in the car," Eva said in the hospital car park.
"Would it be possible for you to take me to my mother's house? Nobody knows the address; the house is on the other side of town; you can't risk being seen with me in the car. I need to change into something clean before I go back to the hospital."
"What would your mother say if she saw me in her house? Why do you have to go back to the hospital?"

"Don't worry, my mom has other problems at the moment and won't leave the hospital until Bonelli is stable. Besides, she's in no position to judge anyone."

"What do you mean by that? Is your mother going to stay with Mr. Bonelli? Why?"

"Because he is my biological father, and I believe he is also my mother's one true love."

"What, Mr. Bonelli, is your father? Well, that explains a lot."

When they arrived at the Leblanc family's magnificent villa, Eva was completely spellbound. Uncertain whether she could enter the house, she instinctively stayed in the car until Valentin opened the door and took her by hand. Still visibly upset, she asked to get out of the car and then clasped him tightly in her arms.

"Come with me," he whispered.

"You haven't even told me how you feel."

"Maybe it's because I don't know how I feel either. I wouldn't know how to describe this emotional chaos. But I'm glad that Bonelli survived the accident. Losing two fathers in the space of a few weeks would have been difficult to cope with. He risked his life to save mine."

"It's an innate behaviour of a father—the love for his son, the love he's shown you all these years by your side, the loyalty, being with you, even if only for a few minutes during a car journey—that was his only opportunity to be close to you and see you grow up."

"Yes, it's true; he was more present than my parents. As fate would have it, I discovered this secret today. I was afraid of losing him when he was lying on the floor in a pool of blood," he says, visibly shaken by the accident.

At the hospital, Valentin asked to be taken to see his mother. In the meantime, Mr. Bonelli had been moved to intensive care, and his condition was still critical. When he arrived at the entrance to the room, he saw his mother kneeling in front of the bed, holding his hand in hers. It was a profound image of a love that had been hidden for who knows how many years. What Valentin was experiencing with Eva was something his mother had been going through for years, which was no doubt why she was trying to shield him from it.

"Mum," Valentin whispered before she cut him off.

"So as not to cause a scandal, we decided to have a secret love affair; those were hard years for both of us. He was always secretly close to me and wanted to be by your side all these years. Driving you was the only way he could see his son grow up. I ruined all your lives just to keep a company's image clean," she sighed tearfully.

"You with your morals of avoiding scandal. Is that why you tried to keep me away from Eva? You must know one thing: you won't succeed; we will find a way to live our love like a normal couple."

"I know how you feel, and I can understand if you hate me for it, but please, let's not talk about it now. Ricardo needs us, and I want to be with him. At this moment, I know I don't want to be anywhere else but with him," Valentin's mother said, as Mr. Bonelli suddenly moved slightly until the connected monitoring equipment started to beep. In a panic, Valentin ran into the corridor to get help as a nurse approached him at a leisurely pace.

"Looks like someone's trying to wake up; let's see," the nurse said, looking at the equipment.

"Ella..." Mr. Bonelli murmured.

"Yes, he's waking up; I'll call the doctor right away. I think we need to sedate him again; his body needs absolute rest."

"Where is Valentin? We've had an accident," muttered Mr. Bonelli.

Moved, Valentin approached the bed, took his hand, and whispered, "I'm here with you."

His face filled with tears as the doctor injected more sedatives into his drip and checked his vital signs.

"He needs rest; please go home; it's been a hard day for you too. We have everything under control and will call you if anything changes.".

As they reached the exit, they saw several journalists standing outside the hospital. But that's not all: on closer inspection, Valentin sees a journalist talking to his mother's driver. She had to be the one who had been with him in the restaurant, just as Eva had told him. But the lady suddenly notices that Valentin is watching her and quickly ends the conversation, while other journalists take pictures from all sides.

"Where shall I take you?" asked the chauffeur.

But before his mother could answer, Valentin said:

"Please take us to my parents' house and return to the company or finish work when your shift is over," and then: "Mr. Bonelli and you are the only drivers who know the address of my parents' house. If we catch journalists at the door, there will be consequences for you too.".

When Valentin arrives at his parents' house, he makes sure that the maid is not there so that he can speak to his mother alone.

"I'll stay with you tonight if you like," he suggests.

"Sure, that would be great; your room is ready as usual."

"Before I go to bed, I want to talk to you about your chauffeur, and please don't interrupt me."

"Why, what's wrong with my chauffeur?"

"Your chauffeur is in direct contact with a journalist from Hellomagazine, a tabloid. He's been seen with her several times, even in intimate company. A week ago, I also received a letter addressed to the boss's secretary. Guess who suggested we work together? From Hellomagazine, good payment for exclusive news exchange.".

"Which of the two secretaries was the letter addressed to?

"There was no specific name on the envelope. It just said 'to the boss's secretary'."

"Do you think we should keep an eye on the secretaries too?"

"Maybe the one you forced on me. You don't need to worry about Eva."

"Please don't make me feel any more guilty today. I couldn't take any more stress today.

"I just want you to keep your eyes open when you get back to the office. And please change your driver."

"You know, Valentin, after the good work you've done with Algata Pharma and other clients, I'm toying with the idea of stepping back more and leaving the work to you. As soon as Ricardo is out of hospital, I would like to go on a long trip with him. What do you think?"

"I think it's a very good idea. What does he mean to you? How do you feel about him? What kind of love do you feel for each other?"

"Well, you've bombarded me with a lot of personal questions. I could describe loving Ricardo as an obsession, a fierce passion, the certainty of not being able to live without this person, and the knowledge of being reciprocated in this feeling, regardless of whether we could be together or not. To be able to say, 'I love you' to someone with a twinkle in their eye is a privilege not everyone has. I think you know what I mean. But enough with the sentimentality; I need time to find some clothes that will allow me to sneak into the hospital unnoticed by the journalists. I also need a rental car that I can change every other day.".

"Mum, are you listening to yourself? You sound like a mafia boss on a secret mission."

"Who knows, maybe I am," she replied with a smile.

The next morning, Valentin had to reorganise without his favourite driver. Not knowing which of the company's drivers he could still trust, he and his mother decided to rent two small cars in order to remain incognito for a while. While Mrs. Leblanc disguised herself to avoid being recognised at the hospital, Valentin decided to drive to the office.

"See you in the bunker in an hour," he wrote to Eva.

Driving a rental car was very unusual for Valentin, and especially for his mother, who was spoilt by her luxurious life, but suddenly it seemed that she was no longer interested in all this goodness. In the space of 24 hours, Valentin had seen a side of his mother he had never seen before. He was used to seeing his mother as a strict businesswoman, always matter-of-fact, with few emotional outbursts, and now he was confronted with a completely different kind of woman who seemed caring, enamoured, and tender. Over the years, this man had managed to access the best part of his mother, the part she never showed to anyone else. This proved how important he was to her, regardless of her social position.

"Have I told you today how much I love you?" Valentin whispered into Eva's ear.
"Let's see, let me count... Well, that's exactly three times in about ten minutes. But tell me, how do you feel today? How does it feel to have a father who is still alive when you lost yours a few weeks ago?" Eva asked curiously.
"Well, not only do I have a new father, I also have a new mother. In the last 24 hours, my mother has shown character traits that I didn't know she had."
"Today you're holding me tighter than usual. What is happening to you?"

"The connection with you is getting stronger every day. I think we're in the same situation as my mother and Bonelli."

"With the difference that we won't end up like them," she said firmly, kissing him tenderly on the lips.

"It is curious that I said the same thing to my mother the other day."

"It means that we know exactly what we want and are waiting for the right moment to do it."

"My mother has decided to take a longer break. I will now have to devote more time to the business. With you by my side, we'll be successful," he said confidently.

"You mean with the grenade from your office? That's what they call it here at the company. I think you've forgotten who's at your side in the company."

"You're the only person at my side, and I'll talk to you about all the decisions that need to be made with each customer. When we reach the level of satisfaction with all our customers, as we did with Algata Pharma, then in a few years we can sell the company and decide where we want to live with our children.".

"But how, you're not going to run this company for generations?" she asked in surprise.

"I want to live happily with you, to see my children and grandchildren grow up; that's my wish. My parents have already provided for the next generations; we have the security to live the way we want to.".

In this modern age of superficiality, finding a young man with traditional values like Valentin was like looking for a needle in a haystack. But Eva had found him without having to look for him. They had simply found each other. Their souls had met by chance. Something that is almost unthinkable today, yet people still fall in love in this way in the 21st century.

When Eva returned to the office, she found several missed calls on the answering machine. Some of them were from David. Her mobile phone had no reception in the bunker, but there were also several missed calls from him on her phone's display. Something important must have happened with all the times he had tried to contact her.

"You finally called me back. There was a sign on your door this morning; what's going on?" he asked irritably.
"Well, in my position as secretary, at a time when my boss is going through all sorts of things, you can't just expect me to sit in the office. I was on a call; my boss is probably taking a long break after her son's accident; she's emotionally affected. It's more than understandable, having lost her husband just a few weeks ago. What do you have to tell me that's important?"
"Steven told me that the junior boss's secretary was seen in your boss's chauffeur-driven car. Don't you find that strange? I mean, after we saw him in the restaurant with the journalist, the letter addressed to the secretary turned up, and now they're travelling in the same car... and she, the grenade, was all over the tabloids with the junior boss."
"Stay away from the coffee gossip with Steven; we'll talk about it at home tonight. I'll see you at lunch when you can talk about normal things," Eva said pointedly.

After the phone call with David, Eva began to plan her new working structure for the coming weeks without her boss, so she printed out the list of client portfolios and the relevant sales statistics, then stuck them all on the board with magnets to get a clearer idea of which client Valentin could have offered similar solutions to Algata Pharma that would have led to another positive sales turnaround. Given what Valentin's efforts had achieved with the client in Montreal and with Algata Pharma, it was reasonable to conclude that the concept he had proposed was more viable than his mother's. His mother's decision to take a break came at just the right time. After work, she went out for lunch.

A few meters behind her, in front of the canteen, Eva sees David talking excitedly on the phone. With a gesture, she tells him the colour of his face while he talks brusquely on the phone.

"By the colour of your face, I can guess who you were talking to on the phone," she said amusedly.

"And with whom?" he asked, a little surprised.

"Your mom, of course!"

"Yes, of course. But now we'd better hurry and get something to eat; I'm very hungry."

It wasn't often that she found herself with a disgruntled and hungry husband, but Eva made the best of the situation.

As David's colleagues sat quietly in their seats, enjoying their lunch, she took advantage of the quiet moment to ask questions about Sila's pregnancy.

While Robin excitedly talked about all the details of the ultrasounds and buying the first baby clothes, Steven began to list the negative things associated with having children. At the top of the list was the fact that a wife has little time for her husband and he feels neglected. She seemed to have found the most inappropriate topic for the day.

"In other times, men didn't question how much time their wives spent with their children. But today, unfortunately, a woman finds herself in a difficult position when her adult husband needs more attention than a baby and she has to decide whom to give more time and affection to. Especially because a child cannot understand why an adult man needs so much attention. The father figure needs to be a role model, not a rival... Don't you agree?" Eva asked in a rather sharp tone.

"No," Steven replies defiantly.

Much to Eva's surprise, Valentin was standing in her office after the lunch break, looking curiously at what she had pinned to the board.
"Darling, why did you print out all these diagrams?" he asked.
She put her lips seductively to his ear and whispered, "To prove to you that your strategy is more successful than your mother's."
"You're flattering," he said, touching her lips with a kiss.
"You haven't told me why you're in my office."
"Look at the envelope I left on your desk."

She quickly picked up the envelope, opened it, and took out some pictures.

"How did you get these pictures?" she asked in surprise.
"Bonelli, my father, has a cousin here in town, Carlos Bonelli, who works for a security company. After my mother told him yesterday that she had doubts about her driver, he asked him to follow my secretary and my mother's driver. This is the result, showing the two of them with the Hello magazine journalist".

"You know, David told me this morning that his colleagues have also seen them together. What are you going to do now?"
"Lure them into a trap. But we have to wait a few days; I don't want to put my mother under any more psychological stress."

"How is Mr. Bonelli?"
"I can't remember ever seeing him so happy. My mother never leaves him for a moment. I think if he keeps it up, he'll be able to leave the hospital soon."
"What are they going to do when he's discharged? I mean, I don't think they can go on holiday right away."
"My mother has decided to take him to the country house for a month and then fly to the planned holiday destination for at least three months. They'll be back by Christmas."

"You talk about it as if it's the most normal thing in the world to see them together.

"I don't know how to explain it to you, but somehow it's the same; I love to see them together; I love to see that my mom is able to show love; I love to read that feeling on their faces."

In the afternoon, David left work early to go shopping for golf equipment with a colleague. The relationship between Eva and David seemed to have become habitual, neither of them doing anything special for the other, at least not as often as they used to. Afraid of provoking David's suspicions, Eva decided to prepare a special dinner when the doorbell rang. Late in the evening, the postman delivers a small, light parcel. Without reading who had sent it or who it was for, she tore off the wrapper and opened it curiously. The contents left no room for speculation other than a possible delivery error, so she put it on the table and continued cooking.

"What a delicious smell," a voice called from the corridor.

David had just gotten home and was happily carrying his shopping into the kitchen when he saw the parcel on the table.
He quickly picked it up and looked inside.
"Whose parcel is this?" he asked with a hint of uncertainty in his voice.
"I don't know; I think it was delivered by mistake."
Without hesitation, he opened the window and threw it out.
Stunned, Eva looked at him and said, "Say, have you lost your mind? It was clearly a mistake; we could have taken it back to the post office; the postman didn't speak the language very well anyway. Now these pretty pink baby woolly socks are lying in the car park without having found their owner. I wonder who's waiting for them.
"Don't worry about that. They weren't meant for us anyway, and we don't have time to go to the post office anyway."

"You didn't even say hello to me," Eva said.

With a guilty look, David approached her and nibbled a little on her earlobe.

"Better now?" he asked, picking up his golf equipment to show her.

"You're really into this sport, aren't you?"

"Absolutely, I think I love it almost more than you do," he replied amusedly.

"I'm starting to believe that, you know?"

With some consideration, having neglected her for the past few weeks, David walked over to his wife, picked her up, sat her down on the table, spread her legs, pressed her against him, and tried to kiss her.

"Hey, our food's getting cold; let's postpone it," she said, pulling out of his grip.

"Dinner can wait; I'm in the mood now," he said, pushing himself between her legs.

Already a little irritated by the situation, Eva tried to release her grip when she noticed her husband's state of arousal, which reminded her of her duties as a wife.

Unwillingly and without resistance, she gave in to her husband's desires. The days when she would be alone with Valentin seemed far away.

The next morning, Eva went to the office in a bad mood, not knowing that Valentin had a firm plan to expose his secretary and his mother's chauffeur. Given the good health of his biological father, Mr. Bonelli, they decided to carry out the plan the very next day, a Friday evening, after work. Carlos Bonelli and his colleagues were part of the plan; his mother and his biological father, Ricardo Bonelli, had organised everything down to the last detail.

Before the lunch break, Valentin went to Eva's office to tell her in person and found her rather dejected.

"Hey, look at you; you seem depressed today. Has something happened?" He asked, tenderly holding her face in his hands.

But she burst into tears and clung to him. "I don't know how much longer I can put up with this love triangle. Every day that passes makes it harder for me to go on like this," she sighed.

Touched by her emotional state, he held her tightly in his arms.

"I feel the same way, but we have to try and hold on a little longer. When my mother comes back from her holiday, we'll find a final solution. I promise you that. Your parents are coming to visit in three weeks, so you'll have some time to recharge your emotional batteries."

"Oh God, my family, I'd almost forgotten about them in all the chaos of the last few days."

"The chaos will soon be over. Come, sit down; I want to show you something."

Valentin proudly placed two sheets of paper with strange drawings on his desk.

"What are these strange scribbles?" she asked helplessly.

"Tomorrow night my secretary and my mother's chauffeur will be exposed; that's the plan," Valentin explained.

"You're going to meet them at the Tosca Restaurant on the Ottawa River? Just the two of you?"

"Yes. I will drive to the meeting point in a rental car; no one will recognise me, and I will meet them outside the restaurant, where my men will be positioned on three buildings in front of and beside the restaurant to film this meeting. As soon as my men beeped, I knew the journalists were waiting to take pictures of us. So I'll try to hug and kiss them."

"And what is Carlos Bonelli's role?"

"He will be stationed in the car park in front of the restaurant to intervene as soon as the photographers start taking pictures. Nobody knows about this meeting except the people organised by Carlos Bonelli. If the photographers are there, it means that my secretary has invited them.".

"I can't wait to see how this turns out. Let me know as soon as you're ready. I'll be home alone because David's playing golf."

"It's getting dark early in the evening; what do you say I pick you up afterwards and nibble you in the car? Nobody knows the rental car."

"I say, I'm already hot for the idea of being nibbled on in the car."

"I love you," he said, kissing her hand charmingly.

The next morning Eva had more butterflies than concentration. Valentin was already on fire in her imagination and making himself felt in her body.

The only distraction from these hot thoughts: work. But the boring day seemed to have no end.

When David arrived at her office an hour before the end of the working day and brought her the car keys, she breathed a sigh of relief as she could already see the romantic evening she would spend in the car with Valentin.

"Steven and I are going to leave a little early tonight because we have a game, so you'd better take the car. I don't know what time we'll be ready. Don't expect me for dinner," he said cheerfully and left the office.

To freshen up before the meeting with Valentin, Eva decided to leave the office a little earlier than usual. The closer the meeting got, the more she wanted to see him.

With quick steps, she headed for the exit and reached the now half-darkened car park. On this dark, eerie evening, she quickly got into her car and drove off, but as she left the company car park a few meters away, she saw Mrs. Leblanc's driver, still out of uniform during his working hours, standing by the side of the road with a bag in his hand, obviously waiting for someone. Curious, she stopped behind some parked cars and turned off the engine to watch him without running the risk of being noticed.

A few minutes later, a black van with foreign number plates comes out of the corner of a building at high speed, but she can't tell from a distance what country it's from. Could it be from overseas? But that wasn't so important at the moment; much more important was why it had stopped in front of Mrs. Leblanc's driver and, above all, why he had gotten into the car. With an uneasy feeling, she decided to follow him. After a few kilometres, she noticed that the van was heading towards the Ottawa River. Her uneasy feeling grew so much that she tried to call Valentin on her mobile phone. The call went unanswered. Looking around, she recognised the area around the Tosca restaurant and noticed that the van had suddenly slowed down. Without losing sight of it, she quickly looked around for a parking space, but just as she found one, a car drove past her and took one of the empty spaces she had decided to park in.

Still in the lane, in a split second she saw Valentin standing at the edge of the pavement with his secretary, and the van stopped in front of them. Two men in balaclavas got out and walked briskly towards Valentin, and at the same time the secretary, Mrs. Oliveira, took a few steps back, moving away from him before the men reached him, as if she knew what was going to happen. With a quick grab, the men blocked Valentin and held him down, but when he tried to resist, they pulled him up, dragged him to the car, and tried to push him through the already open door. Seeing this, Eva panicked and began to honk the horn, while the secretary, Mrs. Oliveira, ran away as if nothing had happened. Determined and without a second thought,

Eva stepped on the accelerator with all her might until she crashed into the van at full speed.

Chapter 8 Glory Days

"Do not expect me to be your best friend just because you saved my son's life. But the fact that you risked your own life to do so makes you a hero in my eyes, so I'm promoting you to personal secretary and sole coordinator of my son's business affairs. You may return to your office now."

Those were the only kind words Mrs. Leblanc had for Eva after she had suffered a few bruises and a broken leg trying to save Valentin's life. At least those words were kinder than the ones David found for her when he arrived at the hospital accompanied by the police and couldn't understand what had made her crash her new car into the parked van.

"It was a coincidence that I was there; I just wanted to order a pizza from the Tosca restaurant as I was alone for dinner. I was just about to park when some idiot took my space. When I saw another free space, I got distracted by looking left and right and collided with the van, which was parked quite centrally in the road, and lost consciousness in the collision," Eva told the policeman in a convincing tone as the doctor applied the plaster cast to her leg.
"Well, then all that remains to be clarified is why she collided at such high speed. Isn't that right?" the policeman asked his colleague.
Eva promptly replied, "Well, just imagine if the next idiot tried to take my newly found parking space, then adios pizza! Unimaginable with the hunger I had after work."
Annoyed, David shook his head several times. "When she's hungry, you can't control her. I've known her since kindergarten."

Eva also knew David from their days in the sandbox, so she knew exactly what she could and could not say in a given situation. The police officers took her at her word, but David was angry because he feared the insurance company would refuse to pay for the damage they had caused.

"To end the evening on a positive note, I would like to announce that Mrs. Leblanc will pay for the costs incurred as a result of the accident, in gratitude for the fact that this coincidence saved her son's life. As far as she is concerned, the case is closed for us. We wish you a speedy recovery," the policeman said and left the room with his colleague.

Eva's parents, who had already travelled from Spain, picked her up early from work to accompany her to the doctor. With her leg still in a cast, she was only able to work half a day. The truth was that she was supposed to be off work for four weeks to allow the fracture to heal, but she didn't want to stay home without seeing Valentin.

"I don't know what your boss told you, but even here in Spain you are now a heroine, even worldwide, because the pharmaceutical company Ritel is internationally recognized. recognized. Your father bought several newspapers, and we proudly showed them to everyone," said Carmen, full of praise.

"Mrs. Leblanc also told me that in her eyes I was a heroine. Coming from that woman, I think it's a great compliment," said Eva, amused.

"We've been here a few days now, and you still haven't told us what happened that night. We're eager to hear your version of events. ¿Sabes?" Eva's mother said curiously.

"Come on, Mum..."

"Come on, we're all ears," Marion replied.

"As you've probably read in the papers, I was near the pizzeria when I crashed into the parked van. As I was knocked unconscious, I don't know exactly what happened, but I do know that this accident prevented Valentin Leblanc from being kidnapped. Apparently, Valentin Leblanc was almost on board the van at the time of the collision, while the kidnappers pushed him against the side of the van, and he was slightly injured in the collision. Security guards nearby intervened before the police arrived. It eventually emerged that the kidnapping had been organised by several people close to Leblanc, including his secretary and Mrs. Leblanc's personal driver, who apparently knew each other."

"I don't even want to imagine how it would have turned out if you hadn't gotten hungry for pizza and no one had noticed what was going on," Eva's mother said.

"Please, Mum, let's change the subject."

"Did your boss's son at least say thank you?" asked Eva's father.

"His face was the first thing I saw when I came around. He didn't take his eyes off me until the police and the ambulance arrived."

"Eva Maria Fernanda Rodriguez, I know that look," says Eva's mother in a suspicious tone.

"But come on, Marion, you with your suspicions..." Federico intervened between them.

"I always said her husband was a madman and not the right man for her. Who knows, maybe one day she'll listen to me and meet her prince charming," Carmen replied.

"¡PorDios! Carmencita!" scolded Marion.

During the examination, the doctor realised that the bruises had not completely healed two weeks after the accident and that Eva's leg still needed rest, so she was ordered to rest for ten days.

"But why am I on sick leave for ten days? It's not necessary; I'm fine, really," Eva asked.

"A little rest will do you good; believe me, enjoy your family; you'll have plenty of time to work when you're back," the doctor replied.

"Thank you, Doctor; now we can enjoy the time with our daughter to the full," Eva's father said in the little English he spoke.

"By the way, do you know that in the last two weeks you have become one of the most famous people in town?" the doctor asked Eva.

"I would say the most famous in the world. Even here in Spain, she's in all the newspapers," replied Eva's proud father.

When they got home, they immediately realised that David had not returned, so Eva asked her sister to empty the letterbox. However, she was surprised by an unusual piece of mail, and her attention was immediately drawn to a letter bearing the seal of Ritel Pharmaceutical.

What could this letter say that she had not already heard from Mrs.Mrs. Leblanc in the office?

"Attention, Mrs. Eva Rodriguez."

Subject: Formal Invitation to Your Honourable Reception.

"Dear Mrs. Rodriguez,
We are delighted to invite you to our special celebration of honour to be held on the 17th of September at the Leblanc family estate.
We are sure that you and your family will enjoy the celebration and would be delighted if you could join us. Please confirm your attendance by 10 September.
We look forward to welcoming you in person and thank you very much.

Ella and Valentin Leblanc"

"And what does the letter say?" Carmen asked curiously.
"It's not a letter, it's an invitation to a ceremony of honour," Eva replied.

"An invitation to a ceremony of honour for you? What are you going to do?" asked Marion.

"The invitation is not just for me, but for all of us, including my family. The ceremony is on 17th September, and we have to confirm by 10th September."

"But the party is the day before we leave. And 10 September is today! Why did you send the letter so late?" asked Eva's father.

"Well, to be honest, we haven't emptied the letterbox for almost a week."

"Then hurry up, call, and confirm that we'll all be there!" said Eva's mother enthusiastically.

"But Mum, I need to talk to David first to see what he thinks."

"A wife doesn't have to ask her husband's permission. Remember that, Eva Maria Fernanda Rodriguez," Marion said proudly.

"Marion, what are you trying to say? You're just a chronic feminist," said Federico, irritated.

Eva called Mrs. Leblanc's office to thank her for the invitation and to confirm her attendance. But there was no answer.

"It's late; Mrs. Leblanc must have left," Eva said regretfully. But the same number rang again, and Velentin was on the other end.

Visibly moved to hear his voice, Eva clears her throat and quickly fires off a few words: "Mr. Leblanc, ehmm, my whole family is here. Thank you for calling me back. All of us, me and my family... ehmm, I just wanted to say that my family is happy to accept your invitation."

"Eva, did you hear yourself? You sounded embarrassed and confused at the same time.. How do you talk to your boss?" asked Carmen.

"You're always criticising me. Help me cook instead and shut up."

"Mum does the cooking..."

"Then just shut up!"

"Bitch alert?" shouted a voice from the entrance hall.

In all the chatter, no one had noticed that David had come home.

"Did I miss something?" he asked curiously.
"You missed something; the Leblancs have invited us to a party in Eva's honour!" Marion said proudly.
"You mean us, me and Eva?"
"No, I mean all of us!" she replied.

Slightly perplexed, David was silent for a moment, then took a bottle of water, filled his glass, and simply said, "When is this party, and who are the guests? I have no intention of making the front page of the local paper."
But everyone there looked at each other in silence until Carmen burst out, "I told you, he's just a weirdo," and laughed.

Two more weeks in a cast, ten days off work, and seven days until her party of honour—that was the balance sheet that evening. The front page of a newspaper would have been the least of Eva's problems that day, considering that her family, her husband, her lover, and her lover's entire family were gathered at a party where, apart from her and Valentin, at least two other people knew about her forbidden love. How was she to behave all evening? How could she look Valentin in the eye while sitting next to her husband and pretend to be a caring and loving wife in front of everyone?
But while Eva racked her brain with all sorts of worries, David simply asked, "Can we go in two cars that day, as there are enough people here who would like to stay with you at your party? You know I also have an important golf match that day, which I confirmed six weeks ago, and I'd like to go."
That seemed to be David's only problem, but Eva's mother, visibly irritated, was already trying to say something when Frederico interjected: "Marion, let's go to the hotel now, please; it's been a long day for everyone."

At dinner, Eva noticed that David was absentminded .

"You're already annoyed by my family's presence, and they've only been here for two days; how's that going to go for the next eight?" She asked, irritated.

"You react to my mother, so I have the right to react to yours. Don't you think? Besides, your sister also seems to have inherited your mother's long tongue. It feels like having your mom as a 'double pack'."

"All right, you haven't had a good day. I'll go to the sofa and put my leg up. You try to come down."

For Eva and David, life as a couple became more and more a habit of living together and sharing tasks from day to day. Moments of intimacy became rarer and less desirable. The first eight months of expat life were filled with all kinds of events, new commitments, and the discovery of new passions. In David's case it was golf, and in Eva's it was Valentin, a passion that increasingly disrupted their marriage.

The next morning, Eva was waiting for her family at breakfast when she received a message from Valentin:

"Good morning, darling. I think of you and live with you every day, even when we are not physically together. If you were here now, I would embrace you with all my strength. I don't know how I will get through all these days without seeing you."

Seized by endless longing, and before her family had even gathered for breakfast, she called him back.

"Remember in Toronto when you asked me to run away with you? Now would be the time for me," she said, just before the doorbell rang.

Eva's family members arrived early in the morning, happy and ready to go, determined not to let Eva's leg cast ruin their day. The day began with a shopping trip, for which they came up with a bizarre idea.

"Surprise!" shouted Carmen as she pulled the wheelchair out of the lift.

"You're crazy! Where are Mom and Dad, and where did you get the wheelchair?"

"The hotel had two of them, and we asked if we could borrow one. Let's have breakfast in a patisserie and then go shopping."

"Let's go!" said Eva and sat down in the wheelchair.

After a sumptuous breakfast, the four of them set off in search of a luxury boutique.

For this honourable occasion, Eva had to wear the most beautiful dress, possibly one that would cover her cast leg. When she saw the exorbitant prices in the shop windows, she decided to try on a dress in a shop that offered seasonal discounts.

"This dress is the last one left in size XS, and as we couldn't sell it, it's heavily discounted. The purple will look great with her brown hair. Would you like to try it on?" the saleswoman asked.

Full of enthusiasm, Carmen picked up the dress and said, "Yes, of course, she'd love to try it on, wouldn't she, sis?"

"Are you taking the words out of my mouth?" asked Eva, irritated.

"That's the greatest talent she inherited from her mother," Federico pointed out.

"Federico?!" scolded Marion.

With her leg in a cast, Eva needed help in the changing room, so Carmen helped her put on the enchanting dress.

"You look like a princess, but what elegance," said the shop assistant. She continued: "Take this long-sleeved bolero and try it on; you'll need it in the evening because it's already quite chilly in mid-September."

Slowly, Eva put on the black velvet bolero, looked at herself in the mirror, and then turned to her family. Her mother, visibly moved, nods her head in agreement.
"And now let's take a trip; let's see what's on my list of places to visit: Parliament Hill, the Houses of Parliament and the magnificent Victorian buildings, and museums like the National Gallery of Canada," says Federico.
"But don't tell me you're going to see it all today..." Marion added uncertainly.
"If there's anyone to worry about here, it's me; look at the state I'm in," said Eva.

Once on the hill on the south bank of the Ottawa River, Eva took in the surroundings. After almost a year in Canada, she had never visited Parliament Hill. The last time she had seen the building was on the other side of the river with Valentin, gazing into the distance as he buried his face in her hair, melting every cell in her body. With her eyes closed and a light September breeze on her face, she savoured this memory for a few more seconds when her mother pulled her arm: "What are you doing, sleeping standing up? Come on, get in your wheelchair, and let's visit this beautiful place."

As they entered the atrium, they were overwhelmed by the beauty of the stone sculptures and painted panels depicting Canada's political, economic, and social history. The glass panels on the ceiling feature images of the French lily, the three maple leaves that symbolise Canada, and the English rose.
Glass panels with floral representations of the Canadian provinces and sculptures under the windows depict aspects of the Canadian Constitution.

The public galleries of the Senate and House of Commons were furnished with red cushions, gold-leafed ceilings, and artwork that reminded MPs of the country they served. New culture, new wonders to be discovered. The four of them stayed to admire them until closing time.

"What's on tomorrow?" asked Eva on the way home.

"A tour of Ottawa?" asked her father.

"Done!" replied the rest of the family.

When she got home, Eva sent Valentin some photos of the day, which he commented on immediately. But she didn't get a chance to write back because David arrived at the same time.

"What a surprise!! You've brought pizza for dinner!" she said excitedly.

"Yes, so we don't waste too much time cooking; I've got a little golf match tonight, remember?"

"Yes, I'm happy for you. So shall we start eating so you can go straight away?" she asked.

"Give me five minutes, and I'll be there."

But during those five minutes, Eva picked up the phone.

"I miss you so much. Come see me in an hour; I'm alone," she wrote to Valentin.

The dinner between David and Eva was limited to the essentials, then David packed his gym bag, kissed her on the mouth, and left the house. "Don't wait for me; I might be late tonight," he said at the end.

Of course, she wasn't worried about the time her husband would spend on the road, because as soon as he left the house, Eva wrote a message to Valentin, quickly tied a plastic bag around the cast, and jumped in the shower to freshen up.

154

Dressed in a tracksuit and basketball cap, Valentin was soon at the door. It was the riskiest thing they had done since their relationship began, but the moment they saw each other again and their bodies touched erased the last whispers of reason.

Silently, he held her in an endless embrace. Nestled in his arms, she slipped a hand under his sweater and stroked his bare skin as he cupped her face in his hands, looked deep into her eyes, brushed the strands of hair from her face, and kissed her deeply.

"Since I've known you, my eyes have seen only one image, and my mind has only one thought: you and the love I feel for you," he whispered, continuing to kiss her.

Slowly but surely she removed his jumper and ran her tongue over his skin down to his neck, making him moan.

"And what other thoughts do you have?" she whispered, also touching his nipples with her tongue.

He kissed her passionately on the neck, then slid his hand under her dress along her thighs and stopped on her buttocks, making her moan.

"Only you make me glow," she whispered.

He carefully led her to the nearest chair, kneeled in front of her, slowly pushed her dress up, went face down, and pulled her pants off with his teeth, causing her to moan lustfully. Without a thought for the cast on her leg, she got off the chair and sat down, right at the peak of her arousal.

In the middle of the night, Eva realised that David had not yet gone to bed. She looked around the flat, a little worried, and found him asleep on the sofa. Next to him was a half-drunk bottle of wine.

When did David start drinking alone? Was it because life as a couple was getting boring by the day? Certain that she wouldn't get an answer that night, she went back to bed.

The next morning, David left the house early and without a word, leaving breakfast ready. Eva, who had spent the night brooding over the situation, didn't notice that he had already left. Wracked with guilt, she called him on his mobile to see how he was doing.

"I saw you drinking half a bottle of wine by yourself. Is everything all right?"
"It was the bottle your parents brought; it was standing there looking at me, and then I thought, well, if you're looking at me so insistently, I'll have a sip," he said jokingly.
"Aha, the bottle even talked to you," she said in an amused tone.
"I'd rather say it; the wine talked to me, and after I'd drunk half a bottle, it even sang to me."
"Judging by the amount left in the bottle, I'll take your word for it. Today we're going on a city tour by bus; my parents wanted us to. Would you like to join us in the city after work?"
"No, I'm still tired from last night; I'd rather wait for you at home."

The trip started in Ottawa in glorious weather, but Eva quickly realised that she hadn't even seen a small part of the place where she'd been living for the last few months. The first stop was the Canadian Museum of Civilisation, apparently the most visited museum in the country, with a focus on archaeology, history, folklore, and ethnology.
The next stop was Rideau Hall, the official residence of the Governor General of Canada. The prestigious building of the Canadian president was located on Sussex Drive in Ottawa and covered 32 acres of land.

"I am beginning to feel the fatigue of travelling with my cast. Now I understand why the doctor ordered total rest," said Eva.

"Next time, just leave your cast at home," said Carmen, amused. "The next stop is the Byward Market, Ottawa's largest public market. We'll take a long lunch break here," told the driver over the microphone.

"Finally..." Eva sighed.

After an eventful day, Eva was taken home and tried to relax, but as she sat on the sofa, she realised that half the bottle of wine was still where David had left it. The temptation to take a sip was strong after reading several sentimental messages from Valentin.

"I want to take your hands and put them close to my heart so you can feel what happens to me when you look at me." read the first message. With tears in her eyes and a melancholy heart, she looked at the second message.

"Without you, I feel the emptiness inside me.".

But while she was wiping away her tears, David entered the apartment.

"Darling, what's the matter? Why are you crying? Does your leg hurt?" He asked worriedly.

"I don't know; I'm just exhausted. The city tour was probably too exhausting," she replied, trying to justify her emotional state.

"That's what I thought; I didn't dare say anything so as not to seem rude."

"But darling, what are you trying to say? You're never rude."

"I could try and massage your leg a bit if you like," he asked.

"No, it's all right; you've had a hard day too, especially with the alcohol left over from yesterday. I'll put my legs up a bit, and we'll just relax."

With her heart set on another man and in the arms of her still husband, she lay back and closed her eyes.

Two men who could touch her in a different way, two completely different men who made her feel two completely different things.

The day of her tribute was fast approaching, and Eva was still struggling with the discomfort of her cast. After all these days of visiting museums, cathedrals, the Rideau Canal, Parliament Hill, and the famous Alexandra Bridge, she felt as if she had run a marathon, not just a sightseeing tour.

But a new day was dawning, and her family was looking forward to seeing her early in the morning. Punctual and full of energy, they rang the bell downstairs as she squeezed into the lift with little enthusiasm.

"¡Buenos dias!" The three of them greet her cheerfully.

"Your energy is giving me a stomach ache today. I warn you, today is the last day we'll be travelling; I need to rest."

"Don't moan; a pensioner would have more energy than you. Let's go and have a big breakfast," said Carmen in a good mood.

"You talk like a peasant. My feast is in two days. Tomorrow you'll have to go without me, and I don't care what you think," Eva said angrily.

"Alright, then we'll make the best journey we can today."

"And that would be?" Eva asked, irritated and curious at the same time.

"Ottawa in a double-decker," Carmen replied with a broad grin.

Stunned, Eva looked at her parents and said, "Why don't you say anything? I see. So you're involved in the planning? You want me to come to my party half dead; is that your plan?" she shouted.

"Come on, get in the car; you screech like a bitter old maid. We'll have fun, and from tomorrow we'll just relax. Agreed?" said   Marion.

When they arrived at the Canada Aviation & Space Museum, where the flight was to take off from, the four of them waited their turn.

Eva's father, realising the difficulties with her leg in a cast, decided to fly with her. Carmen and Marion were flown together in another plane.

Full of adrenaline, with the wind at their backs and the roaring engine of a 1940 Waco, they flew over Ottawa and marvelled at the breathtaking beauty of the city in a unique experience.

"Have you ever seen anything more beautiful?" Federico shouts into Eva's ear.

"Thanks for making me do it," was her only reply.

After a single day's rest, Eva's parents arrived at the house on time to drive to the party in two cars, as agreed. David quickly carried his gym bag to the car and helped his wife with her crutches.

"With or without the cast, you have the most beautiful wife in the world," Eva's father said proudly.

"A father's love knows no mistakes," David replied with a grin and got into the car.

After a 20-minute drive, they arrived at the Leblanc country house and were greeted in the forecourt by Mr. Bonelli and two of his employees. After shaking hands with everyone, Mr. Bonelli walked over to Eva, hugged her, whispered in her ear, "I'm proud of you," and led her out onto the terrace, where, in the magic of a warm late summer evening, everything was ready for the event. The tables were festively laid, with bowls of ice and champagne in several corners. Silk lamps and soft music added to the atmosphere. Mr. Bonelli rang the small bell he held to signal the arrival of the guest of honour, and the music stopped and applause broke out.

Mrs. Leblanc and Valentin stood in front of Eva and her family and shook hands to show their hospitality, but Eva's face turned red when she met Valentin's gaze.

"You look lovely," Mrs. Leblanc said to Eva.

"Thank you," she replied shyly, then the family was led to the head table, and the sumptuous buffet of seasonal produce, perfect for such an occasion, was opened. Valentin and his mother sat down at the same table.

A very embarrassing situation for Eva. To the delight of everyone present, they were able to communicate in the same language, as Valentin and his mom also spoke Spanish.

"Why do you keep looking at your watch?" asked Carmen, turning to David, which caused all eyes to turn to David, who replied, visibly embarrassed: "I know it's an embarrassing situation, but I have a golf match in an hour that was scheduled five weeks ago, before the circumstances with the leg in plaster happened."

"That's not a problem for us, is it, Valentin? The important thing is that our guest of honour can stay here," Mrs. Leblanc said in a pleased tone.

"Of course, the rest of the family will stay here as long as they like," David replied.

"That is very generous of you," Carmen replied, causing amusement around the table.

Over dinner, Mrs. Leblanc spoke in an unusually familiar way about her childhood, details that Eva, after all these months of working with her, didn't know. Not even Valentin had ever told her that her mother came from a poor family and that her tenacity helped the whole family to prosper.

This simple way of communicating created a familiar atmosphere around the table. Eva's parents and Mrs. Leblanc chatted as if they had known each other for years.

While the waiter brought delicious dishes to the table, Eva and Valentin took advantage of the distraction and looked at each other for a few seconds. The eyes of two lovers crossed, full of longing.

But before the dessert arrived, David stood up, kissed his wife on the forehead, and said goodbye, to the obvious disapproval of Eva's family.

With the skill of someone who knows how to change a situation, Mrs. Leblanc broke the silence by drawing attention to the dessert: "Our desserts include a typical dish from their country. Would you like to guess what it is?"

"Churros?" asked Carmen.

"Churros are not a dessert, you little one!" replied Federico, causing hilarity around the table.

A few seconds later, Mrs. Leblanc clapped twice to get the waiter to bring the trolley of desserts closer. At that moment, the band played 'a whiter shade of pale', Mrs. Leblanc's favourite song, and some of the guests began to dance in this romantic mood.

"Why don't you invite Mrs. Rodriguez to this slow dance? With a cast on her leg, it would be the perfect music," Mrs. Leblanc asked, turning to Valentin.

The two looked at each other in surprise, but Valentin held out his hand and asked her, "May I?"

Touched, she nodded her head in the affirmative.

On crutches and accompanied by Valentin, Eva reached the dance floor and then slowly drifted off in Valentin's arms while the rest of the family were busy with dessert.

Silently, with their eyes closed, they savoured the moment until the song ended.

Having eaten and drunk like there was no tomorrow, Marion and Carmen were snoring in the back seat after only ten minutes in the car.

Federico shook his head a little uneasily, then turned to Eva, who was sitting next to him, and asked her in a calm but direct tone, "How long has Valentin Leblanc been in love with you?"

"Dad, what are you talking about?" she asked in surprise.

"Well, regardless of the fact that I'm also a man, you can see from afar that he's in love with you. Be thankful that your mother and sister filled themselves with champagne; otherwise, you wouldn't have been able to tame those wicked tongues."

Chapter 9   Noxious Letter

"I loved you before I met you. I love you, and I will love you until the end of my life, and if there is an afterlife, I will love you there too," Valentin whispered in Eva's ear as they returned from Montreal by helicopter.

Mrs. Leblanc and her lover Bonelli will be travelling for three months. Valentin, with Eva at his side, has taken over the management of Ritel. A big responsibility for the two of them and a unique opportunity to spend the whole day together inconspicuously.

"I haven't told you yet that when my father Bonelli saw your husband leaving the ceremony, he ordered the band to play 'a whiter shade of pale'. As it was his and my mother's love song, she understood the signal immediately and urged us onto the dance floor.".
"Well, I kept something from you too. On the way back from the party, my father wanted to know how long you'd been in love with me.
"And what did you tell him?"
"Nothing that would change his mind."
"We're screwed..."
"Not until my mother and sister find out. Although my sister would probably be happy."
"Do you think your father will keep this a secret?"
"My father wouldn't betray me for anything in the world," Eva replied firmly.
"In fact, it would be our job to reveal everything at the right time."
"We will."

When Eva came home after two days away, she found a table set and flowers, and at the same time David came out of the bathroom with a wet upper body and a towel tied around his waist.

"Hey honey, I didn't hear you come in... I'm ready for action," he said, raising his eyebrows with a grin.

But Eva took two steps back and said firmly, "No, come on, I've had a hard day. Get dressed and come and eat."
"You're getting frigid, poor Leblanc, having to put up with you all day as a secretary. I can already imagine the daily routine: No, not that, and this has to be done this way... blah, blah, blah'. He must be longing for the evil grenade.".

Without getting upset but still offended, Eva affirms, "The advantage of working with a fridge is that you can concentrate 100% on your work. His mother must have thought about what she was doing when she gave me this job.".
"Absolutely, she's an intelligent and perceptive woman."
At the table, they reviewed the highlights of the last two days.
"I haven't told you yet; Robin didn't come into the office today; Sila's water broke; it looks like her baby will be born prematurely," David told them.
"Oh no! It was supposed to be born at Christmas. What are they going to do?"
"The doctors have decided to give Sila a lung puncture and have a Caesarean section. Unfortunately, I don't know anything more. The only thing I know is that I also have to do his job because he took four weeks of paternity leave because of the premature birth."
"Good, then you know what it means to come home exhausted and not wanting to do anything. In a few weeks you'll be so hysterical I'll call you impotent."
"Never!" he replied proudly.

The next day, Eva was preparing some important work documents when her mother called her on her mobile phone. In a desperate tone, she tried to explain what had happened.

"David's father has apparently had a heart attack after receiving a letter; I'm afraid you'll have to catch the next plane."
"What kind of letter? How could that happen?" asked Eva worriedly.
"I don't know; Leonor hasn't told me anything more."
"I have to go now."

Flustered, she left everything on the desk and ran to the lift, but when the door opened, David was standing in front of her.
"Did you hear what happened?" she asked.

"Yes, and that's why I'm here. I need to get on the next flight to Barcelona. My father is in critical condition."
"All right, let's go. I'll inform Mr. Leblanc; I'm sure he'll understand in a case like this," she said frantically, dragging him into the lift.
"No, I'm going alone; otherwise, there'll be three empty seats in the company. I'll be fine, don't worry," he (David) said, then gave her a quick kiss and just walked away.

Shocked by this terrible incident, Eva called her mother-in-law Leonor to find out what had happened: It is inconceivable that a man could have a heart attack after reading a letter.
"Cristiano opened a letter that wasn't addressed to him, and suddenly he had severe chest pains. That's all I can tell you. Excuse me, I have to go to his room."

After a few emotionless words, Leonor ended the conversation without giving any more information.

Eva, who had always believed that only Leonor could see Cristiano, had to change her mind. But what could have been in the letter that had landed him in intensive care?

Back in her office, she told Valentin what had happened.
"How could your husband leave without you? If his father died, what would he say at the funeral? How would he explain his wife's absence?" asked Valentin.
"I'm asking myself the same thing," Eva replied helplessly.
"Did he even say how long he would be gone?"
"No," was her reply, sadly.
"Then I'll look after you while he's away. From tonight, you'll sleep with me until he gets back from Barcelona," he told her, taking her in his arms protectively.
"If I stay with you for so many days, it will be difficult for me to go home," she said, looking at him with a loving gaze.
"Then stay with me," he whispered, kissing her on the forehead.

But their conversation was interrupted by David's phone call.

"I'm already at the airport, and I left my car in the terminal. You'll need to pick it up with the spare key; I'm sure one of the drivers can take you there."
"You are at the airport without having gone home first? Didn't you pack your bag?" she asked, surprised at the speed of the journey.
"Yes, of course I passed home. I put a few things in my gym bag and hurried to the airport. My parents have some clothes for me too, but that's not so important right now. My dad is getting worse, so I hope I get there in time."

In tears at the frustration of not being able to see Cristiano one last time, Eva clung to Valentin.

"David's father is a true angel who had far too much patience with a difficult woman like Leonor at his side. I'm sorry for him. He always treated me like a daughter."

"Your husband had the chance to take you with him, but he didn't. I will take care of you."

Of course Eva believed Valentin's words and felt protected; he had often shown her that he was reliable. A man who knew what he was doing, who was at the height of his masculinity, and who clearly recognised his role as a man.

"I have to get the car before it gets dark and leave it in the car park of the apartment building so that no one notices we're gone."

"Give me the car keys; I'll make sure it's picked up and taken home," Valentin said lovingly.

In an agitated mood, Eva was driven home by her driver after work. When she arrived at the flat, she looked around, tidied up a bit, turned on the timer to make it cosy, and then took a shower. Feeling a bit more relaxed, she sat down on the sofa and picked up her mobile phone. She immediately saw a message from Valentin on the display, giving the meeting point where he would pick her up. Was this a new chance for them to try life together for the first time? It seemed as if there were forces turning everything in her favour.

No sooner had she arrived at the meeting point with Valentin than her mobile phone suddenly rang, and she had an uneasy feeling when she saw her mother's number on the display.

"I hope you're sitting down, because I'm afraid I don't have any good news," Marion said, her voice choked with tears.

Feeling uneasy, Eva approached the tree on the pavement, holding on lightly to keep from falling as Valentin ran towards her.

"Eva, can you hear me? Cristiano died before David could get here!" Marion shouted.

"Yes, I can hear you," she sighed in Valentin's arms.

"Why didn't you fly with him? What will people think now?" Marion shouted even louder.

"He didn't want to take me; now he'll have to explain to the others. But where is he? Why didn't he call me?" She asked in tears.

"I thought you understood that men don't have a say. In a harmonious relationship, it's always up to the woman to make the important decisions. He had just arrived in Barcelona when he got the call; his relatives were waiting for him at the airport. His mother called me and asked for you.".

"Mum, you with your feminist views. I'm trying to call David now.".

Marion ended the call to give Eva time to collect herself and call her husband. But at the same moment David called, just as Eva was getting into the car with Valentin.

"Darling, I don't know if you know this, but my father didn't wait for me. He died while I was still in the air. It's all my fault," he said, completely shaken. Eva was beside herself with despair and began to sob loudly, while Valentin stood beside her and held her tightly.

"Don't say that; if anyone is not to blame, it's you. Did you even get to see him?" she asked.

"Yes, but only briefly," he replied with a sigh.

"Where is your mother? And how is she?"

"She's here with me, with the rest of the family. We're leaving the hospital in a few minutes."

"Shall we call her later?"

"I'm ready; let's talk tomorrow."

The suddenness of Cristiano's death and the way it happened shook Eva to the core and plunged her into deep grief. Two deaths in the space of a few months, a serious accident that almost cost Bonelli his life, and the attempted kidnapping of Valentin. What was going on around her?

"I don't know what to make of everything that's happened in the last few months; there seems to be a curse on our families," she said, wiping away her tears.

Valentin stroked her hair lovingly as she lay on the sofa with her head in his lap.

"I don't see this time as a curse, but as a time of change. My father was unhappy and decided to leave this world; no one was to blame for what happened to him. The accident that almost cost Bonelli his life ensured that he and my mother could live out their love before it was too late and brought out the part of my mother that had been locked away for years. The attempted kidnapping made my mother accept you by my side even before our love became official. She was the one who wanted to meet your family and had organised your ceremony. This bereavement in David's family will surely have other effects that time will reveal.".

"Do you know that you are very wise for your age?"

"I know what you're trying to tell me: that many men today seem to be all the same, that everything is lumped together, and we're all categorised as immature, insensitive, and not very masculine. You know what I think? That some men can be mature at 25, and others can still be childish at 50. It always depends on how you grow up, how you live, the values you're taught, and the people you interact with. All this influences our character and the way we respect ourselves and others, and how we treat others.".

"Not a day goes by that I don't think how lucky I was to meet you," she said with an affectionate look.

Touched, he leaned forward and kissed her eyelids as she took his face in her hands.

Valentin had prepared breakfast for both of them early the next morning, but before they ate, Eva looked at her mobile phone in surprise when she realised she hadn't received any more calls from David.

"Darling, you seem down. Is everything all right?"

"Yes, it's just that David hasn't been in touch."

"Surely he must be unwell with the bereavement."

"I'm sure he is. Tell me, how are we going to get to the office this morning? I mean, without being seen together."

"Do you see the key next to your handbag?" he asked with a grin.

"Yes, what key is that?"

"The key to the car I borrowed for you yesterday while you were at home. You can use it to go home and get your car to go to the office, so David's work colleagues won't notice anything suspicious. I suppose they've got big mouths, from what I've seen in the canteen."

"Oh yes, they do."

As she still hadn't heard from David, Eva tried to call him late that morning while Valentin was in a meeting. But the call went unanswered, and she received a text message:

"We're at the funeral parlour; the preparations for my father's funeral were completed a few minutes ago. I'll call you later."

It wasn't much, but at least she'd heard from him. But this strange feeling wouldn't let her rest, so she decided to call her mother.

"¿Qué pasa, cariño?" Eva's mother answered before she could say anything.

"I don't know; I just have a bad feeling about this situation. Have you been to the funeral parlour yet? David hasn't been in touch much and doesn't tell me much."

"Well, it won't be an easy situation for him. His father died suddenly, and his mother has a nervous condition. We're going there this afternoon to pay our respects.

"Do you know what was in the letter that caused his heart attack?"

"No. We only heard that Leonor burnt it."

"That's strange. Don't you think so?"

"Since they've been known to have a screw loose, nothing about this family surprises me anymore. I'll call you when we get back."

Having no choice but to wait for more information, Eva resumed her work when David called her.

"What's the news? What was the letter about that gave your father a heart attack?" she asked, hoping for an answer that would clear things up.

"Why are you so obsessed with that letter? I don't know what it said; my mom burnt it before I could even see it, saying it wasn't important.".

"I know your mom; she would never have done that unless there was a very specific reason."

"Who knows if the letter was to blame or if it would have happened anyway? Let's not talk about it; your mom is no less toxic than mine."

"How do you feel?"

"I can't explain; it all happened so fast I haven't had time to process it."

"Do you realise the position you've put me in by leaving me here? Regardless of the fact that I've known your father for 20 years, what do you think people will think of me?"

"Who cares what people think? Now excuse me, but I must go back inside."

David coldly interrupted the conversation, which hurt Eva so much that Valentin found her crying. A mixture of guilt and a lack of understanding that David was taking everything so lightly made her feel bad. Was it David who had changed drastically in the last few months, or had he been like this all these years and she hadn't seen it through the rose-tinted glasses of love? Whichever version was plausible, the fact was that she had developed a problem with this kind of behaviour.

"Darling, don't you want to take a few days off to relieve the emotional stress? It hurts me to see you like this," Valentin said, taking her in his arms.
"Kiss me," she ordered, pursing her lips.
Valentin promptly gave her a deep kiss, followed by a second and a third.
"Is it better now?" he asked, shocked.
"You couldn't have done better."

But between the many kisses, Eva's mobile phone rang.

"There weren't many people at the funeral home. Your mother-in-law looked emotionless, as if she had been mummified, and she stood in front of the body without a single tear; she didn't even have a handkerchief in her hand in case her eyes got wet," Marion said, stunned.
"I'm sure she was stuffed full of tranquillizers."
"Then it must have been her husband too. I don't mean to interfere, but your husband had the same attitude as his mother.
"Maybe he took tranquilizers. Who knows?"
"Your sister and I just think you're too naive. I won't say any more about it, or you'll tell me I have a bad tongue."

When Eva had finished talking to her mother, she turned to Valentin and said, "You can tell me what you want, but it doesn't make sense to me. I don't know what's got into David or his mom, but I have the impression that they have something to hide."

"If they've deliberately decided to keep something from you, then it's not worth thinking about because you'll never know. Rest assured, I'm on your side; I can imagine you were fond of that poor man, but he's gone now, and they've decided to keep you out of it.".

"You're right, when David returns, I won't continue this conversation. You and I have plans for our future, and I just want to concentrate on that."

"That's a good plan," he replied, kissing her forehead.

After a busy day at work, Eva met Steven in the car park at the end of the day and pretended not to see him, as she had no particular sympathy for him.

But he saw her and walked straight up to her.

"Hey Eva, how are you? How come you're not at home after your father-in-law died?" he asked in a tone that immediately irritated her.

"Well, to be honest, my place is neither here nor at home, but at my husband's side in a situation like this, don't you think?" She replied sourly.

"We men don't always have to stick to our wives; we live in different times now; you don't seem to realise that."

Irritated by his answer, Eva looked at him as if she wanted to hit him with her eyes and said annoyed: "Oh yes, of course I am aware; we are in the age of lost values, disrespect, and the lack of or incomplete use of brain matter."

Without further ado, Steven hurried off to his car, while she increasingly felt that she no longer understood what was going on in the world. So she shook her head, got into the car, and drove home to see if everything was all right.

As soon as she arrived at the car park, she met the caretaker, who stopped her before she could enter the building.

"Mrs Rodriguez, I haven't seen you for a long time. I wanted to ring your doorbell because a parcel and some baby shoes were found here in the car park a while ago. Your husband's name was partly written on the parcel, but it's impossible to identify the sender because the parcel was damp. I'd like to give it to you."

Without comment, Eva followed him into the room with all the cleaning supplies, and he pressed the parcel into her hand.

"Judging by the bad taste in the choice of these shoes, I could guess where they came from: I bet my mother-in-law sent them to put pressure on my husband to get me pregnant? That bitch. Anyway, thank you, but you can throw them in the bin. Have a nice evening.".

The caretaker looked at her in silence and with a certain bewilderment and nodded his head.

Relieved that no one had noticed that David had thrown the parcel out of the window, she walked briskly back to the flat. Everything was just as she had left it the day before, but the feelings changed from day to day each time she entered the apartment, like a time bomb ready to explode at any moment. Grief over Cristiano's sudden death turned to anger at David and his mother as the hours passed. The more she thought about them, the more she noticed a certain similarity in their characters, and she didn't like it at all.

Valentin was waiting for them at the usual meeting place. There were some sports clothes for her in the car. Their destination: the huge garden of Villa Leblanc.

"What are you doing in your tracksuit tonight?" she asked in surprise.

"What are we doing in our sportswear tonight? ... Look over there; I've brought some for you too," he replied with a grin.

"For me? Where did you get them? I didn't leave any training clothes at home with you."

"Do you remember the day we went to the farm? It was the day my father had his accident. You had brought some clothes in a bag and left them there in a hurry. Bonelli had given them to me."

"I didn't remember those clothes. Did you keep them at home the whole time?"

"Yes, I did. Every night when I went to bed, I held them close and smelt them," he said lovingly.

"You are not of this world. What have I done to deserve all this love?"

"Darling, to love and to be loved are both wonderful feelings, but not everyone is able to grasp the many nuances and differences. Everyone feels love for someone or something in their own way, some more, some less, some loudly, some quietly."

"I love the way you love me and your understanding of love and your respect for values and individuals," she said.

Arriving at Villa Leblanc, they entered the house briefly to allow Eva to change and were surprised by the delicious aroma and the table set for two in the dining room in front of the majestic fireplace.

"Did you plan this too?" she asked, overwhelmed by so much natural warmth towards her.

"He lifted her lovingly, spun her around, and whispered, "I love you."

"The sauna is ready, Mr. Leblanc, as you requested. Would you like to go in?" the housekeeper asked.

"Thank you, but we'll go to the sauna after dinner; now we'll take a few steps in the garden. I'll see you later," replied Valentin.

Eva and Valentin walked hand in hand in the huge garden, which was the size of a park and bordered a nature reserve. Happy to show her around, he led her through the different areas until they reached the centre of the park and stood in front of a children's playground with a slide, a swing, and a tree house.

"This was my kingdom," he said with a grin.

"I can't believe how new the games are; it looks like they've only been put in a few days," she said admiringly.

"My mom made the gardener look after them carefully because she wanted my children to play with them one day," he said.
just before her phone rang.

Apparently David had remembered that he had a wife on the other side of the world. Eva jerked back and forth, looking at Valentin as if to ask permission to answer the phone, but he nodded as if he understood what she was trying to tell him.

"Hello," David said tearfully.
"Hello, how are you? It doesn't look good tonight," she asked sympathetically.
"Today is the first day I've really realised what's happened, and I've had a nervous breakdown."
"Damn, have you at least been to the doctor to get something for it?"
"No, my mom's got enough drops at home to kill an army.".
"Now I understand what my mom was trying to tell me this afternoon," she said in a reassuring tone.
"What did your mom say?"
"That's not important. You'd better tell me what you've arranged for the funeral."
"The funeral is tomorrow at 3pm in the Basilica of Santa Maria del Cam. I'm sorry I didn't take you with me, because there are things that could have been organised differently," he said despondently.

There were things that could have been organised better... Was that the only reason why Eva's presence was irreplaceable? Eva began to give weight to David's words. It wasn't her presence as his wife that was important in this moment of despair, but the fact that someone was taking care of things. Was it the daily comforts that David was missing and not his wife? Or was it she who saw more and more negative things in him?

That evening, full of love and serenity for herself and sadness for him, Eva decided not to pay any further attention to David's words and simply said to him, "If there's anything I can do for you, I'll be happy to do it from here.

"I'm a bloody fool, and you're still the same good girl, kind and willing to do anything. I know what I have in you."

Another casual remark that confirmed that the comfort David had in sharing his life with her was everything to him and probably went far beyond any feeling of love. Despite everything, she remained calm and said to him, "Let me know if you need anything."

Like the rest of the house, the Leblanc's tastefully decorated sauna area left nothing to be desired. A potpourri of fragrances awaited them during the sauna infusion—a dream out of 1001 nights. Almost hypnotised by this magical scent, Eva hadn't noticed that Valentin had already undressed and was standing naked next to her.

"Won't you join me?" He whispered in a seductive voice.
Still a little dreamy, Eva turned to find him standing naked next to her.
"More than joining you, I'd like to eat you right now."

Valentin took Eva's words as an order, lifted her up, and sat her on the bar, which was already stocked with drinks and ice. He then took an ice cube, put it in his mouth, pushed her hair back slightly, and ran the ice cube down her neck. This provoked an immediate reaction from her. She wrapped her legs around his waist and tilted her body backwards as if inviting him to take the ice cube somewhere else. So he pulled up her top, exposing her torso, then went to her breasts with the ice cube, lingering on her nipples and making her moan.

"I've never been in a sauna before, but from what I've read, the ice is used after the sauna, not before," she whispered in a demanding voice, trying to pull herself up to kiss him. But he gently placed his hand on her chest to bring her back to her previous position and ran the ice cube down to her navel, leaving the rest of the ice there.

"Shall I stop then?" He whispered, touching her lips with his thumb as she lightly bit his finger, then he pulled her against him until their bodies were even closer together. Their eyes, burning with desire, met; he put his hand on the back of her neck and brought his lips close to hers; then he took a small piece of ice in his mouth and ran it over her lips, glowing with passion; then he lost himself in a fierce kiss, then lingered. Expecting to go on and glowing with passion, she looked at him and asked, "Why did you stop?"

But he picked her up and carried her into the sauna. "We'll continue here," he said, pulling off her clothes.

The next morning, Eva met Steven again in the car park.

"Good morning, Eva, Are you in a better mood today? It looks like you walked here today; is there a problem with the car?" He asked attentively.

"But this morning we're curious again, since when do you care about my mood and how I get to work? You know we live about 800 meters from here; a nice walk in the morning is good for your physical and mental health. Don't you think?"

"Uii... bad mood day... If you need anything, you know where to find me," he said and walked on.

Obviously Steven didn't know that David's father was being buried that day. Who knows what other unkind words he might have found for them? A man who was capable of neglecting his family in this way, of being overwhelmed by his duties as a father, and yet who was very demanding of his wife. A man who knew how to get the most for the least. But apparently he wasn't the only one, for David had recently become more and more like him. Had he taken a leaf out of Steven's book, or was he showing his true colours?

When she arrived at the office, she tried to call David, as he hadn't answered her messages. But it took a while before he answered. Full of sadness and anger, she is unable to adopt a neutral tone towards him.

"Why don't you answer the phone? And above all, why don't you answer it yourself on such a painful day for everyone?"

"Maybe because I don't feel like talking to anyone right now?" he replied aggressively.

"OK, let's forget it. It's not a good basis for communication.".

"Yeah, I'd say so too. Maybe we'll talk about it when I've calmed down," he replied, ending the conversation.

She was just trying to be close to him, and he was refusing to make any attempt.

Unhappy with the whole situation and not understanding why David had treated her like this, she decided to call her mother.

"Hey, sis, what's with the sad voice? What's wrong?" Carmen answered her mom's phone.

"Where is Mom? Why are you answering?"

"I'm standing in front of a flower shop waiting for mom to buy a funeral cushion for your father-in-law's funeral."

"At least I've got some news after the others left me in the dark," Eva said with relief.

"Don't say I didn't tell you your husband was a madman; you seem to be the only one who hasn't realised it. I wonder how much longer it's going to take."

"Come on, don't exaggerate; just because you don't like him doesn't mean he's a madman."

"If donkeys had a choice, they'd choose straw over gold. That's what you're doing—settling for straw when you could have gold. You're so

179

much like a donkey that you haven't even noticed that your boss is in love with you," Carmen said casually.

"Are you calling me a donkey? No seriously?" Eva said in a completely different tone.

"Yes, I am," her sister replied, laughing out loud.

Marion's voice could finally be heard in the background as she left the shop, and Carmen immediately picked up the phone.

"Have you been fighting again? I heard you all the way to the flower shop. You two are like cats and dogs," Marion grumbled.

"Maybe it has something to do with the fact that your daughter's tongue is more poisonous than you thought."

"Today is not the day for bickering. It's a sad day for everyone. The funeral is in a few hours, and I can imagine how you feel in this situation forced upon you by your husband, but I want you to know that we respect him for your sake, and none of us will ask him any questions about it."

"Maybe you will, but I don't know if I'll give him my opinion," Carmen said, interrupting the phone call.

"Carmencita, I love you, but you will keep your mouth shut in the future! That is an order!" Marion returned when.

The ringing of the phone in the office interrupted the conversation.

Mr. Wilson from Algata Pharma in Toronto was in a hurry to get an appointment before Christmas. That's how quickly the months passed between the many events.

"Mrs. Rodriguez, it's a pleasure to hear from you again, and it would be an honour to present you with the preliminary financial statements. We have had many successful years at Ritel, but this year has opened up new horizons and expectations for the future. This deserves to be celebrated. Are they coming to us in Toronto, or are we coming to them?" he asks enthusiastically.

"Well, I'm very pleased to hear that; the junior boss seems to have brought a wave of good fortune."

"Indeed!"

"Would you give me a few days to sort this out? I could tell you in advance that I would like to return to Toronto."

Upset and at the mercy of her emotions as the time for the funeral approached, Eva felt tired and in need of some fresh air, so she decided to take a walk in the company garden. At lunchtime there was absolute silence around her, as if the whole workforce had gathered in silence to eat. But almost at the end of the garden, she heard quick footsteps behind her and stopped for a moment. Listening more closely, she realised that the sound was coming at high speed, so she turned and stood motionless at the sight, as if she had seen a ghost.

"You fucking whore!" the person shouted, pushing her so hard that she fell to the ground and hit her head hard on the pavement, knocking her unconscious.

Chapter 10 Insufficient proof

"How long will this amnesia last? She's been in the hospital since yesterday and doesn't recognise anyone," Eva's father asked desperately as the doctor examined her.

Since the incident in the company garden, Eva has been in a state of amnesia due to the violent impact of her head on the ground. The people who found her in the company garden called the police, and it was only because of the commotion that Valentin came out and saw her lying unconscious on the ground. David, who was in Spain at the time because his father had died, was contacted by the police by phone during the funeral and got on the next plane with Eva's father.

Now he had to deal not only with the guilt of leaving her alone in Canada but also with the anger of his in-laws.

"This kind of amnesia can last up to 24-30 hours. Don't worry, the head injury is not serious, so let's assume she went into shock. Her vital functions are fine; she has an appetite and will recover soon," the doctor said confidently as
David sat stunned at the bedside.

Frederico turned to him angrily and asked, "Are you sure you are up to these responsibilities as a husband? I don't want to offend you, but I have the impression that you married too young and that life has put you in situations that have tested you. First the move to Canada, then Eva with her leg in a cast, then the loss of your father, and now Eva with amnesia.".

"There are difficulties in all marriages," he replied simply.

After visiting hours, David and Federico left the hospital, each in their own state of mind and each trapped in their own silence. What they didn't know was that Valentin would be with them all night and into the next morning. The doctors at the Saint Vincent hospital did everything a member of the Leblanc family could wish for, including a candlelit dinner in the neurology ward.

But Eva fainted during the meal. Valentin, in a panic, ran into the corridor and called for help. The ward doctor and a nurse rushed into the room, checked Eva's pulse and pupils, and tried to revive her when she suddenly let out a loud scream. The doctor immediately tried to calm her down, but she mumbled loudly with her eyes closed and started waving her arms.

"She's trying to tell us something; did you understand what she said?" the doctor asked Valentin.

"Yes, but I don't understand her—something about olives or something," Valentin replied.

But suddenly Eva opened her eyes wide, looked at Valentin, and shouted, "Mrs. Oliveira!

"Who's Mrs. Oliveira?" the doctor asked.

"My ex-secretary who is in prison," Valentin replied.

"No! She pushed me to the floor!" She cried and fainted again.

"What the hell is going on? Help her!" shouted Valentin, terrified, and grabbed Eva to lift her up.

The doctor quickly injected something into her vein and then put the blood pressure cuff on her while Valentin sat on the floor and held her. After a few minutes, she slowly tried to open her eyes and took Valentin's hand.

"Valentin," she said softly.

The doctor looked at Valentin and smiled. "She's back," he said.

"Would you like to tell us what happened?" the doctor asked.

She nodded her head in silence.

"I wanted to get some fresh air. My whole family was in Barcelona for my father-in-law's funeral, so I went for a walk in the company garden. It was very quiet and peaceful around me until I heard noises behind me. Suddenly I realised that they were not far from me, then I turned around and there was Mrs. Oliveira, but she looked different. I was standing in front of her without being able to say a word; everything happened in a matter of seconds; she shouted at me, and at the same time she pushed me violently, with a force that was out of this world.".

"We must call the police immediately," Valentin said worriedly.

"But if this Mrs. Oliveira is in prison, how could she be with you?" the doctor asked, a little confused.

"I don't know; I just know it was her," Eva said confidently.

Hoping to solve the case, the police did not take long to arrive. Two policemen entered Eva's room, which was already full of questions...

"We were there when you fainted in the company garden, so we're familiar with your case," said one of the officers.

"Would you believe me if I told you that the woman who pushed me to the ground with insane force was Mrs. Oloveira, Mr. Leblanc's ex-secretary?" She said hopefully.

"Yes," replied the policeman, looking at his colleague.

"Yes? What does that mean?" asked Valentin, confused.

"Yes, we believe that Mrs. Rodriguez was telling the truth. Mrs. Oliveira is not a woman either," replied the policeman.

"What?" asked Eva with a snotty look.
"What exactly do you mean?" asked Valentin.
"Well, she was born a man... you know what I mean?" said the policeman.
"That explains her strength when she pushed me to the ground. But why is she, or he, still at large?" asked Eva, irritated.

"Well, I don't know where to start, but after the attempted kidnapping of Mr. Leblanc, all the perpetrators were sent to prison, and Mrs. Oliveira was originally sent to a women's prison. During an investigation, it turned out that she only looked like a woman 'on top'," the policeman said.

After the policeman's incredible confession, Eva looked at Valentin and asked, "Does he mean that the so-called 'grenade' still has a penis?"
Valentin nods.
"Didn't your mother know that Mrs. Oliveira was a trans woman?" she continued.
"Would you have thought she was a man?" asked Valentin.

Without answering Valentin's question, she turned to the policeman.

"Could you please tell us what happened next?" she asked.
"Since we don't have prisons for transsexuals and Ms. Oliveira, who had committed a crime, lost her right to stay in Canada, a judge decided to send her back to Brazil, where she was put in a men's prison."

"But why is she back here?" she asked helplessly.

"Brazil is the deadliest country in the world for trans people. There is a lot of violence against transsexuals. Many are murdered every year, which is probably why Mrs. Oliveira moved to Canada. Once in Brazil, Mrs. Oliveira was brought before a judge. The law didn't consider the offence against Mr. Leblanc in Canada serious enough to send Mrs. Oliveira to jail, so she got off with a fine, got a new passport, and came back to Canada," the policeman said.

"Great, then we can prepare for the next problems," Valentin said sourly.

"Don't worry, Mrs. Oliveira is no longer at large. A judge has approved the final sex change operation, which will take place in two days' time, after which she will be transferred to the women's prison," the policeman replied.

"Was it that easy?" Eva asked in surprise.

"Mrs. Oliveira wanted it. Unlike the other offenders, she only got three years in prison, which is much better than being murdered in Brazil," the policeman replied.

"But why did she get off with so little?" asked Valentin.

"Of all the accomplices, Mrs. Oliveira was the only one for whom there was little evidence; the other two played the most important roles."

"The letter to the chief secretary, do you remember?" Valentin asked Eva.

"Yes, I remember that letter; it came from a well-known press centre, Hellomagazin."

"The main perpetrators had only taken advantage of Mrs. Oliveira; only a small part of the planned income from the kidnapping was planned for her, so the evidence was not sufficient for a longer sentence," the policeman replied.

"But why did Mrs. Oliveira come to the company and attack me?" asked Eva.

"Well, you had ruined her plans. Mrs. Oliveira was going to use the money from the kidnapping to pay for her gender change," replied the policeman.

"Well then, everything seems to have been cleared up. The patient needs to rest now," said the doctor.

After an eventful evening, Eva fell into a deep sleep. During the night, the doctor visited her again to make sure her memory was stable and found her asleep in Valentin's arms, who signalled with his thumb that everything was fine.
"I think that's exactly what she needs right now," the doctor whispered, blinking.

The next morning, Eva's father was unexpectedly on the ward and met Valentin in the corridor.
"Mr Leblanc? Right?" asked Federico.
Valentin looked at him in surprise and beamed.
"Your daughter is looking forward to seeing you," he said and ran out of the ward.
"Daddy!!!" cried Eva as he entered the room.
"You're back at last; you scared us!" He said with tears in his eyes as she ran towards him.
"Thanks for coming; I've missed you," she said, overwhelmed.

"I was here all the time, but you ignored me."

"What did you always tell us when we were children? Don't talk to strangers!" they said, laughing together.

"Since when do bosses visit their employees in hospitals?" Federico asked curiously.

"I don't know what you mean," Eva replied.

"Mr. Leblanc was here on the ward, didn't you know?" he asked.

"No. The police were also here last night; that could be the reason."

"The police? Why?"

"Because I suddenly remembered everything. Even the person who pushed me to the ground."

"Did you know the person who hurt you?"

"Yes, it was Mr. Leblanc's ex-secretary, one of the three accomplices in the kidnapping."

"But what does this have to do with you?"

"Long story: apparently I interfered with the operation, and she was deported back to Brazil as a result."

"I hope nothing more happens now, because I'm afraid her husband couldn't take any more stress."

"What has all this got to do with David?" she asked in surprise.

"Oh... I just think you got married far too soon, and he may not be ready for the responsibility. But maybe I'm just imagining things because I'm your father."

Sadly, she suddenly looked down at the floor without answering.

"Am I right?" he asked, surprised at her reaction.

"Dad, I'm just tired. Let's talk about something else. How long are you staying in Canada?"

"Well, that depends on how fast I can get my spare clothes dry," he replied with a grin.

"What do you mean, your spare clothes? I'm on the edge of my seat."

"Your husband and I went straight from the funeral to the airport and then to you without stopping. And without any suitcases or clothes, of course."

"Oh no. Did you have to buy new clothes for me?" she asked regretfully.

"Darling, it's not your fault, and it's also a real highlight for me. For the first time in years, I get to choose my own clothes. Do you know what I mean?" He said, his eyes persuasive.

"Oh yes, Mum... You see, your marriage isn't perfect either."

"That's right, it's not perfect, but..."

The round interrupted the conversation. The doctor approached Eva's bed with a beaming face.

"Can I go home already?" she asked directly.

"We'll keep you under observation today, and if your condition remains stable, you can go home tomorrow. What do you think?"

"Do I have any other choice?" she asked.

"I'm afraid not... let's see how your blood pressure is today," the doctor said.

During the examination, there was a knock at the door. David had also found his way to the hospital. Unsure if Eva would recognise him, he entered the room cautiously and looked at the doctor.

"Mr. Rodriguez, come in quietly; your wife knows who you are again," the doctor said, making everyone laugh.

Visibly relieved, David ran over to Eva and hugged her.

"You gave us a fright, you know that?" he said.

"Yes, I think someone told me that earlier today," she admitted.

"Can you really remember everything?" he asked.

"Yes," she grinned.

"Do you remember how the accident happened?" he asked.

Meanwhile, the doctor packed up his things and headed for the exit, then turned to David and said, "Your wife still needs to rest!"
"Do you remember how you lost your memory?" David asked again.
"I was violently knocked to the ground in the company garden," she replied.
"I didn't know you had made enemies in the company. How can something like that happen?" he asked, perplexed.
"You remember the famous grenade, don't you?" she asked.
"Of course, I think everyone in the company remembers it. But she's in prison; what's the grenade got to do with your memory?"
"Perhaps you should sit down," Federico said to David.

A little confused, but full of curiosity, David sat down next to Eva's bed and looked at her.

"I'm all ears," he said expectantly.
"It's not her," Eva said.
"OK. Now I don't understand anything," David said, scratching his chin.

"Mrs. Oliveira is transsexual, so she couldn't serve her sentence here in Canada because there are no prisons for transsexuals. She was then sent back to her native Brazil. In Brazil, a judge ruled that there was not enough evidence against her for a prison sentence, and she was fined. After being scared to death in her country because of the tense situation with transgender people, she got a new passport and came back to Canada.".
"Are you saying she has breasts on top and a bird on the bottom?" he asked, confused.
"That's right."
"But what does all this have to do with your accident?"

"Well, I'm the one who interrupted the kidnapping with the accident, thus destroying the dream of a lot of money."

"Incredible story; wait till the boys find out; they were all so keen on the grenade," he said with a grin.

Federico looked at him indignantly and shook his head.

"The boys won't know; keep it secret. You know how loud Steven is. How long do you think it will be before the whole company finds out? He's worse than Hallomagazin and the press put together. I'm warning you!" Eva said angrily.

But David looked as if he didn't know why she had reacted that way, until Federico said to him, "I think it's natural to keep silent in a case like this without being asked. Regardless of the fact that my daughter is personally involved, Mrs. Oliveira should not be discriminated against because of her sexual orientation and her desire to change her identity.".

"In my home, as in most families, I was taught that there are only two sexes: male and female, and anything else is a sin," David replied.

"My boy, you can believe me when I tell you that bisexuals, transsexuals, gays, and lesbians were already a problem in the Middle Ages. Only today there are more possibilities and fewer taboos; you can easily have an operation from man to woman and vice versa, and in some cases it's even subsidised by some health insurance companies.".

"You see? That's sick!" David replied definitively.

Annoyed, Eva covered her ears and shook her head several times.

"Darling, how would you like to go shopping? I can go home tomorrow morning, and I would love a full fridge. My dad is with me," Eva said to end the conversation nicely.

David's eyes lit up, as if happy at the suggestion, then he ran to her and kissed her on the forehead.
"Shall I go back to work tomorrow? Your father's here," he asked carefully.
"Of course, I'm in top form."

As soon as David had left the room, Federico turned to Eva and said, "I bet you still don't realise how immature your husband is.".
"Dad, you're acting like Mum and Carmen right now," Eva replied.
"Maybe you're right, and this isn't an appropriate topic of conversation today. Let's go down to the Klinink garden; a bit of fresh air will do you good."

Punctually in the evening, and after visiting hours, Valentin came to her with two pizzas and churros.

"Please tell me you remember who I am. I'm dying to kiss you," he said in a seductive voice before she could even say hello.
"How long has it been since we kissed?" she asked jokingly.
"Oh no! You don't remember us?" he asked uncertainly.
"Of course I do; come here and kiss me!"
"You scared me!" he said, hugging her tightly.
"Apparently I've scared everyone here today. But I have to admit, even without the memory, I felt safe around you," she said with a grin.
"Then why didn't you kiss me for so long?"
"You don't just kiss strange men like that," she said, amused.
"Unthinking but sensible, your parents did a good job," he said in praise, and finally kissed her.

"What else have you brought? The smell is familiar," she asked.
"Pizza and churros. Finding the best churros in Ottawa was a big job, so let's eat before it gets cold, as much as I'd like to keep kissing you."

Valentin lovingly set the small table, unwrapped the pizza, which had already been cut into pieces, and placed it on the plates.

"You knew which pizza I like?" she asked in surprise as he pushed the ham and olive pizza in front of her.
"Of course I did; you already told me. I also know your shoe size; I spied on you while you were sleeping," he said in an amorous voice.
"You're not from this world. No kidding!" she said, touched.

They spent their last night in the hospital cuddled together in the small hospital bed, but even that didn't seem to bother them. Within a few months, Valentin had become, without many words, a loving partner, a passionate lover, a protector, a reliable and responsible man who was obviously comfortable with his masculinity and expressed it with full energy. This is how they found each other—a dream man and a woman who was already taken, waiting for the right moment to live their happiness without restrictions.

On the day of his discharge, Federico entered the ward early in the morning to pick up Eva, and David was already there, beaming at the door of his room.

"What are you doing here so early? I thought you were going to work today," Federico asked in surprise.

"I'm allowed to start a little later today; I didn't really want my wife to have to take a taxi home," he replied.

With a look of satisfaction, the two men entered the room and found Eva ready to be picked up, the ward doctor standing next to her with a letter in his hand.

"Can we take her now?" Federico asked in his imperfect English.
"Of course, please keep an eye on her for a few days. We'll do another CT scan in two weeks' time, and then the matter will be closed for us," the doctor replied.

After the unplanned hospital stay and David's early return, Eva realised at home that the timers were still active. She looked around quickly. Had she forgotten something?
"What are you rushing around for?" her father asked suddenly as she walked through the apartment.
"Nothing, just looking around."
"Looks like someone was afraid of being left alone. Since when does your husband need a timer in every room?" asked Federico.
"That was me..."
"You were afraid to be alone here? That surprises me," said Federico.
"You seem to have forgotten that I was alone in a foreign country. I didn't even know how long David would have stayed away."
"I think I know someone who would never have left you in such a situation. When I arrived at the hospital this morning, I saw Mr. Leblanc on the ward again, talking to a nurse, but he didn't see me.".
"I don't know what you're talking about."
"It doesn't matter. When the time comes, you'll know what I'm talking about."

A glance up, a slight shrug of the shoulders, and she ran straight for the fridge.

"Daddy, I think we need to go shopping anyway. Would you come with us?" She asked with a sweet look on her face.

"I have nothing better to do. Let's call a taxi, and we can go straight into town for lunch."

"We can do that, but only if you promise me we won't do a sightseeing tour."

"I promise," he replied with a grin.

In the city, Eva and her father were taking a relaxed stroll when they suddenly bumped into Martha. But she didn't look happy.

"Hey Martha, aren't you feeling well? You look serious."

"I'm fine, but how are you? I heard about what happened at the company."

"And what exactly did you hear, if you don't mind me asking?"

"Well, I only know Steven's version; apparently there's also a crisis between you and David, and he left you here when he flew to Barcelona. You know, it's similar with us; I have to put a lot on hold to keep things running smoothly."

"Mhmm, interesting," Eva commented, emotionally neutral.

"Well, as they say, once a woman has forgiven a man, she doesn't have to reheat his sins for breakfast." Federico said.

"Daddy, you're just brilliant; you always have the right quote for every situation. Shall we continue?" She asked, looking at her watch.

Deep in thought, Eva walked on beside her father. Where had Steven gotten the idea to say that there was a crisis between her and David? Was it already obvious to others, or had David confided in Steven? Whatever the answer was, it meant nothing to her because Steven couldn't take her seriously.

"You seem pensive," Federico said, interrupting her circling thoughts.

"Well, you heard Martha's words, didn't you?"

"Are you going to put such fractions of conjecture on the gold scale? There's no evidence for such a statement."

"Not really, you're right."

"Look, I'd like to eat here; I wanted to last time with your mother and Carmen," Federico pointed to a French restaurant.

"We can do that; I've never had French food before. How long do you plan to stay in Canada?"

"Two more days, then I'll fly away; by then you'll be back in top form."

"I'd love to keep you here; it's so nice to spend time with you," she said gratefully, hugging him tightly.

A pleasant surprise awaited them at home in the afternoon. David, who had come home early from work, had started cooking and set the table for three.

"Sit down; I've cooked something delicious for you," he (David) said beaming, then ran over to Eva and kissed her on the lips.

"Wow, it looks like you've gone to a lot of trouble," she said praisingly.

"Yes, that's what good husbands do," he replied in a proud voice, then took a bottle of non-alcoholic champagne and filled the glasses for everyone.

"What exactly are we celebrating?" asked Federico.

"We're toasting the family," David replied.

But somehow it didn't all add up, so Federico called David a mink. There were many characteristics that could be attributed to this personality, notwithstanding the fact that he was raised by an extremely toxic mother. However, he only had two days left in Canada, and this precious time with his daughter was more important than David's maternal trauma. Did David need a woman to care for him because his mother had failed to do so in his childhood, and had he found in Eva a loving, reliable woman who could make up for what he had not received from his mother? Was this what David needed?

"You haven't told me much about what happened after the funeral. What will happen to your mother now? She's all alone," Eva asked, turning to David.

"Well, her cousin from Granada is going to stay with her for a while; they are the same age and both widows. But let's not talk about sad things today," David said cheerfully.

"Whatever you like, it never seems to be the right time for that kind of conversation anyway.".

Despite a few tense moments, the three of them managed to spend a reasonably pleasant day, so the evening ended with conversations about childhood and fond memories, and David then drove Federico to the hotel.

In the meantime, Eva decided to take a nap, and when David came home, he found her already in bed and joined her. But she kept her eyes closed, and he snuggled up against her.

"Are you asleep?" he whispered, slipping his hand under her pigiama top and stroking her bare breasts before she could answer. With her back to him, she winced slightly, but David didn't let that stop him from continuing.

"I know you're angry with me, but I want to make it up to you. I've missed you," he whispered.

"I've missed you too," she replied quietly, fulfilling her duties as a wife.

When David left the apartment the next morning, she immediately called Valentin. She quickly realised that the first night she had spent with David in days was not just a burden for her.

"It was impossible to fall asleep without you; I could feel you without you being there. The bed felt as empty as my heart. I took the pillows in my arms and snuggled up. Your scent comforted me for a moment. Some of your clothes and shoes are still here," he said sadly.

"It was even worse for me; I wish I'd spent the night alone. I don't want to fall asleep with anyone else but in your arms.
"When I think we won't see each other again until Monday at work, I go crazy."
"Did you really think we wouldn't see each other until Monday?" she asked with a hint of provocation.
"Why, did you have other plans?"
"Of course. The day after tomorrow I'm taking my father to the airport, and David has a golf match after work. Would you be free for a rendezvous at the country house at 2 p.m.?"
"Are you serious?" he asked excitedly.
"Absolutely! Clear all your other appointments from your diary. I want you all to myself."
"I'm all yours."

But Federico interrupted the love talk. Just in time for breakfast and with a map of the country, he stood at the door.

"It looks like you're planning an attack on me... we said yesterday 'no city tour'," said Eva, irritated by the map in Federico's hands.
"Mira Carino, there's no town on this map," he pointed.
"If there's no city marked, what are you planning?"
"A bicycle tour to the Pink Lake. The right car and bikes are waiting for us downstairs," he said, raising his eyebrows.
"Dad, you're an overactive pensioner, you know that? No wonder Mum is sometimes overfed."
"At your age, a leisurely 2.3-kilometre bike ride around the lake doesn't overexert you. Besides, I had already done a lot of research at home about the lake. Did you know that some of the fish that live in the blue-green lake are thought to be prehistoric, apparently due to a

lack of oxygen at the bottom of the lake? One unique fish that lives there is the three-spined stickleback, which appears to have evolved from a saltwater fish to a freshwater fish. Swimming is prohibited for both humans and animals. We'll leave after breakfast."

"It looks like I don't have any say in this, does it?"

"Yes, you do. You can decide where we go for lunch after the trip."

"Great, that's very generous of you," she replied with a touch of sarcasm.

After half an hour's drive, Eva and Federico arrived at the Gatineau Park car park. The stunningly beautiful autumnal trees around the lake melted into the blue-green water. Eva looked admiringly at her father and said, "Thank you for letting me come here."

In several stages, they reached the lookout points across the lake where they could see the many species of birds. They could walk down a flight of steps to the shore.

"Let's park the bikes here," Federico suggested.

From the observation points, they walked down to the shore, where the clear and shallow water allowed them to look over the bottom and see the numerous three-spined birds. All around them was absolute silence.

"What a wonderful sight," she said enthusiastically.

"Yes, it is. Time is what we can never get back. And therefore the most precious thing we have. If many people realised that every day is one less day of life, they would probably live differently than just chasing after professional success and material things. Fast-paced, overworked, tense, and irritated, most of them miss out on the beautiful moments.".

"I believe that in order to re-educate people about certain values, the media world should be abolished. Technology is both a blessing and an escape. I don't want to imagine what it will be like in 20 years.".

"Well, maybe someone will come up with the idea of taking everything back to the Stone Age," Federico said amusedly.

"No matter where this process or development leads, my children will get an old school education and learn exactly the same values that you have passed on to us. I will make sure of that.

"Then I'm curious to see if your husband will join in, because his mother hardly gave him anything. He can be grateful to have had a good father. I wouldn't want to be in that poor man's shoes; he certainly didn't have a happy life with the impossible and selfish Leonor. No wonder he died so young," Federico said regretfully.

"I can hear the sadness and anger in your voice—the same feelings that have been with me these past few days.

"We have to look forward and take responsibility for our lives, knowing that life is up and down; nothing goes smoothly and often not according to plan, but that's what keeps us alive. In the lows, we get the best impulses and ideas, we create experiences and successes, we rebuild ourselves, we learn from them, but we do not remain flawless. As long as we live, we learn and remember these words." (Federico)

"Daddy, you are the wisest, most loving, and best father anyone could ever wish for," she said, holding him in a long embrace.

In the late afternoon, Eva and her father returned the rental car and bicycles and took a taxi home. On the way home, she rested her head on her father's shoulder and held his hand tightly between hers. A bond that needs no words. She and her father had always been one heart and one soul.

"Let's cook together; your husband doesn't seem to be back yet," Federico suggested.

"That's a great idea. Spanish evening?" she asked.

"Spanish evening!" he confirmed.

Time flew between cooking and tasting wine, but David didn't seem to be in any hurry to get home.

"Aren't you going to call your husband to find out where he is?" asked Federico, a little irritated.

But when Eva picked up the phone, she saw several messages on the display. One from Valentin and one from David.

"Don't wait for me; we have a long meeting at the office; I'll eat later.".

"Let's have a drink; David has to stay late at the office. I'll make up the sofa bed for you later; I want you to sleep here tonight.".

"If that's what you want, then that's what we'll do."

Eva and her father were sitting on the sofa, full and well-fed, when David returned. Good-humoured and hungry, he stood in front of them and looked at them.

"You look strange; have you had anything to drink?"

Now Eva and her father looked at each other and laughed to tears.

"I had a good guess. Does anyone need a lift to the hotel?" asked David, who still had his jackets on.

"My father will sleep here tonight. Schaumal, the sheets are already there," she replied.

A little irritated, David looked at his wife and said, "Then let's hope he doesn't feel disturbed in the morning," and ran into the kitchen.

The next day, David was picked up by Steven so that Eva could drive her father to the airport. There was an empty bottle of wine in the living room, next to the couch.

"Dad, did you finish that bottle?"

"Yes, I did; it was by far the most relaxing night I've had in a long time. I slept like a baby," he said, still half asleep. "We have to leave soon because your suitcase is at the hotel. Do you remember?"

"Let's go now; I have to take a shower. Hurry up, hurry up!"
"I thought it would end like this," she said with humour.

Saying goodbye at the airport was harder than usual for Eva after a few intense days with her father.
"Promise me I'll see you at Christmas," she shouted with tears in her eyes as her father ran into the check-in area.
"I promise!"
As she walked back to the car, she was glad to be spending time with Valentin because he was waiting for her at the country house.
From the narrow road leading to the villa, she saw the smoking chimney. She quickly parked her car in the courtyard, got out, and saw him coming towards her.
Only their eyes spoke; only their lips were filled with love. No words were necessary. Silently, he picked her up and carried her to the door.
"I love you so much that there are no words to describe this feeling," he said.
"Your words touch me deeply. I love you too," she whispered as he set her down at the door and led her by the hand into the house, where the warmth of the fireplace and the many candles greeted them.
"Was your father able to relax on the plane?"
"Somehow I can't quite put my finger on it, but he was different this time," she said emotionally.
"Yes, that's what I thought. That must be why he left this letter for me at work yesterday," he said, placing the still-sealed envelope in her hands.

Chapter 11 Arrangement

"**H**ave you ever watched someone have sex?" Steven asked casually at the end of the day as David waited for Eva.

"I'm not sure what you mean," David replied, confused.

"I mean, watching other couples having sex?"

"No. To be honest, I've never thought of that. Have you?"

"So it never occurred to you...? Is that why you've never done it or haven't had the opportunity?" asked Steven Penetrant.

"But you seem familiar with the subject. Have you ever done it?"

Without hesitation, Steven took his mobile phone out of his pocket and showed David his chat history.

"I've seen this young woman before at the golf club; is that possible?" asked David, pointing to the profile picture.

"Yes, she and her partner are a bisexual couple," Steven explained with a smile.

"And what's that got to do with you?" asked David, who still didn't quite understand what this was all about.

"You can read the chat history if you like," he replied, picking up his mobile phone.
David eagerly read the messages without commenting.

"Why don't you say anything?" asked Steven.

Without showing any emotion, David handed the phone back to him and asked, "What do you want me to say?"

"Just what you think."

"At what point in this chat do you want to be praised? At the point where you write to her that you and your wife live in the same house but are no longer together? Or that you are in an unhappy marriage but are making arrangements to avoid paying alimony for her and the children?"

Suddenly David sees Eva coming their way and hands his phone back to him. Steven puts it in his pocket and walks quickly to the car.
"Was Steven in a hurry today?" she asked, after he had run off before she had gotten to the car.
"Apparently he had to take the kids somewhere," David lied.
"Since when does he take his kids somewhere? I thought there was a regular division of roles in his marriage to Martha," she teased.
"I'm not interested in other people's marriages."
"Perhaps you should know that Martha assumes we're in a marital crisis after you flew off to Barcelona alone after your father died," she scolded.
"Yes, it was a mistake to leave you here, but there's nothing I can do about it now. Now please let's go; I have to go to the laundry.".
On their way home, Eva and David went into town to pick up their trousers.
"There, look! Isn't that Martha with the girls?" Eva called loudly as he parked the car.
"Yes, it looks like it," he replied, getting out of the car quickly as Martha walked on with her children.

After a moment and with his hands full, David returned to the car to find a less than friendly Eva waiting for him.

"Why are you so angry?" he asked.

"Steven's an arsehole," she replied.

"I'm not going to get into any more conversations about Steven and Martha. They're adults and responsible for their own happiness," he replied admonishingly.

"In fact, Martha's probably the one who's at the end of the stick."

"Even if that were the case, it's not your problem. He's behaving properly towards me; the rest is none of my business."

The next morning, after a tense evening and a restless night, Eva sat down with Valentin in the meeting room and waited for the rest of the participants to arrive.

"Your father's letter has been bothering me for days," Valentin said.

"I keep holding the letter in my hand, reading it, and hearing my father talking to you; it's a strange feeling."

Dear Valentin,

I have always tried to stay out of my daughter Eva's family affairs, but recent events have caused me to reconsider and take a stand.

I'm sure you're wondering why I'm contacting you. Well, as a man, I can tell when a man looks at a woman and expresses all the love in that look.

I am not talking about David's look at Eva, but your look, the way you look at my daughter Eva.

I could already see what your gaze expressed at the ceremony for Eva that took place in your villa in the country. When I saw her several times in the hospital a few days ago, I realised that I could trust you. Perhaps I don't have the right to write these things to you, but the accident Eva had when she was alone in Canada forces me to do so. Perhaps it is fear or the instinct of a father who sees things that are not obvious to others, but I feel that I can allow myself to ask you to look after my daughter and protect her in the way that you can.

Thank you

Federico

"His trust overwhelmed me. He doesn't know me, but he relies entirely on his instincts," Valentin said thoughtfully.

"In fact, my father is a very instinctive person. Something's been bothering him about David lately; somehow he's made it clear to me, but I can't figure out what it is."

"Maybe you'll find out later, but until then, please kiss me," he asked her and gave her a peck on the cheek.

As Eva walked into the car park at the end of the day, she saw David and Steven talking.

"And which one was the wildest?" David asked Steven, not realising that Eva was standing right behind them.

"Can I see who was wilder?" she asked curiously.

Surprised, Steven quickly put his phone in his pocket and took two steps back as David watched without comment.

"You look at me as if I've said something forbidden. Who would be so wild, apart from Steven's twins?" asked Eva naively.

The men looked at each other in relief and laughed.

But on the way home, Eva still wanted to know what they had both been looking at on Steven's mobile phone and asked determinedly, "What was Steven showing you earlier?"

"The twins are playing, just like you said."

"Somehow I never believe Steven one hundred percent," she said incredulously.

"Well, you have your own opinion of Steven, so I'm afraid I can't help you."

"He just radiates suspicion."

"Just because he radiates suspicion doesn't mean I have to tell you everything that's been said between us. Don't you think?"

"It's all right; I didn't mean to intrude."

"I'm going golfing with the boys in an hour; I hope that's OK with you," he said carefully.

"Sure, I was planning to go jogging too."

"What? You want to do sports too?" he asked in surprise.

"Sure, why not?"

A few minutes after David left the house, Eva put on her sports clothes and set off. A few streets away, Valentin was waiting for her in a dark corner. Fearless and full of joy, she ran towards him, sure in her heart that she was doing the right thing, especially after her father's letter to Valentin.

Arriving at the car, Valentin looked through the still-closed windshield. She looked in, leaned in, and pressed her lips to the windscreen.

"Why kiss between glasses? When it really tastes better?" he called.

Eva released herself from the windscreen and quickly jumped into the car. He took her face in his hands and kissed her deeply.

"Have I told you today how much I love you?" he asked, continuing to kiss her.

"Mmhh, I don't think I can count how many times..." she replied, pulling him close again.

After the long kisses, Eva looked at him and asked, "Do you want to spend your time here in the car?

"No, there's a nicer place I've been thinking about, and it's not far from here."

Without revealing where he was going, Valentin started the car. After a few minutes, they arrived at the Villa Leblanc, drove through the massive metal gate, and stopped in the conservatory.
After getting out of the car, Valentin blindfolded Eva and led her into the warm conservatory.

"What smells so good in here?" she asked enthusiastically.
Valentin then took the scarf from her eyes and asked, "Will you be my guest today?"

Full of enthusiasm, she looked at the table set for two for a candlelit dinner and nodded in agreement.
"What have I done to deserve this?" she asked, overwhelmed.
"I could give you many good reasons, but I'll only give you one: I love you more than anything, and there's nothing I wouldn't do to see you happy," he replied, pulling her hand towards him to kiss it.

Surrounded by many rare plants, palm trees, and exotic climbers, in a romantic setting, Eva and Valentin were enjoying their dinner when suddenly her mobile phone rang.
"Aren't you going to answer it?" asked Valentin.

She glanced at the screen and saw Martha's number.
"I don't think it's important; she probably wants to vent about her husband," she replied, and she put the phone back in her jacket pocket.

But then it rang again.
"Eva, please help me!" Martha screamed in panic.
The sound of a child crying could be heard in the background.
"What's happened?" Eva asked worriedly.
"Moira is having an asthma attack and has lost consciousness. I can't reach Steven; the ambulance is on its way. Please help me."

"I'll be right there!" said Eva without hesitation.

Valentin stopped a few meters from Martha's house and let Eva out. The ambulance was already at the door. Eva rushed to the house, but when she got inside, little Moira was lying on the floor, turning blue. With tears in her eyes, Martha picked up Alexa and handed her to Eva: "Please take care of my little girl; my parents are on holiday.".

Eva immediately carried little Alexa out of the house, stood on the pavement, and called a taxi. Martha's desperate sighs could be heard across the street. The sigh of a mother afraid of losing her child.
After a few minutes, a taxi arrived, and Eva got in with little Alexa and tried to call David.
He couldn't be reached either.
"Please take me to Golfworld," Eva ordered.

After a quarter of an hour's drive, they arrived at the large, dimly lit car park of the golf club. Eva looked around tensely and immediately spotted her car in the car park.
"Please stay here and wait for me," she told the taxi driver, taking little Alexa with her.

But as she made her way to the entrance, crossing an even darker area of the car park, she heard strange noises. Attracted by these sounds, she looked around and spotted a car that looked like Steven's in a dark corner and stopped for a moment. As she turned to leave, she heard more noises and saw the car shaking.
"I'm scared," Alexa said.
Eva cautiously moved closer to the car to see if it could really be Steven's car.
"It's Daddy's car," little Alexa whispered as the car started to shake again.

A shaking car with steamed up windows. And an unavailable husband, which couldn't be good.

With hurried steps and the little girl still in her arms, Eva walked to the taxi, left little Alexa in the front seat next to the driver, and asked him to wait for her. Then she entered the club and saw David and Robin sitting at the bar, chatting to a few people.

"What are you doing here?" David asked in surprise.

In silence, Eva took a golf club from an abandoned bag and quickly ran out.

But David and Robin sensed something was wrong and ran after her, but it was too late. Furious, Eva stood in front of Steven's car and smashed the golf club against the windscreen until screams could be heard from inside the car. David and Robin held Eva down as the other club guests arrived in the car park.

"What the hell are you doing? Are you mad?" David shouted as he pulled Eva away from the car.

Amid the commotion, the taxi driver approached Eva with a crying Alexa as Steven and two women got out of the car.

"Daddy?" cried little Alexa.

"You bloody bastard!" screamed Eva, taking the little girl back into her arms.

"Let's go, please," said the taxi driver.

"Stop right there!" David shouted as Eva and Alexa got into the taxi.

Angrily, Eva slammed the door and said to the taxi driver, "Drive away!"

When Eva saw several missed calls from Martha and one from Valentin on the way home, she feared the worst and called Martha back immediately.

"My child," Martha sighed incessantly.

"Mum..." cried Alexa.

"What is wrong with Moira? Martha, please tell me how Moira is!" cried Eva.

"She's been resuscitated and taken to intensive care. I'm with her."

"Thank God! I'm taking Alexa home with me. Please keep me informed."

"Were you able to find Steven?" she asked then.

"We'll talk later; the little one needs my full attention at the moment." She had barely hung up with Martha when the next call came from Valentin.

"I can't say much because little Alexa is with me, but it was a very dramatic situation; I'll tell you what happened in person later," Eva said.

When Eva came home, the first thing she did was look after Alexa. The child seemed quiet and withdrawn because of what had happened. All the way home, Eva wondered if she had noticed what was going on between her father and the two women in the car, but she didn't dare ask.

"What would you like to eat?" Eva asked politely.

But Alexa looked sad and just shrugged.

"Look, how about a couple of scoops of ice cream?" Eva asked, opening the freezer.

A sparkle immediately went through her beautiful blue eyes, and she smiled.

"OK, I see, let's get started," Eva said and filled two tubs with ice cream.

A few minutes later, David came home and went into the kitchen. But when he tried to open his mouth, Eva looked at him angrily and told him to be quiet. After the ice cream, the child seemed satisfied.

"I'm tired; do you have a big bed? I want to sleep with you," Alexa asked.

"I'm tired too, so let's cuddle up together."

"But where will David sleep?" she asked, a little confused.

"Oh, he can sleep on the couch; he's a big boy now," Eva replied with a shrug.

"Daddy always does that," Alexa said.

Eva, not expecting such an answer, took the little girl by the hand, walked across the living room to where David was already sitting on the couch, and asked him to put the blanket on the couch.

"The little girl has been through a lot today; she's going to sleep in my bed," she told him curtly.

Without comment, David went into the bedroom, took the duvet, and lay down on the couch.

The next morning David and Eva met very early in the kitchen.

"Can you tell me what's going on?" David asked innocently.

"Moira almost died of an asthma attack yesterday and had to be resuscitated while her dad was screwing two women in the car at the same time! That's what happened!"

"Bloody hell!" said David angrily.

"Is that all you have to say? You disgust me!"

"What's that got to do with me?"

"You know exactly what your boyfriend is doing, and you support him. You probably even enjoy Steven's great stories. Get out of my sight!" she said and walked back into the room to Alexa.

Visibly dejected, David left the house while Eva looked after Alexa. David's behaviour towards Steven's evil deeds made her think. Recently, the character of the person she had married for love had changed a lot, and not for the better. Had it always been like this, and had she never noticed? Had her father had a premonition about David's change of character, and was that why he had asked Valentin for help? Either way, she didn't like the immoral and selfish behaviour of David's friends. Where had good family values gone?

What was the point of getting married and having children if you had to run away from all those obligations? Did she have the right to think badly of Steven after falling in love with Valentin? But all these thoughts were interrupted by Martha's phone call.

"I don't know how to thank you," Martha sighed.
"That's what friends are for. But tell me how Moira is."
"She was transferred to the children's ward half an hour ago and is out of danger."
"That's great news! Alexa is still asleep; I think yesterday was a traumatic experience for her."
"What do you mean? Her sister lying unconscious on the floor or her father shagging in the car?" asked Martha bitterly.
"So now you know too..."
"The whole town knows. The photos of the smashed windscreen are in the newspapers. And my future ex-husband has been banned from the golf club. You are by far the bravest woman I know!"
"How are you?" Eva asked sympathetically.
"My daughter is alive, and that's all that matters to me. Steven has to leave by the end of the week; the marriage is getting divorced. Who knows how long he's been doing this behind my back? The trust is definitely broken," she said in a confident voice.
"How will you manage on your own? The children are still quite young.
"My parents will be back in the early afternoon to pick Alexa up from you if that's OK; everything else will be put off until the weekend. We'll see the divorce lawyer next week."
"Wow, you are a very strong woman; it shows in your actions and determination, and if I may say so, I totally agree with you on your decision. I would have done the same if I were you.".
"Somehow I had the feeling for a long time that Steven had become strange, but you don't want to admit certain things. Just think what a great life he had; he didn't have to worry about anything but his

work. I looked after the children and the house all day. When he came home in the evening, dinner was already on the table. Every other day, right after dinner, he packed his gym bag and left the house. Full service, like a hotel, that was his life. Whether I live alone in a relationship or alone with the children, it makes no difference," said Martha with conviction.

"You sound confident and convinced that everything will work out the way you want; I'm sure of it.

"Men are not to be underestimated these days; I think some men's day-to-day behaviour is Oscar-worthy," Martha said with some sarcasm as Alexa called from the bedroom.

"Your daughter needs me; I'll talk to you later," Eva said and said goodbye.

In the early afternoon, after Martha's parents had picked up little Alexa, Eva tried to reach David.

After several unsuccessful attempts she decided to go to the office, but when she got there she found a rather stressed Valentin, whose diary was full as the end of the year was approaching and the daily work would soon be too much for him to handle alone.

"Hey Amor, what took you so long?" he asked as she put down her bag.

"Well, a lot happened between last night and this morning," she said, holding the newspaper in front of him.

"It's fortunate that the little girl is well again. But what am I supposed to do with the paper?" he asked, a little confused.

"That was her father when I finished with his car," she pointed at the photo with her index finger.

Wide-eyed, he read the text of the advertisement.

"Were you the rioter? What's your name?" He asked, a little panicked.

Amused by Valentin's reaction, Eva replied, "I can't be on all the front pages, you know. From heroine to rioter would be too scandalous. The police have made the names anonymous. Are you relieved now?"

214

"I wouldn't care, but I think my mother would have had a heart attack if her son's future wife was not only divorced but involved in a little scandal," he said with a grin.

"I'm glad you don't care," she said, relieved.

"But what the hell happened in that place that made the beast in you start to destroy?"

"Well, it was pretty intense, and I think it was the right thing to do. A gesture of solidarity with a woman who had been betrayed for who knows how long and was about to lose her child," she said proudly.

"Knowing you, it must have been really violent, but what triggered your reaction?" he asked curiously.

With her arms crossed, Eva went to the window and looked out silently and thoughtfully, then she turned to Valentin and asked, "Have you had sex with several women at the same time?"

"What kind of question is that?" he replied a little indignantly.

"Did you, yes or no?" she asked seriously.

"What do you think? You've known me for a while."

"Well, I think that men are an underexplored area and that many are able to hold on to a woman without problems and without feelings, out of convenience, the so-called'safe 'harbour', and lead a parallel life where all options are possible."

"Why do you only think of men? Women can do that too, can't they?" he asked, slightly offended by the statement.

"But women often get to a point where they separate from men because they just want to find themselves. They decide for themselves without having to blame a third person for the failure of the marriage.".

"But that's not the point. What happened last night is obviously still very much on your mind. What happened?"

"When I arrived at Martha's, little Möira was lying on the floor, completely blue and being resuscitated. In front of me was a distraught mother holding one little girl in her arms and watching

215

the dramatic resuscitation of the other. The feelings are indescribable. She had tried to call her husband several times, but he didn't answer the phone, so I took little Alexa in my arms, ran out of the house, and called a taxi. We went to the golf club, and then it happened," she said, turning to the window.

"Yes, but then what happened?" he asked.

"The car park wasn't very well lit, and as I was walking towards the entrance of the club, I suddenly heard strange noises coming from a darker corner, then I turned and saw Steven's car. The windows were steamed up, and it looked like it was shaking, so I walked closer to get a better look, and then my blood rushed to my head as I realised what was going on in the car. Furious, I took the girl back to the taxi, ran into the club, and saw David and Robin talking to others; then I grabbed the first golf club I could get my hands on and ran back to Steven's car.".

"Wait, you smashed the windscreen with a golf club?" he asked incredulously.

She nodded her head in agreement. The good-natured and patient Eva was now losing her cool.

"And then?" he asked.

"Then Steven and two women got out of the car at the same time, while the taxi driver brought little Alexa back to me. Meanwhile, David and some of the club guests arrived in the car park."

"Did you see the little girl with her father and the two women?" asked Valentin, horrified.

"Yes, but I don't think she understood what was happening."

"Is that why you want to know if I've ever slept with more than one woman? Are you afraid something like that might happen to you?" He (Valentin) asked sympathetically.

"I know your parents raised you with solid values, but this incident and my father's actions with the letter addressed to you have raised a lot of questions in my mind."

216

"You know, I think you should be able to tell the difference between men who don't want to love you but can't let you go and men who consciously choose a woman because that woman is all they want. And that's you for me; I just want to belong to you for the rest of my life," he replied.

"I believe everything you've just told me, not because your tone is convincing, but because you prove it to me and make me feel it every day," she said, moving.

The caring Valentin stood up, ran to her, and wrapped his arms around her in a warm, secure embrace that needed no further words... Until he was interrupted by David's phone call.

"Sorry I'm late, but we had a very long meeting; there's a state of emergency here because of Steven's incident," David explained frantically.

"In what way?"

"Well, Steven has asked our team leader for a transfer, and Martha kicked him out of the house after yesterday's action; he has to move out by the end of the week."

"Too bad for him; he must be lucky to have such a good-natured wife like Martha," Eva says irritably.

But David was silent and remained mute on the line.

"Are you still there?" she asked.

"Yes, yes, I'm here. I'll meet you in the car park in an hour, OK?"

Just in time for closing time, David stood alone in the car park, gazing thoughtfully into the distance as Eva walked to the car. Unsure of Eva's possible reaction, he instinctively skipped the kiss, which turned out to be a good decision because Eva was just waiting to poison him; all he had to do was say the wrong word... And sure enough, he said it...

"Steven could have charged you with criminal damage; didn't you think of that? That could have been very bad for you. Have you read the papers?" He said it in a reproachful tone.

"Are you telling me that the problem was my reaction to his disgusting behaviour and not his behaviour?" she asked indignantly.

"I just think you had no right to behave that way," he replied emotionlessly.

She swallowed nervously several times before she found an appropriate response to David's poisonous conversation.

"Do you think his behaviour is appropriate for a husband and father of two small children?"

Shrugging his shoulders, he simply said, "Everyone should live as they see fit."

After David's answer, Eva realised more and more why her father had turned to Valentin. David revealed more and more negative traits from the toxic upbringing he had experienced at home. How would the next few months of living under the same roof work out? The distance between them was growing day by day, and Eva had already separated from him in her heart.

"By the way, Robin and I are going to help Steven move his things out of the house tonight; he's found a new flat at short notice," he finally said.

"If you drop me off here, you can go straight there," she replied, slamming the car door shut.

The next morning, Eva and Valentin had several meetings away from home, but she did not yet know that he had booked a place for lunch at the Riviera Ottawa restaurant. The first time they'd been there together, they hadn't known much about each other except that they had a strong physical and emotional response when they kissed and touched. Neither of them had ever felt such desire for another person, and yet they both agreed that they wanted to be together forever.

"We did it," she said excitedly as the driver pulled up outside the restaurant. Like a true gentleman, Valentin ran to the car door, opened it, and offered her his hand to get out, then sent the driver away.

"Yes, we've been here before. Do you remember when?" He asked her with a smile.

"You kidnapped me on the pretext of a date you'd made up. I remember every detail of that date. When I close my eyes, I can see us standing by the river and you burying your face in my hair. My life has never been the same since that day."

The restaurant manager greeted them at the entrance: "Welcome, follow me to the reserved seat," he said, leading them to the exact spot where they had sat together for the first time.

"Same place, same woman; you wouldn't have believed me a few months ago," he said.

"What was I to think? You're the son of the company owners, and I'm a married expatriate who's only been working in the company for a few days as your mother's assistant. It sounds like a scene from a film."

In his silence, Valentin looked her in the eye, slipped his hand into his jacket pocket, and pressed a small parcel into her hand. Surprised, she looked at the package and opened it.

"So, do you want it?" he asked hopefully.

"Wait, where did you get this old ring? I've seen it before," she asked with some surprise.

"This ring belonged to your grandmother, your father's mother," he replied.

"What? It can't be; it must be something similar because the box looks new," she replied.

"Here you go," he said, handing her a small envelope.

"You're making me nervous; what's in the letter?" she asked, overwhelmed.

"You remember the letter I got from your father, don't you?"

"Yes, not a day goes by that I don't think about that letter. But what does it have to do with this?"

"The letter I showed you first wasn't the only one; there was a second letter for you in the parcel and a note about the ring."

"But what is my father trying to achieve? I thought he wanted to save me from being disappointed by David; that's why he turned to you.

"Your father arranged our engagement," he said, pointing to the letter, but she couldn't believe it. How could her father arrange an engagement with Valentin when he knew she was married to David? It wouldn't make any sense.

"Don't you want to read the letter?" he asked her as she held the envelope tightly in her hands.

"Right now?" she asked excitedly.

"Yes, right now."

My dearest Eva,

After Cristiano's death, I discovered some things that worry me and will come to light in time. I'm sure you're wondering why I gave Valentin my mother's ring, but the answer is simple. Even then, in the country house, during your ceremony of honour, I knew immediately how you felt about each other, and believe me, he can't hide his feelings for you. You need a man who will honour you and treat you as you deserve, a man who understands and fulfils the role and duties of a husband, a man who will stand by you through thick and thin, and yes, a man who loves you passionately and who is obsessed with you, as I am with your mother. I know you are still bound to David by the marriage certificate, but your heart is not with him.

Your heart will lead the way until you reach your destination. Follow your heart.

With love.

Dad'.

"So you had the letters and the ring with you all this time and didn't tell me?" she asked.

"Yes."

"You also have a piece of paper with the ring; what does it say?"

Valentin took the note from his jacket pocket and handed it to her.

"You haven't even taken your jacket off," the waiter said as he went to fetch the menus.

"And what's worse, we haven't even looked at what we want to eat," Valentin replied with a smile, and the waiter left them alone.

After the waiter had disappeared around the corner, Eva opened the menu.

"I'm very special; recognise the moment..."

Surprised, Eva looked at Valentin and remarked, "My father has always loved riddles, but I never thought he would involve us in a riddle of his own creation.

"I have recognized the moment, and today is the right time for me; even if you are still bound to your husband by a marriage certificate, you are all I want. Please become my wife as soon as circumstances permit. I love you more than anything."

Deeply moved, Eva tried to hold back her tears, but just as she was about to answer, David called her.

"Answer it," Valentin advised her, "it could be something urgent."

Unenthusiastically, but aware of her marital duties, Eva answered.

"My mother wanted to surprise me, and she's at the airport in Ottawa," he announced excitedly.
Unable to say a word, Eva stared at Valentin for a millisecond before she fainted.
"Hello? Hello?" a voice shouted from the mobile phone now lying on the floor.

Chapter 12 High visitor

"I'm bored; when can we go into town?" complained David's mother from the living room.

"Mum, please be patient. I have a few things to do, and then we can go," David replied in an irritated tone.

"You took a fortnight's holiday to spend time with me, not to do housework. Why do you have a wife if you have so many things to do?" asked Leonor.

"I married Eva because she's a very good woman. It's Christmas in a few weeks, and there's a lot of work in the company. You know, she has a very responsible job that allows us to live very well. Besides, it's not her fault that she's been sent to clients all week, so someone here has to help with the housework."

"Aren't you worried that she might cheat on you when she's away from home for so long? Besides, I'm a guest here, and you're on holiday, so she can take care of the rest of the house herself at the weekend when she comes back."

"Mum, Eva is a very good woman, but honestly, have you seen her? Men don't cheat with a woman like that, you know what I mean? She's too good... and yes, as a husband I can take care of the household; she also shares her salary with me," he replied, no less venomous than his mother.

"Then let's go out now; you can do the laundry later."

"All right, let's go," he finally replied.

These were some of the values David had been taught by his mother to prepare him for social and family life: lack of appreciation, zero empathy, selfishness, and lack of respect for his partner. Just as she had behaved during her marriage to Christian, she demanded that David treat his wife in the same way.

During the one-hour Ottawa Winter Tour, David and his mother enthusiastically drove through Ottawa and Gatineau, the perfect tour for someone like Leonor, who hadn't even thought about bringing the necessary winter clothing for a stay in Canada because of the surprise effect.

From Parliament Hill to Rows Lake, from the Riedeau Canal to Lansdowne Park, the first part of the tour included sightseeing.

"It's cold here, isn't it?" she asked during the first break.

"Well, we're not in Barcelona. If you'd said something, I could have at least borrowed some of Eva's clothes; there are plenty of hats and warm fleece vests."

"For God's sake, it's not that bad," she replied, shoving her hands into the pockets of her thin jacket.

After a short break, they moved on to the next part of the tour, the Canadian Museum of Nature, the Canadian War Museum, and the Canadian Museum of History, but even these wonders didn't seem wonderful enough for Leonor, who was happy to move on to the last part of the tour: the National Gallery of Canada, Notre-Dame Basilica, and the Royal Canadian Mint, which Leonor found really interesting and not at all boring, especially since, unlike classical museums, you don't visit a mint every day. The Canadian Mint not only mints the Canadian dollar but also 74 other currencies, as well as commemorative silver and gold coins.

"I really liked it; you can go to museums everywhere, but something like this is really fascinating," says Leonor as they leave the mint.

"At least something positive happened today," he replied with a little sarcasm.

With all the madness going on, Eva was glad she wasn't stuck at home. Having fainted at the announcement of Leonor's arrival,

Valentin decided to keep her away and booked them both on a surprise business trip to Vancouver.

Eva knew only too well what a fortnight's stay with her mother-in-law meant for everyone's peace of mind, especially two whole weeks under the same roof, as Leonor felt entitled to spend the whole fortnight at Eva and David's place to avoid being alone since Cristiano's death.

Equipped with laptops and everything they needed to get back to work, Eva and Valentin were flown by company helicopter to the Shangri-La Hotel in Vancouver. Vancouver is Canada's largest port and a stop for cruise ships of all sizes. Vancouver's waterfront offers beautiful views of the Pacific coast, a variety of water and beach sports, fantastic boat tours, and is also a major location for the film industry, nicknamed 'Hollywood North'. About two hours away is Vancouver Island with its many scenic and cultural attractions, the capital Victoria, famous for its English colonial charm, and the town of Langford, 15 kilometres away, as well as Goldstream Provincial Park with the famous Goldstream Falls and Niagara Creek Falls, where the water plunges 47 meters, the old Niagara Trestle railway bridge, and the gold mines. Valentin's leisure program was tightly planned. These days were to give the two of them the opportunity to set the course for a future life together, as they had never been alone for so long.

"When I look around me, I feel like I've landed in paradise," enthuses Eva at the harbour.

"Then it was the right decision to bring you here," says Valentin.

"To be honest, I wouldn't have cared where you took me as long as I was with you. But being here with you is the best thing that's ever happened to me," she replied with a look full of love.

"Oh yes, you can say that again," he replied, hugging her tightly.

Soft as a feather, Eva stroked Valentin's bare skin under his pullover as a cruise ship sailed into the harbour, lightly biting his lower lip.

Longingly, he cupped her face in his hands and pressed his lips to hers in a deep kiss, then slipped his hand under her jumper.

"Now it's getting dangerous," she whispered with a laugh.
"And especially interesting for the audience. Shall we continue?" he asked.
"You mean all the way to the Shangri-La Hotel?"
"Yes. You know we're only staying there for two more days, right?"

She looked at him in surprise and denied it with a shake of her head.

"Why are you in such a panic?" he asked, amused.
"I thought we'd be away longer," she replied gloomily.
"We will be. We're going to Vancouver Island the day after tomorrow, to a beach club resort, and we'll stay there until our flight back to Ottawa."
"What?" she asked in astonishment. When did you arrange all this?"
But before he could answer, Eva's mobile phone rang insistently.

She looks at the screen and stops laughing.
"Spending time with my mom is quite exhausting; be glad you come to work instead," said David, exhausted.
"I think it's good for all concerned that I've been sent on a business trip, because with all the things your mom gets upset about, the air at home could have been even more explosive."
"You know how she is. One minute she seems happy about something, and the next she thinks the same thing is bad, but that's how she is," he said as if it weren't so dramatic.
"Oh yes, I know. She liked me for a few months at the beginning of our relationship, but then she didn't. And it didn't matter what I did. If I did too little, then I hadn't done enough; if I tried to do more, then I was doing too much as a woman; but if I tried to find a middle ground, then the middle ground was shit too. It went on for years.

And as soon as you did anything other than what she wanted, her blood pressure went up and the drama started," she said sarcastically. "That's the way she is; you can't change her," he said sympathetically. "If you can't change her, you have to put up with her," she replied, ending the conversation.

Leonor's judgements and criticisms had made her life difficult for years. Misunderstandings, arguments, and painful situations alternated with constant comparisons with other people who were obviously always better than her. The manipulative behaviour and constant games against poor Christian, which probably led to his death, and the lack of compassion did not make her a model mother and wife.
"Amor, you look depressed," Valentin said, pulling her out of her thoughts.
"It's amazing what you can sometimes put up with as a partner for years, and then suddenly you can no longer tolerate certain things."
"I think at some point you have to make decisions to stay mentally healthy, and that doesn't just mean deciding against a person, but against a whole life."
"That's the way I see it, especially since I've been living here in Canada. In Barcelona, apart from David, I spent most of my time with my family and a few friends. Workmates were workmates, and apart from the office or company parties, there was no other contact. But it was here that I realised how naive I was about the world, and although I had to put up with an impossible mother-in-law like Leonor for years, I experienced far worse here. The indifference and insensitivity of people like Steven make me feel so outraged that sometimes I feel I don't fit into the world.".
"Our family will have deep values; anything else is out of the question for me, no matter what the system tries to impose on us. I will not allow anyone to take away my identity and my values.".

"I see you as the rock of our family; I feel safe with you; I couldn't imagine a better partner and father for my children," she gushed, hugging him tightly.

"That is the nicest thing anyone has ever said to me, and I see the same in you," he replied, kissing her deeply.

The evening was not so friendly between David and his mother, especially after he expressed his wish to go to a golf match.

"We see so little of each other, and you leave me alone in the flat in the evenings; other parents are treated better!" Leonor commented reproachfully.

"The other children too!" he replied, closing the door behind him.

Offended, Leonor ran after him, shouting into the corridor, "Does your wife know you're going out alone?"

Stunned, David looked at her before the lift closed and said, "Suddenly it seems I'm being inconsiderate and disrespectful to my wife just because I want to exercise. Am I supposed to have a guilty conscience?"

Offended, Leonor turned and went back to her flat.

The next morning, in the semi-dark suite, Eva was still lying in bed, moving slowly, half asleep, wrapped in the blanket, as if her body was searching for something her soul had already found. A feeling of warmth pervaded her body, and her breathing quickened. Then she groaned. The feeling of warmth turned into desire; her hands slowly slipped under the blanket and grasped Valentin's head, dangling in her belly. Overwhelmed with desire, she took his hair in her hands and controlled the intensity of his movements until he made her cry out.

"What have you done to me?' she whispered in seventh heaven.

Burning with desire, he pulled her to him and whispered, "Who says I'm done yet?"

After the hot start to the day, the two of them headed out to see their local clients, for the three clients in Vancouver had also seen a significant increase in sales since Valentine's takeover, and this was to be celebrated as the year drew to a close.

With his elegant business suitcase and a beaming Eva at his side, Valentin confidently entered Pharmaver's meeting rooms, where the management was waiting for them. The sales figures for the last 10 months were displayed on the prepared screen. The managing director, Mr. Conell, asked them to sit down.

"I think the figures speak for themselves, don't you?" said Mr. Conell.

"Absolutely, I couldn't be happier," Valentin replied enthusiastically.

"Your mother was always a great negotiator, but with you, I get the impression it's an innate skill. You are made for success.".

"Having received the same feedback from all my clients over the past six months, I am firmly convinced that I have inherited the good genes from my mother," says Valentin.

"That seems to be the case. To thank you, we would like to take you and your wife out for lunch. What do you think?"

Honoured that Mr. Conell thought Eva was his wife, Valentin looked at her and said, "What do you think, darling, would you like to stay for lunch?"

"I'd love to," she replied.

"Excellent! Then let's take a tour first, so I can show you around the company."

The time with the nice Mr. Conell at Pharmer flew by.

After an extensive tour of the company and a delicious lunch, Eva and Valentin went straight to Kanadian Medical, where the managing director, Mrs. Nowak, a very attractive woman in her mid-forties, was waiting for their interviewee. Her large blue eyes scrutinised Valentin from the moment he walked through the door, an examination almost as thorough as an X-ray. Pleased with her crisp interlocutor, Mrs. Nowak left her comfortable chair and walked over to Valentin in her high heels and dress, which was far too tight for such a meeting, to shake his hand.

"Mr. Leblanc, it is a pleasure to meet you in person; you have literally exploded our turnover, and we look forward to working more closely with you," she said with a greedy look on her face, as if she wanted to eat him up. Then she also looked at Eva, "And you young lady must be the secretary." She continued, shaking her hand briefly.

"Mrs. Rodriguez is my future wife," Valentin added.

Surprised, Mrs. Novak looked at Eva more closely and remarked briefly, "Really?"

"Shall we take a look at the turnover for the last six months together? Cura Care is also expecting us in two hours; we have a full schedule today," Valentin said, setting a time limit.

"As you wish," she says with a penetrating look.

After a quick overview, they realised that the figures were much better than those of the big pharmaceutical company. Surprised, Valentin turned to Mrs. Nowak and praised her: "Considering how big the company is, the turnover has increased enormously in the last six months; that's incredible!"

"Yes, and we are very proud of it. The close and intensive cooperation with our business partners makes it possible," she stressed.

"So let's toast to these successes," Valentin suggested.

"Champagne is only available in my office, where we celebrate our successes with business partners of a certain calibre," she said in an inviting tone.

"Oh, I think orange juice would be fine," he said, picking up the bottles from the other side of the table.

"Did you notice how that horny milf was looking at you the whole time?" asked Eva as they left Canadian Medical.

"Yes, an extraordinary woman, isn't she?" commented Valentin with a grin.

"Extraordinary? It's a wonder she didn't eat you up right away and declare me her cleaning lady."

"Well, they always say that men are pushy, just want to have fun, and are unfaithful, but as you can see, women can do that too."

"Yes, there seems to be some truth to that, and she certainly likes young men."

"She's confident, attractive, and knows what she wants. Not all men get on with women like that; in fact, I'd say most men are a bit afraid of women like that these days.".

"It's because women have taken on more and more of the male role in recent years and men sometimes look beyond their masculinity," she said.

"You could talk about this for days without coming to a definitive position. Not to mention what the other genders that have come along identify with or not.".

"Oh yes. Difficult subject."

At exactly 4pm, the driver pulled up in front of CuraCare, an unusual building from the outside. Eva and Valentin were greeted by Mr. Martino and his secretary and made their way into the high-tech meeting room. A projector with a remote control coming out of the ceiling, a white projection screen, and chilled champagne accompanied the meeting.

"I take the chilled champagne as a sign of a successful year," said Valentin Positiv.

"One of the most successful years since the company was founded," added Mr. Martino.

"This makes me and my family very proud," said Valentin happily.

"Somehow you both have Latin roots; could it be?" asked Mr. Martino.

They looked at each other and laughed, then Valentin asked, "You too, right?"

"Yes, me too. You speak Spanish too?"

"Yes, we both speak Spanish, and so do our parents," Valentin replied proudly.

"Really? Your mother speaks Spanish, and she never told me?" asked Mr. Martino in surprise.
"My mother is a mysterious woman," Valentin replied with a grin.

"Well then, let's have a tapas evening to end the day on a high note," Mr. Martino suggested invitingly.

In her party mood, Eva had missed several calls from David, who had already sent her a couple of text messages. When she realised it was getting late for the tapas round, she was gripped by fear. Knowing her mother-in-law Leonor as well as she did, something must have happened.
"Sorry I'm late; I've had one client after another, and I've just got back to my hotel room. Has something happened?" she asked.
"Actually, everything is fine, except that my mother has fallen in love with Ottawa and she's thinking of moving here," David said casually. But there was no reply to David's statement.

"Hello, are you still there? Come on, it was just a joke," he said after silence on the other end of the line.
"I can't stand jokes like that," she replied seriously.
"You know, I was at Steven's for a bit this afternoon; he's met a nice woman; he seems to have come to terms with the fact that he and Martha are getting a divorce."

"Are you listening to yourself? He has a new girlfriend exactly four days after he was caught with two other women in his car. What kind of man is that?" She asked shocked.

"You have to remember we're not in the Middle Ages anymore. The way relationships are formed has changed," he said reproachfully.

"Yes, you're right, the way relationships are formed has changed, but in a negative way!"

"Just because it's different doesn't mean it's negative; everyone has their own way of looking at things."

"You answer as if Steven's behaviour is the most normal thing in the world."

"It's best if we just leave it alone; it sounds like you're still living in a wonderland and don't understand how interpersonal relationships work in the 21st century. You'd better tell me how work is going, and when you come home, the organisation is a bit problematic without you.".

"I see, so that's what I'm good at... in organizational matters," she replied in a melancholy tone.

"Women are unbeatable and irreplaceable for that," he replied simply.

"In fact, I've received a request from two other clients near Toronto who want to renew their contracts; they're not far from here and would be willing to receive their business partners on Saturday morning as long as it's before the end of the year, so my trip could actually be extended without notice. I hope you and your mom can manage on your own by then," she lied fearlessly.

"Oh, go ahead; I think it will be adequately compensated. We'll manage."

After the phone call with David, Eva felt even more unable to adapt to certain things; in fact, she didn't even want to try because she had been taught certain values by her parents and nothing in the world would convince her to behave or think differently just to please others.

"Hey Amor, what's on your mind tonight?" asked Valentin as Eva stood in front of him with a tense face.

"I'd like to extend our stay here if that's all right with you. There's no reason to go home so soon unless it's necessary."

"Are you serious?" he asked, pleased.

"Yes."

He looked at her lovingly, as if inviting her to a dance above the clouds, then picked her up and twirled her around.

"You make me the happiest man in the world," he whispered, kissing her.

"And you make me the luckiest woman. How about we end this successful day with a dip in the pool?" she asked, unbuttoning her blouse.

"Great! We can end the day the way we started it," he said enthusiastically.

The next morning, Eva and Valentin were flown to Vancouver Island via the breathtaking Goldstream and Niagara Creek Falls.

"Arrival in paradise!" the pilot shouted over the intercom.

Overwhelmed by the stunning scenery and distracted by the loud noise of the helicopter, Eva didn't realise Valentin was trying to give her something until he gently touched her shoulder.

"The package looks familiar," she said, her eyes wide.

Valentin asked the pilot to mute his headphones for two minutes, then turned to Eva.

"No one can disturb us up here, and no phone call can reach us, so I'll ask you again: Will you be my wife as soon as circumstances allow?"

"Yes, yes, I will!" she replied, and he quickly placed the ring on her finger.

"Forever," she said.

"Forever," he exclaimed.

After a long kiss, they realised that the helicopter had already landed and that someone was waiting for them at the airport.

"Valentin!" a voice shouted from a distance.

But Eva and Valentin turned at the same time and saw two people in the distance.

"Isn't that your mom?" she asked.

At the end of the airfield, Mrs. Leblanc and her life companion, Mr. Bonelli, waved and ran towards Eva and Valentin. It was a very emotional moment for Valentin and his mother, but especially for Bonelli as the biological father in this constellation.

"You look gorgeous, as always," Bonelli said to Eva and hugged her, while Valentin and his mother shared a long hug.

"I've missed you terribly," Valentin's mother said, overwhelmed. Then she went over to Eva, gave her a big hug, and said, "I'm glad to see her.

"I'm happy to see you too," Eva replied.

"Now that we're all here, let's go to the Beach Club Resort," Valentin said.

"Did you know they're on the island too?" asked Eva, a little confused.

"Yes, of course, they invited us."

"So everyone knew except me?"

"Yes, and for a very special reason," he replied with a beaming expression on his face.

Mrs. Leblanc approached Eva and handed her a parcel. "This is for tonight; I hope it suits you," she said.

"This is for me? And... For tonight?" Eva asked, increasingly confused.

"Yes, for tonight, we'll meet down at the beach at seven o'clock," she replied.

Valentin promptly took the package from her and led her to the bungalow while her mother and Bonelli continued on their way.

"Aren't you going to tell me what's going on?" she asked.

"It's a surprise," he replied.

But when they arrived at the bungalow, Eva opened the parcel and marvelled at its contents. There was a beautiful dress, matching sandals, and an autumn stole.

"Wow, do I have to wear all this tonight?" she asked, overwhelmed.

"Yes, all of it," he replied.

On a warm autumn day, just under 20 degrees Celsius, Eva and Valentin walked hand in hand along Canada's most beautiful beach, surrounded by a breathtaking, wild landscape, the salty air enveloping the scent of the rainforest, and only the sound of the long, gentle waves kissing the beach to be heard. Small, inaccessible islets dotted the long bay.

"I can't find the right words to describe this beauty," she said.

"Yes, I understand; I often feel the same way when I look at you," he replied with a smitten look.

"You're a charmer," she said, moving closer to kiss him.

"What did you notice about my mother?" he asked.

"That she hugged me warmly, like I was family."

"Just that?"

But a call on Eva's mobile interrupted the conversation.

"Hey Marta, why are you crying?" Eva asked worriedly.

"I hope I didn't disturb you. You can't imagine what's happened," she sighed.

"Is it because of the children? How are the little ones?" she asked worriedly.

"No, it's about the bastard who moved out a few days ago and is already living with a new woman he's obviously just met."

"I'm sorry to hear that. If there's anything I can do for you and the children, I'll be happy to do it."

"Apparently he met her at the new golf club. After the three of them were banned, they moved on to the next club," she said excitedly.

"What do you mean 'the three of them'? I thought only Steven was banned."

"No, David and Robin aren't allowed in the club either. Didn't you know that?" Martha asked in surprise.

"This is the first I've heard of it."

"We'll never know what happened; the three boys are close; they would never betray each other," she said through clenched teeth.

"I have that feeling too, and I know one thing: David's attitude to family life has changed dramatically, and not for the better."

"Welcome to the world of superficial feelings, which is spreading like an unstoppable epidemic due to the influence of social media."

"Unfortunately. I think that in 20 years there won't be many people who know the meaning of the words family and love. We are heading for an era without values.

"Do you think things will get worse than they are now? I've already played the arse card with Steven; just the thought that it could get worse scares me," said Martha, full of doubt.

"We have to hold on to our values and pass them on to our children, no matter what happens and no matter what happens in society, otherwise we risk dying out.".

"My mom is calling in the background; we'll hear each other then. Take care, my dear," Martha said hurriedly.

Eva and Valentin walked hand in hand along the path, she in her stunning dress and he in his elegant suit, until they reached a small cove. What they saw there moved them both to tears. On a torch-lit path lay a white carpet leading to an altar. In front of the altar was an arch of orchids and spouts. There was sand and candles all around. A table for four sat under a festively decorated pavilion, warmed by several large fire bowls. After a few minutes, a man with a folder in his hand approached and stood behind the altar, then made a hand signal. Panpipe music began—the magical, goosebump-inducing tones of 'A whiter shade of pale'.

"Wow, what's going on here? I'm beginning to have an idea," said Eva.

Valentin's mother, in a delicate champagne wedding dress, and Mr. Bonelli, elegantly dressed in a blue suit, emerged from a dimly lit corner, their eyes shining, and walked down the white carpet through the torch-lit aisle to the altar.

"I would like to ask the witnesses to stand next to the bride and groom," the celebrant said, pointing to Eva and Valentin.

Moved to tears, Bonelli tried to make the speech he had been dreaming of for years. But his emotions took over, and he limited himself to a short sentence...

"Only in the mysterious laws of love can a logical reason be found. But I'm only here tonight because of you. You are the reason for my existence. You are the only reason for me.".

Valentin's mother, who no longer had any hope of marrying the love of her life, was also moved to tears and said briefly,

"I carried your heart with me; I carried it in mine, and in all these years I have never parted from it. Everything I've done I've done because I love you. Thank you for always being faithful and close to me, for being my rock and my source of strength, and thank you for contributing with love to the growth of our son Valentin. I couldn't have wished for a better husband.".

"In the end, what belongs together comes together," said the officiant at the end of the ceremony.

"Now I know from whom you inherited that long kiss," Eva said to Valentin as the newlyweds savoured their kiss.

"Indeed," he replied with a grin.

After the ceremony, the four of them made their way happily to the pavilion, where a waiter greeted them with a glass of champagne.

"To love!" Valentin exclaimed, raising his glass.

"We still can't believe this has happened to us," said Valentin's overjoyed mother.

"We didn't expect you to understand our decision, but we really hope you'll be happy with us," said Bonelli.

"And if I may, I would also like to express our wishes regarding the wedding gift," said Valentin's mother.

As it was a surprise for Eva, they had not had the opportunity to buy any presents.

"We're sorry we didn't bring a present," said Eva, her face flushed.

But Vantin's mother, who had now changed her priorities about what was important to her, looked at her and said, "You can't buy what we want. Maybe we're asking too much, but we only have two wishes.

"Do we have to do anything for you?" asked Valentin jokingly.

"No. We would be happy if you called your father that too. We know that you have known and loved someone other than your father for many years, but your real father is still alive," she said.

"And the second? What is your second wish?" he asked.

"My second wish is that we all get along and act like family. I know your situation is still complicated by Eva's marriage, but we recognise your relationship as official, and as far as I know, Eva's father would want that too."

After these words, Eva and Valentin looked at each other in complete astonishment, then apologised and left the table for a moment.

First the surprise of the wedding, then the request for a wedding gift, which concerned not only Valentin as a son but also Eva, who had already been accepted as a future member of the family, and, as is customary in a good family, Valentin did not want to make any important decisions without first talking to his Eva.

In the pavilion, Bonelli stood beside his new wife and held her hand. Beaming, Valentin and Eva approached hand in hand, and as Eva went to her seat, Valentin turned to his father.

"To call you father is not only a matter of respect for me; it's an honor. In all these years, not a day has gone by without you being by my side. Whether I was happy or sad, you always had an open ear for me and remained loyal to me in everything I did. You can't imagine how many times I wished I had a father like you, and in my heart I always saw you as a father. You have been a gift to me all these years, and today I want to be one for you. Father," Valentin said emotionally and hugged him.

Valentin's mother moved to tears, stood up and joined him in the embrace, then turned to Eva and held out her hand. And what about our second present?" she asked.
"Well..." Eva replies as her phone starts to ring.

During the dreamlike family ritual on Paradise Island, Eva had almost forgotten that a less loving family was waiting for her at home, so she quickly left the pavilion to speak to David. An excited David answered the phone.

"Hey, I thought you'd be in bed by now, but you sound really restless," Eva said in a relaxed tone.
"Me restless? You would be too if you were here!" he shouted on the other end of the phone.
"Why? What happened?"
"I was picked up by the police on the golf course and taken to the police station."

Chapter 13 Surprise!

"**H**urry up, we're going to be late for the staff meeting," Eva shouted as David comfortably chewed the last piece of bread.

"Don't stress yourself; you're acting as if the introduction of homosexuals into the workplace is a big deal. Do you know how many of them work in companies of all kinds?" asked David casually.

"Do you know how many of them, as you call them, are still discriminated against in the workplace in the 21st century? How often and how naturally, depending on their profession, can they come out without having to reckon with consequences or harassment? I'm not just talking about gays, but also lesbians and bisexuals, and yes, if we want to, the so-called 'diverse' ones too. Do you really think they would all have the same career opportunities as straight people if they came out?"

"Fortunately, our junior boss, the mother sweetie, is understanding of all kinds of sexual orientations and has even organised a welcome party for them, which all staff are obliged to attend. That's annoying!"

"There's nothing to add to your comment," she said.

When he arrived at the company, Valentin greeted his 200 employees in the large conference room. Built like a grandstand, the room offered space for employees and guests. Equipped with loudspeakers and a podium with a lectern, the room could be used for all kinds of meetings.

The decision to introduce the two outgoing employees to the entire workforce and ask for solidarity was taken by Valentin after the two employees expressed their desire to be treated like everyone else.

"Discrimination causes stress, and stressed employees are often sick and less productive. Being constantly seen as 'different', having to

241

pretend not to stand out, takes its toll. That's why I'm here today to tell you that in this company, everyone can be who they are without fear of discrimination. Sexual orientation or gender identity, as well as race and color, are treated equally in this company, and everyone is given the same career opportunities. Discrimination or harassment on the grounds of sexual orientation, gender identity, race, or color will be dealt with by warning or dismissal. Just as everyone has the right to be who they want to be, everyone must respect all company rules during working hours, regardless of sexual orientation, gender identity, origin, or skin color," Valentin clarified, as the enthusiastic employees confirmed the rules with a round of applause.

"Now let us welcome our new colleagues," Valentin said.

The meeting was well received by all the staff and ended successfully late in the evening. Only David's mood had not changed.

"How long will this mood last? I feel you've become more and more like your mother over the past few months. Why is that?" she asked, annoyed.

"You know, we live in a more modern country here; I've adapted accordingly and broadened my horizons; my perspective is just different, and you don't like it. You'd better get used to it."

"What should I get used to? To the fact that you are expressing more and more of your mother's toxic personality traits, or to the fact that in the future I will have to interrupt my business trips because you are in police custody?" she asked, exhausted.

"Oh, the police have gone too far; just because those two whores from the old golf club thought Steven was holding them in the car against their will, Robin and I have been dragged through the mud too. The two of them got into the car with Steven voluntarily and then turned the tables to save face.".

"Let's stop talking about it; it's getting too silly for me."

"It's better that way; we're talking past each other anyway."

At home, Eva and David avoided each other. Their differences grew from day to day, but neither of them showed any interest in finding a solution together.

The next morning, Eva threw up several times. All the stress with David and the emotional tension caused by her longing for Valentin weighed heavily on her, but when she arrived at the office, Valentin took her in his arms.

"You look exhausted; has something happened?" he asked, kissing her forehead.

"I think all this stress is starting to get to me."

"For me too, this is the most difficult situation I've ever been in. My days and nights are still filled with longing for our time in Vancouver. Lying alone in my bed again has become unbearable, but love gives me a lot of strength and hope.".

"After every journey and every intense moment together, the pain is even greater. Fortunately, David is busy with many other things and doesn't notice how I am.".

"You look very pale; I'll get you a breakfast roll from the canteen," he said affectionately.

Seven weeks before Christmas, the desks were full of paperwork, and the numerous daily emails and faxes were piling up fast. It wasn't a good time for drama or physical weakness, but Eva felt battered and at the edge of her emotional strength. In all the confusion, she had almost forgotten that Mr. Wilson and his beloved Mrs. Mayer would be arriving in the next two hours and that she was responsible for completing the program.

"Here, eat something; I've brought you a light sandwich," Valentin offered.

Hungry, Eva quickly bit into the sandwich, which came out faster than it went in.

"Good thing the paper bucket was right at my feet," she said with relief as the sandwich poured out again.

"Aren't you going to see a doctor? I'm getting worried."

"Mr. Wilson and Mrs. Mayer will be here in two hours; we're on a tight schedule; I can't afford to miss it. Maybe my stomach just needs a cup of tea and some rest," she says optimistically.

Eva and Valentin wait for their guests in the visitor center. Mr Wilson and Mrs Mayer stride through the main entrance, beaming.

"It's a pleasure to see you again! We are absolutely delighted with this area," says Mrs. Mayer.

"We are really pleasantly surprised, and if today's figures are as good as the location here, then nothing stands in the way of a long-term contract with them," says Mr. Wilson happily.

"Excellent! Then let's start managing the company," suggests Valentin. From production to sales and marketing, discipline and structure reigned in all areas and on all levels of the company. The numerous, well-equipped meeting rooms and lounges were available to employees on all floors of the building. The large canteen on the ground floor was the focal point for staff gatherings, with each room or area designed to maximise comfort during leisure time and performance during working hours.

"Just amazing," said Mrs. Mayer.

"The presentation will take place today on the screen in our main meeting room. It was in this room that we had the honour of introducing our gay employees to the rest of the company team yesterday. It was impressive how they were received when you think about discrimination against homosexual employees in the workplace. It's not a given," said Valentin.

"You seem to be doing a good job, my dear," said Mr. Wilson, patting him on the back.

"I have to admit I'm lucky to have the right support for it," Valentin replied, turning to Eva.
"Your support seems to be different today," Mrs Mayer observed.
"My stomach has been in knots all morning; the stress seems to have found an outlet," Eva added.

But Mrs. Mayer looked at her again and said, "Please don't take this as an intrusion, but have you had a pregnancy test yet?
"A pregnancy test?" Eva asked through gritted teeth.

But of course Eva hadn't thought about that; after all, she hadn't had sex with her husband David for weeks, but she had sex with Valentin at every opportunity and in every conceivable place.
"That would make a nice Christmas present..." smiled Mr. Wilson as Valentin stood silently next to his desk with the remote control in his hand, ready to start the presentation. Those present, however, were preoccupied with the subject of pregnancy. Young in years but mature in character, Valentin performed brilliantly in the negotiations and eventually won a five-year contract with Algata Pharma.
"Where's the champagne?" asked Mr. Wilson.

"On our dining table. Shall we go?" asked Valentin.

The best moment of the day turned into a nightmare for Eva, who was afraid of throwing up at the table and couldn't decide what to eat—luckily the staff brought champagne first.
"You can't drink it until you know what's making you sick," warns Mrs. Mayer.
"Well, I'll have toast with mineral water," says Eva resignedly.

After a successful afternoon and a successful lunch for Eva, it was back to work. Valentin's positive influence on sales and customer acquisition had been unbroken for months; he had been underestimated for too long; now he could prove everyone wrong.

"I am thinking of hiring an assistant to make your work easier, someone who can pre-select and take care of everything related to faxing. As my personal assistant, you no longer have time for that. The large number of customer presentations and the increasing number of personal customer contacts require your full commitment and efficiency.".
"That's a great idea," she enthused at the suggestion.
"Do you really think you could be pregnant?" he asked suddenly.
"Well, since we've been out of control so much, I wouldn't be surprised. But I feel much better after lunch, so I think it was more the stress.".
"What if you were pregnant?" he asked with a hint of hope in his voice.
"We'll worry about that when the time comes. Right now all I can think about is the work that needs to be done.".

At the end of the day, Eva found herself sitting on the sofa with David, staring into space.
Being married to someone and feeling like a stranger at the same time was a feeling she had never experienced before. The situation weighed on her more and more.
After Steven's infidelity, there were fewer and fewer things to talk about, and the subject of her mother-in-law was practically taboo after the holiday under the same roof.

"I've bought two tickets for Indiana Jones and the Kingdom of the Crystal Skull tomorrow; maybe that'll open up some noncontroversial topics; what do you think?" asked David, who knew how important it was to have a well-balanced wife at home.

"Don't you want to go golfing tomorrow?" she asked, surprised.

"I've neglected you a lot these past few weeks, and I want to make up for it, plus we have an all-day tournament in Gatineau on Saturday," he explained.

"Oh, I see, well, why not...?"

"Perfect, then we'll go straight to dinner after work and then to the cinema," he said, cuddling up to her.

Dissatisfied but not refusing, Eva allowed it. For weeks she had managed to avoid her duties as a wife because of all the arguments.

"You look a bit thin; get your strength back; you've been ill for weeks," he added.

"No wonder, with all the stress. The days with your mother here at home have done me good. Want to bet I've got an ulcer?"

"Shhh, relax; I'm with you," he said, hugging her even tighter.

And that was the problem: he was still there, and she loved another man with all her heart, a situation that was sapping her strength.

The next morning Eva continued to vomit; every attempt to eat ended in the toilet.

"Damn, how long are you going to watch this? You must have an ulcer! It's Friday; why don't you go to the doctor and get checked out and take a few days off so you can recover over the long weekend?" grumbles David.

"There's too much work to do in the office; I can't afford any more absences until the end of the year!"

"Then wait until you collapse and end up in the hospital again! Aren't the hospital stays this year enough for you?" He asked angrily.

"Fine, I'll drive you to work now and then go to the doctor. If it's nothing serious, I'll come to work later. Are you happy with that?"

"That's a good plan."

Unsure which doctor to see first, Eva accompanied her husband to work and instinctively chose the gynaecologist.

As the surgery was full and she didn't have an appointment, she expected long waits and had already planned to spend half the day there when a voice called her name over the loudspeaker in the waiting room. Surprised that it was quicker than she expected, she ran to the doctor's assistant, who was holding a cup.

"We need some urine; is that possible?" the lady asked politely.

"Urine?"

"Yes, the doctor wants to do a pregnancy test. You can discuss the results with him later," the doctor's assistant explained.

In the waiting room, time suddenly seemed to stand still. Within an hour and a half of giving her urine, she felt like she had read every magazine available. But then she was finally called into the examination room.

"Before we discuss anything, I'd like to do an ultrasound scan. When was your last period?" the gynaecologist asked.

"My last period? Oh, come to think of it, it's been quite a while," she replied thoughtfully.

"Don't you keep track of your periods?" he asked in surprise.

"No, not really. I've been under a lot of stress these past few weeks. I had one or two postponements, but it finally came."

The doctor politely asked her to undress in the cubicle and then sit down on the ultrasound table. With great concentration, he marked a few points and tapped something on the machine's touchpad.

"I'm afraid your period won't come as quickly this time," he said.

"Why, is something wrong?" she asked worriedly.

"See those two dots there?" he asked, pointing to the screen.

"Yes, the two cysts there, that probably explains my discomfort," she replied cluelessly.

"The two cysts are two amniotic sacs about six weeks old, which explains the positive pregnancy test and the vomiting. Congratulations, you're pregnant!" The gynaecologist said happily.

"What, two babies?"

"It's an unexpected surprise for you, but yes, you're expecting twins."

In the midst of the emotional chaos, and with the ultrasound in her hand, Eva left the examination room and bumped into Martha in the corridor.

"Eva? Hey, what a surprise. What are you doing here?" asked Martha.

"Me? What am I doing here?" asked Eva nervously, but before she could answer, the doctor's assistant called her.

"Sorry, I have to go," she said quickly.

After the blood sample had been taken, she left the surgery without saying goodbye to Martha and quickly ran to the car, afraid of being seen again as she had told David she was going to the GP. Still in a state of emotional chaos, she drove aimlessly, crying, until she reached the Leblancs' country house. From there, she called Valentin without telling him why. The twenty minutes until Valentin arrived seemed like an eternity. Outside in the cold, she paced nervously, staring at the ultrasound image.

"Amor, what are you doing out here in the cold? You look completely frozen; can't you remember which flower pot the key is under? Why don't we go inside?" He said affectionately, but Eva handed him the ultrasound.

He looked at it in silence for a long minute.

"There are two," she whispered and started to cry.

Overwhelmed, Valentin pulled her close and held her in silence.

"It must have happened when David flew to Barcelona for his father's funeral. The babies are about six weeks old," she whispered.

"I can't put my happiness into words. One baby would have made me very happy, but two is indescribable," he said emotionally.

"You can't hide a baby bump forever; do you know what that means? The moment of truth is not far away," she said.

"How can we be sure it's really mine? You have a husband at home too... don't get me wrong, but I want these two babies to be ours, not someone else's.".

"I can understand your worries, but you don't have to drive yourself crazy, because I've hardly been fulfilling my marital duties these past few months, as David and I have been drifting apart because of all the arguments. Besides, David doesn't want children, so he doesn't allow himself any mistakes. Today, however, I organised a paternity test at a specialist laboratory. From the 10th week of pregnancy, my blood will contain enough genetic material from our babies. So you just have to be patient for another four weeks," she said optimistically.

"How will you explain the pregnancy symptoms to your husband?" he asked worriedly.

"I was given a homoeopathic remedy. But the pregnancy symptoms are the least of my problems at the moment. Martha has also been to the gynaecologist; I met her in the corridor as I left the examination room, and I hope she didn't notice my excitement. She has no contact with David, but I'd better tell him that the GP has just sent me to the gynaecologist for a check-up before he finds out from someone else.".

"That's a good idea."

"I also made a decision today. I'll tell David everything as soon as my family is here for Christmas. I think that's the right time. The belly can remain unnoticed for another six weeks, but no longer. The days are numbered.

Valentin looks at his Eva full of hope and says, "I feel like I'm in a dream; I think I'm about to explode with happiness."

After dinner, Eva and David walked to the cinema opposite without saying much, where they bumped into Steven and his new girlfriend, who gave Eva a dirty look, walked past her without saying hello, and waved his head at David.

"One thing's for sure, your boyfriend is definitely into fake dolls; the two at the golf club looked exactly like they were made from a mould, with inflatable boats for lips and silicone pads in the bust. Martha's body naturally looks a little different after a pregnancy with twins," said Eva ironically.

"Martha has risen like a sourdough, which is more in line with reality. It's incomprehensible that she doesn't do anything about it; no wonder Steven doesn't like her.".

Eva did not respond to David's inappropriate comments about Martha's body, instead replying, "Good thing you don't want kids.".

"Even if I did, I'd insist you fix certain things after the pregnancy."
"Excuse me? You never know how your body will react to pregnancy, so I find your comments and demands very superficial, and your wishes incomprehensible. I would be at peace with myself because I love myself as I am. My body, my choice. Take it or leave it," she replied confidently.
"We shall see," he says defiantly.

Eva becomes increasingly aware that she no longer wants to be with David and that it is only a matter of weeks.
"The cinema is almost empty; let's sit in the back," he suggests.

In the dark, the two of them sat next to each other in the back row of a fairly empty cinema. After a few minutes, Eva reached for her popcorn and started to eat when she noticed David's hands slipping under her skirt. Restless, she filled her mouth with popcorn again and continued to chew diligently as his hand slid down to her pubic area.

"Take your knickers off," he ordered.

"Excuse me? Here?" She coughed as the popcorn caught in her throat.

"Yes, here. Looks like we're playing this game for the first time," he said, stroking her unclenched pubic area as she squeezed her legs tightly together.

"No way, we're in a completely foreign country. What if there are cameras somewhere and we're being recorded?" She asked irritably, pushing his hand away.

"Come on, what's going to happen here?" he asked stubbornly, grabbing her hand and placing it on his crotch.

Annoyed, she immediately pulled her hand away when she noticed his excitement.

"Are you mad??" she said in a harsher tone.

"Oh, you can't take a joke anymore; Steven and his new girlfriend are probably having fun in the cinema next door," he said, offended.

"One more word, and I'll leave the room immediately. I've had enough," she replied angrily.

The next morning, David left the house while Eva was still in bed. After going to the cinema, they were both in the same bed, but it seemed as if a wall had been built between them. Eva's reactions to David's words or behavior became more and more violent; she found it uncomfortable to be near him, and the intimacy gave her less and less pleasure; her only consolation was that this would soon end.

After a quick breakfast, she ordered a taxi and made her way to the meeting point with Valentin.

"It's time for the bomb to go off here," she said to Valentin as he lit the fire.
"Think of our babies; if Mum is upset, they will be too," he said, putting the last piece of wood down.
"Kiss me!" she ordered from the stool in front of the fireplace.

On a rainy day, softened by the warmth of the fire, he took her face in his hands and kissed her deeply.
"It's a magical feeling," she whispered as tears streamed down her face.

He kissed her eyelids tenderly to wipe away the tears and whispered, "Love is for the fearless, for those who are brave enough to live it, and that's you. You are one of the strongest and most fearless women I have ever known."

Tenderly, she lifted her hand and touched his face, lingering on his warm, moist lips. His strong arms held her tight and secure; they looked at each other, their tongues touching. His hands slid down her body, his lips travelled down her neck, then he lifted his head and stared at her with eyes bright with desire as she looked at him pleadingly before pulling him between her legs.
Slowly he pulled up her top, brushing the skin of her back as she crossed her legs over his waist and pushed his jumper up.
"Do you hear it too?" he asked dreamily.
"Yes, it sounds like a mobile phone vibrating," she replied.

Eva and Valentin had cuddled up in front of the fireplace and lost track of time when the phone rang urgently.
"Are you Mrs. Rodriguez?" said a male voice on the other line.

"Yes, I am, and who are you?"

"I'm a paramedic; I don't want to frighten you, but your husband fell into a frozen pond while playing winter golf and was taken to the Hopital de Gatineau," said the man in a calm voice.

"But how could this happen? Winter golf is one of the most popular winter sports in Canada after ice hockey; I can't imagine that the ice on the ponds was not sufficiently controlled.".

"Well, it wasn't really the lack of ice control, but the carelessness of the boys who had drilled a few holes in the ice to put beer bottles in, which caused the surface to crack in several places and three people, including her husband, to fall into the water. Thanks to some of those present, the three were able to escape the tragedy," the man continued.

Eva was so shocked she couldn't say a word.

"Are they still there? Hello?" shouted the paramedic.

"Yes, I'm still here. Please excuse me. Is that why you called me?" She asked worriedly.

"No, that's not necessary; he'll stay here for two days for observation and can go home on Monday. But you can make a note of his phone number on the ward, as his mobile phone is no longer working.".

Stunned, Eva took down the number and thanked him for the call.

"I have a feeling that David is regressing," she said desperately to Valentin.

"It seems that he and his friends have missed something in life that needs to be made up for, don't you think?" he asked neutrally.

"Maybe...we married too soon. But he didn't want to do much in Spain."

"Maybe he didn't have the right mates, and now the boys are letting their hair down," he said amusedly.

"Oh dear, a pubescent husband, that's all I needed," she sighed.

But before calling David, Eva decided to calm down and did a few minutes of breathing exercises. The excitement of the incident had thrown her off balance, and David's behaviour was beginning to drive her up the wall.

"Hello, I've heard about the accident. How are you?" She asked in a calm voice.

"Fine, my body is slowly thawing out," he replied.

"The paramedic said my presence wasn't necessary; how come?"

"You see, there are three of us in this room, and we've messed up quite a bit, so we've decided to leave our wives out of it," he said in a semi-serious tone.

"Well, I guess you're in good company then," she said, relieved that she didn't have to join him.

"Yes, we are; don't worry. We'll talk more later."

With a shrug, Eva ended the conversation and turned to Valentin: "I'm afraid you'll have to count on me for a while."

"Too bad, I wouldn't know what to do with you until Monday," he said ironically.

"I've got some good ideas," she said, pushing aside the blanket to reveal her bare skin.

Despite the homeopathic medication, the next morning began with morning sickness, so much so that Eva hardly dared to eat.

The next morning started with morning sickness, despite the homeopathic medication, so Eva hardly dared to eat anything.

"Hey, Amor, I've read that an empty stomach doesn't prevent nausea, and I've brought a few things that can alleviate the symptoms," Valentin said worriedly.

"Have you read about morning sickness?" she asked in surprise.

"Of course I have; I know you can do it on your own, but I want to support you, so I've brought rusks, biscuits, and light toast."

"You're just amazing; I'm sure you'll be the best dad in the world. I can't describe my happiness; I feel like I'm in a dream," she said, moving.

"You make me the happiest man in the world. Women like you, who value love and family so much, are becoming rare. Many women today don't want to commit because they're afraid of ending up in an unhappy relationship, but there are undoubtedly many good men who want nothing more than to find a woman with good values.".

"I'm an adulteress, in case you've forgotten. I'm cheating on my husband with you," she said, knowing full well that cheating is not right.

"I know cheating is a sin for you; I agree. But in our case it's different; we found each other, and our feelings were something very special from the beginning. You can't call a love that deep a sin; I would die for you, and you saved my life during the kidnapping attempt by putting yourself in danger. You don't do that with a fleeting affair. We're not talking about a one-night stand between two complete strangers."

"In a way, you're right, but I feel guilty towards David, and I have a thousand thoughts about how I can tell him that our marriage is on the rocks and that I've fallen in love with another man. Hurting his feelings drives me crazy; no matter how stupid he's been acting lately, I'm sure he loves me very much, and it will be very painful for him."

"To lose a woman like you would be a painful and irreplaceable loss for any man, I'm sure of it. I can't imagine what it would be like to be without you. Every night when I go to bed, I thank God that we met and that I was lucky enough to experience this special love that touches my soul so deeply.".

Eva looked at him with great admiration; she had never thought she could have such feelings for a man, and although she always struggled with feelings of guilt, she was more certain than ever that this man was everything she had always wanted in her deepest desires.

"Even finding a man like you is not a given these days. I think God had good intentions for both of us.

After a reasonably successful breakfast, Valentin invited his Eva to follow him outside. The first warm rays of sunshine after the rainy days accompanied them to the building next to the stables.

"Where are we going?" she asked curiously.
"Have you ever driven a tractor before?"
"No, never. But won't it be too cold?" She asked worriedly.

Valentin deftly opened the huge shutter, revealing a state-of-the-art tractor that looked as if it had just been put on display.
"Holy sh*t!" she blurted out.
"Don't you like it?" he asked uncertainly.
"It's amazing! When I think of a tractor, I imagine something completely different, but something so modern and clean... I didn't expect this."
"Perfect, let's go; by the way, it also has air conditioning and heating."
"But where are we going to go with this huge thing? The grounds don't look that big," she asked, confused.
"You'll be surprised how big it is," he reveals.

Under the sun's rays and in a heated cabin, Eva and Valentin left the yard and followed a dirt track along the side of the house, where an old mill could be seen in the distance.

"What's back there? It looks like a farm," she asked, pointing ahead.
"Everything we eat at home comes from there," he added proudly.
"I thought rich people only bought the best of the best in expensive shops."

"This is the best of the best, no chemicals, the real luxury, if you can call it that."

"It's a miracle that in this day and age there are still people who appreciate such things. But you are my miracle," she said with an affectionate look.

"And the three of you are my greatest miracle of all. My babies already count," he added.

"Are there many staff here?"

"Do you see the three houses behind the mill? Three families live there with their children, and they run everything here."

"What exactly is produced here?"

"Everything. Fruit, vegetables, cereals, spices—they also raise some animals, but not in excess. We only produce as much as we and the three families on the farm can consume."

"This is paradise. And where does the river that feeds the mill end?"

"It's a branch of the Ottawa River; that's where we're going now."

At the other end of the property, Valentin stopped in front of a cabin. From there, they could see directly where the water from the river flowed into the river.

"Wow, so many surprises in one morning; I really wasn't expecting this. But who are you, Valentin Leblanc? The handsome and talented businessman, the polite guy next door, or the farmer? Which are you?"

"I am all three, because it was important for my family to teach me all three. My father, Bonelli, spent a lot of time here with me. My mother made me come here four times a week to help with the children of the farming families on the farm. Bonelli was always with me. Now I know what my parents did for me, and I am eternally grateful to all three of them for what they gave me."

"You must be too."

"Here we are. Would you like to see what the hut looks like? Our lunch is ready," he said, opening the door.

A lovingly laid table awaited them, with freshly baked bread, homemade butter, fresh milk, and fragrant pine branches for decoration. There were several pots of freshly cooked delicacies on the wood-burning stove.

"Wow, with all this food, I hope my nausea is limited," she said, taking off her jacket and sitting down next to the warm fire as her mobile phone rang.

"Funny, it looks like another call from Gatineau," she said, staring at the display.

"Aren't you going to answer it? It could be important."

"David said he'd be in touch at two today, and this isn't his number."

Meanwhile, the phone had stopped ringing, and she was about to put it down when it rang again.

"Mrs Rodriguez? This is the head of intensive care at the Hopital de Gatineau; you must come here immediately!"

"There must be a mistake; why the intensive care unit?" She asks in astonishment.

"Your husband had a pulmonary embolism twenty minutes ago."

Chapter 14 Insurmountable differences

————————◆————————

"Quick, open the letter!" Eva cheered as Valentin held up the letter from the lab with the results of the paternity test.

"Yes, I'd love to, but I'm too nervous to do it now. How about you open it after lunch?" he suggested.

"Unfortunately I can't do it after lunch; I have to take David to a special examination, so I have to leave the office early today. Besides, I'm too curious; come on, give it to me; I'll open it for you."

Excited, Eva opens the letter, holds it in her hand, and stares at it in silence.

"Darling, is something wrong?" he asked.

Emotionally, she folded the letter back up and handed it to him. Valentin, a little worried by Eva's reaction, held the folded letter in his hand for a moment, but then looked at it too. He walked silently to his chair, sat down, and put his face in his hands. Tears streamed down the table.

"Please say something!" she said.

"What do you want me to say?" he asked, his voice breaking.

"Anything. That you're angry, that you're disappointed! It hurts me to see you like this, and I don't know how it happened; I just don't understand it," she said desperately with tears in her eyes.

"You are a married woman; it was naive of me to hope for a different outcome.".

Yes, a result that neither of them had expected. The paternity test showed that Valentin was not the father of Eva's children. And now?

What will happen to all their plans? How will this knowledge affect their relationship? David is dependent on Eva's help for weeks after the accident, an extra burden for everyone, and according to the paternity test, he is probably also the father of the children. How will he cope?

"I'm sticking to my decision; I'll leave David as soon as my parents come for Christmas," Eva said with conviction.

"Your husband needs help now, and it seems that he is the father of your children, even though you reject him. You can't leave him alone; be realistic. Do you really think he would leave his wife and children?"

"I appreciate your loyalty to everyone. Even to David, your direct competitor, for whom you never had a bad word, which proves what a great person you are. But it's up to me what happens to me and my children in the future, and I will not raise children in a loveless family, no matter what you decide. I don't love David; I only love you. Fate has given us a very big and unexpected challenge. David is not mature enough to be a father, and above all, he doesn't want children."

"What about David's health? You forget that he was one step away from death," he reminds her.

"You're wrong, I don't forget, and I spoke to the doctors very intensively during his stay in intensive care. The immersion in cold water caused a redistribution of blood volume due to constriction of the blood vessels, but this was not the cause of the pulmonary embolism; it was the larger pieces of ice that broke under the weight of Steven and another man and fell on his leg while he was in the water. The leg injury caused an undetected thrombosis, which led to the pulmonary embolism, but fortunately it was caught early and treated well. David will recover; he is a young man. Do you think everything will be fine between us after the accident? It's not like that; we live past each other and fight about all sorts of shit. Prolonging this relationship would only rob both of us of our lives."

"It often happens that certain strokes of fate bring two people even closer together."

"That may be the case. But in my opinion, only when two people love each other. But David and I are very different, and after the accident, he's even more afraid of missing out. Theoretically, he's on sick leave for another two weeks, but in practice, he'd be out with the boys every day, and he definitely doesn't want to have kids. My parents will be here in a fortnight; you know I can count on my dad. I'm prepared to move into a flat on my own if I have to, but I'm not going to stay in an unhappy marriage any longer. David also has the right to spend his life with someone who makes him happier. As for me, the result of the paternity test has just turned my whole world upside down, and I can understand your disappointment and feel your pain. Your decision, whatever it is, will not change the way I feel about you; to me, you will always be the father of these children, and I can't think of a better father and husband than you," she said with a beaming smile.

Moved to tears, he stood up, ran to her, and embraced her tightly. Cheek to cheek, they remained embraced in silence; nowhere in the world did Eva feel safer than in Valentin's arms.

"You know, there are men who need a woman by their side for various reasons, and there are men who just love being husband and father and have grown up with all the responsibilities that come with those roles. I love you more than anything; I would die for you, but I think you already know that. I will raise these children with you, regardless of the results of the paternity tests. I will love them as if they were my own flesh and blood, just as I love you," he whispered.

Strong words from a man who identifies with his masculinity and is comfortable with it. Identifying with his role as partner, future father, and pillar of the family. Overwhelmed by Valentin's decision and aware of her happiness, she moved closer to him, their bodies melting together.

"It's not fair," she sighed.

"Shhh... We'll get through this together," he whispered.

That emotional afternoon, Eva sat with David in the vascular specialist's waiting room. He seemed to be getting better by the day, which gave her hope for a positive outcome.

"As soon as this is over, I'm going to have a proper party with the boys. What do you think?" He asked, already in planning fever.

"As long as you stay off the ice, I'm fine with anything else. You gave us quite a scare," she replied, pleased with his will to live.

It wasn't long before the doctor's receptionist called them into the examination room.

"You must have had a good guardian angel, my boy," said the doctor, who was clearly about to retire.

"What do you mean?" asked David after this statement.

"Well, you survived the frozen pond and a pulmonary embolism; that's nothing short of a miracle. But the fact that your vital signs are so incredibly good is an inexplicable miracle. What's more, as of today we no longer need any medication," he said enthusiastically.

"How do you think you can explain something like that?" asked David.

"Life is full of miracles, and even in medicine there are many that cannot be explained, so I'm happy for you."

"I don't know what to say. The only thing I remember is that my father kept trying to wake me up when I was unconscious in intensive care," David said incredulously.

"Then you have your father to thank for waking you up; he seems to have done everything right," the doctor said.

"My father is dead," David replied, staring at the floor.

"You see, these are classic examples of unexplained events. Enjoy your time; you have your whole life ahead of you," the doctor added before saying goodbye.

After they leave the surgery, David insists they go out for a meal in town to celebrate. But Eva is not enthusiastic after the doctor advised him to stay at home until the end of his illness. A trip into town while he is still on sick leave could cost him his job.

"For the record, it's forbidden to do things that have nothing to do with improving your health while you're unfit for work," she says firmly.
"But food is good for your health," he replied.
"How about we order in and eat at home?" she asked in a relaxed tone.
"I'm not enthusiastic at all! But what the hell if there's no other way?" he replied with a shrug.

At least it was a small success, but every day Eva felt more and more like she was dealing with a pubescent boy who was doing nothing but exhausting her strength. Cheeky and stubborn, David tried to assert himself wherever he could.

"Since I assume you want to keep your job, it would be a good compromise if we could enjoy the food we ordered at home without any stress."

"Do you think I'm afraid of this mummy's boy? Do you know how many such jobs there are here? And Ottawa isn't exactly the nicest place in Canada," he (David) replied in a somewhat arrogant tone.

"You know, I don't think anything. I just want to eat in peace without having to discuss things, that's all. Do you think that's possible?" She asked in a tone as if nothing could upset her.

"Oh, never mind; we'll do it your way. We always do it this way anyway."

The classic toxic response, with a touch of victimhood to make Eva feel guilty. It was something David was very good at; after all, it was one of the things his mother was good at, and it was hard for him to get over, part of the upbringing he'd been given.

There was no peace at dinner either, because after the doctor's consultation, David seemed to want to go through all his life plans at once.

"If you don't rat me out to that mummy's boy, I'm going on holiday tomorrow for a few days while I'm on sick leave. I've already got something planned... Just a bit of time off," he said, as if going on holiday while on sick leave was the most normal thing in the world."

"You know I wouldn't betray you, even if I thought your plans were unreasonable."

"Yes, I know; I knew what I had in you when I married you," he added with a smile.

"Where are you planning to go on holiday, if I may ask?"

"Do you know where the 2010 Winter Olympics will be held?"

"Mmhh, it's still 2008... I don't know," she replied, a little taken aback.

"In Whistler, the biggest ski resort in North America!"

"Oh no, not again. Haven't you had enough of snow and ice?" she asked excitedly.

"That would be like asking me if I've had enough of the sun and the sea. No, I haven't had enough. The journey starts the day after tomorrow."

"We can't afford any more accidents before Christmas; my parents are coming in a fortnight," she reminded him gently.

"There won't be any more accidents because I'll be travelling without the boys; I've booked a week's Sky course with supervision and spa for myself. You can have the hotel details if you like."

"That seems like sensible holiday planning in an unreasonable situation, being on sick leave," she reminded him.

"Yes, I'm aware of that, which is why I'm relying entirely on your ability to keep quiet."

"I hope you know what you're doing and that you're recovering well from the strain of the last few weeks. That's all I have to say."

As the months went by, the marriage between the two became more and more a matter of dos and don'ts, much like business partners who are shareholders in a company, each having an equal share in the business and being able to benefit from the profits, regardless of how much one or the other had contributed. The important thing was that each could rely on their partner and that the company continued to function.

"You are a fantastic woman; you can always be relied on, no matter what life throws at you. I really appreciate that side of you," he flattered her.

The next morning in the office, Eva doesn't know how to tell Valentin about David's sick leave without embarrassing herself. David's hasty decision had put her in an awkward position. She had promised

David she would keep it to herself so as not to jeopardise his job, but she could only do that if his employer was someone else. What if something happened while he was on holiday—another stupid accident? After all, David was still on sick leave, and Valentin, the man she loved more than anything, was her employer, and she wouldn't have broken Valentin's trust for anything in the world.

"Somehow you seem unhappy this morning, even though your croassant didn't come out after lunch. Are you feeling ill again?" He asked thoughtfully.

"I'm fine this morning; there's just something I need to talk to you about, and I don't know where to start."

"Is it something to do with the paternity test results or David's check-up yesterday?" he asked in a calm tone.

"It has to do with David's medical examination, although the examination itself was very positive," she added.

"Then what are you so worried about?"

"He's off to Whistler the day after tomorrow for a six-day sky and spa holiday," she murmured.

"And that's a problem for you?" he asked in a jealous tone.

"The whole thing isn't really a problem for me, but for you..."

"Oh, for me... early morning pregnancy humour?" he asked amused.

"In case you've forgotten, his sick note doesn't expire for another ten days, so he's still officially on sick leave."

"Darling, as long as I can spend six days alone with you, I don't give a shit about your husband's sick note if I have to. Do you know what that means to me? This time with you is worth more to me than anything else in the world, and I'd even thank your husband for letting me go on holiday alone," he said happily.

Valentin managed to touch her deep inside with his words; every cell in her body exploded with joy. There was nothing this man would do for her; the love and warmth he radiated warmed her heart on these cold winter days. A sense of belonging, a basic need in a union that was increasingly becoming a shared family life.

"But are you listening to me?" he asked when she didn't answer.

"Of course, I've been listening to you so carefully that your words have touched my heart deeply, and I can't find an adequate answer to describe my happiness at this moment," she said with tears in her eyes.

"How could I make you happier?" he asked.

"I couldn't be happier," she replied with tears in her eyes.

But Valentin pointed to a letter already on her desk.

"What's this? Have you already booked our honeymoon?" she asked humorously.

"You seem to have a lot of pregnancy humour today. Why don't you have a look at this?"

Curious, Eva took the already opened envelope and took out the letter, unfolded it slowly, looked at the short text, and jumped on top of Valentin, who was barely able to hold on to the chair.

"Yay!" she shouted loudly.

"Darling, this is not a final confirmation, and above all, there is no guarantee that it will be different, so I don't want to get carried away yet, lest I be disappointed," he said cautiously.

"It's a miracle; God is giving us a second chance," she said hopefully.

"I thought the same thing when I emptied the mailbox yesterday. I was tempted to write to you several times, but I thought you were busy with David's doctor's appointment."

"Nothing keeps me as busy as my life with you and our children, because you'll see, they are your children, and I have no doubt that they are. It may sound absurd to you, but I feel it, and believe me when I tell you that it's almost impossible that David is the father. "

"The lab has only confirmed that the samples were mixed up by mistake and is asking us to repeat the test, that's all. So please don't hold it against me if I don't look as happy as you do, because I know how painful it was for me when the first letter confirmed the negative results.".

"Look, it says here that they even tried to contact you by email because you didn't leave a phone number. The lab must have realised quite early that something had gone wrong. Didn't you see the email?" She asked in surprise.

"It was sent to my old personal email address, the first account my parents had set up for me, and yes, I hadn't seen it. The letter was in my letterbox the day before yesterday afternoon, and it was posted two days ago."

"And when did the email arrive?"

"The same afternoon I found the letter with the negative results in my letterbox, but I only checked it last night after opening the second letter from the lab."

"You see? We could have saved ourselves a lot of emotional stress if you had checked your emails regularly," she said.

"But in reality, when I think back to our conversation at the time when I was heartbroken by the negative result, I think we did everything right because we decided on the next steps for our life together, regardless of the test result. We have unconditionally decided to have a life together; that is the only thing that matters, and I will love you and the children more than anything, even if a second test result is negative.".

Once Eva was alone in the office, she decided to call her father. One thing was clear to her: he had to be the first to know about the pregnancy and the separation plans. The loving and caring father, the pillar of the family, with him by her side, it would be much easier in her situation as a pregnant woman because Christmas time, the festival of love, would mean the end of her marriage this year.

"Ola, my darling! You don't seem very happy, are you all right?" Her father asked, as if he could see her from afar.

"Dad, you're the only one who can see how your children are through the phone," she replied, touching.

"Well, parents have a sixth sense for their children's problems, and they can see things in advance that you children might not notice until much later."

"I know exactly what you mean; is that why you turned to Valentin the last time before you flew home?"

"So are you going to marry Valentin Leblanc?" he asked directly.

"Yes, I will. But there are other things to sort out first."

"You'll manage; you're not the first, and you won't be the last to decide to divorce. Anything is better than investing more years of your life in an unhappy relationship, and, if I may say so, your mother and sister agree with me, you will get all the support you need from all of us."

"Wow, that's definitely more than I expected. Does that mean... mom knows that you contacted Valentin?" She asked in surprise.

"Yes, of course, she was the one who asked me to do it," he replied, as if it were a matter of course that Marion would support such an action.

"You're not serious, are you?"

"Yes, your mother realised after your last summer holiday here that something wasn't right between you and David. It's no secret that we didn't think David was right for you for a long time, but as always, everyone has to make their own experiences. Well, when David's father died and he left you as his wife, he basically broke up with all of us."

"You know David is not a bad person; he grew up in a difficult family and has his own way of dealing with life," she said as if to defend him.

"We don't think he's a bad person either, but the differences between you in terms of family values, interpersonal relationships, social behaviour, and attitude to life are just serious, and we noticed that many years ago. But you were so in love."

"I understand. Back then you didn't want to end my marriage so that I could have my own experiences, but now you want to help me end my marriage, and you even take the initiative and go to Valentin without asking me. Why did you do that? What made you do it? Maybe the fact that he's rich?" she asked directly.

"Yes, exactly, the fact that Valentin Leblanc is rich, but rich in values that are not so easy to find in today's generation, is this man's greatest asset. The fact that he also has the means to provide you and your children with a comfortable life is, of course, an advantage too.".

"Our children, you say? Well, we still don't know for sure if he is the father of the children."

"The father of what children?" he asked, confused.

"I'm pregnant; I'm expecting twins."

"Santa Maria del Cami! Are you pregnant? Since when?" he asked in amazement.

"Six weeks, but I only found out a few days ago."

"How did David react? He's not very fond of children.".

"David doesn't know anything about it."

"And how did Valentin react?" he asked directly.

"He really wants to be a father. It's not an easy situation for him, but he would raise the children as his own," she explained enthusiastically.

"I had no doubt about that, and..."

..... Federico was silent for a moment as Eva's mother could be heard in the background.

"Dad, what's wrong?" she asked impatiently.

"Please let me talk to your mom; she won't leave me alone," he replied, ending the call.

When she got home, Eva found that David was already in bed. His travel bag was already in the hall, on its way out.

"Hey," he called to her softly.

"Oh my God, you scared me. What are you doing in bed so early? Even chickens don't go to sleep at this time of night," she asked.

"My taxi is coming at 4am tomorrow; have you forgotten?"

"Actually, I knew you were leaving tomorrow, but not at this time. I can't come straight to bed though; otherwise, my dinner will be cancelled and the night will be too long," she replied, hoping that her marital duties would take care of that.

"No need; I was asleep anyway. Please be quiet," he replied simply.

Relieved, Eva closed the bedroom door and went into the kitchen.

David woke up in the middle of the night and ran out of the room. Startled, Eva ran after him and saw him panting in the bathroom by the window.

"What the hell are you doing at the window in this temperature? Are you all right?" she asked worriedly.

"I can't tell you exactly; I feel pressure in my chest, like a pulmonary embolism. I'm scared," he said, sticking his head out of the window again.

"Please let's call an ambulance; we can't risk anything happening here," she suggested.

"No, then my holiday will be cancelled," he replied.

"You and your holiday, what are you doing? You're still on sick leave. Let's at least go to the emergency room; we can take your luggage, and if all is well, you can go on holiday in a few hours," she advised him persuasively.

"All right," he said resignedly.

On the way to the nearest ambulance, David's condition didn't seem to be improving, and the fear of another pulmonary embolism grew by the minute. She hurriedly pressed the accelerator to get to her destination as quickly as possible.

"I can't breathe," he said, putting his hand on her chest.

After a few minutes, they reached the emergency room. Eva got out of the car and rang the bell until a nurse arrived, who immediately took David to the shock room. From that moment on, Eva no longer had a chance to be with him. Crying, she ran into the waiting room and sat down on an empty chair, trembling.

Pregnant, full of fear and uncertainty, she sat there in the middle of the night, looking at the clock, hoping to find out something about David's condition. But the first hour passed without a nurse or doctor entering the waiting room, a very frustrating situation. Thousands of thoughts ran through her mind in a situation where she had to be prepared for the worst. With tears streaming down her face, she fumbled in her pocket for a handkerchief, unaware that a smiling David was standing next to her.

"Phew, that was close; did you see the time? Let's get a taxi to take me from here to the airport. Then you can drive home," he said nonchalantly.

"How to the airport? You said it was close, and now you want to walk to the airport? What's going on here? Why have you been dismissed already?" She asked excitedly.

"By close, I meant the time, nothing else. My back was a bit stiff from lying down, and I felt like I couldn't breathe well. Panic did the rest. Come on, let's run outside."

Without asking any more questions and horrified by David's behaviour, which increasingly reflected his mother's character, Eva walked with him towards the exit, whereupon he happily unloaded his luggage from the car and looked in the distance to see if the taxi was coming. In temperatures of -11°C, Eva stood motionless beside the car.

"Come on, huddle up until the taxi arrives; you look frozen," he said to her and gave her a big hug.

With a kiss on the forehead and full of euphoria, David said goodbye and left her alone in the car park. In a state of complete emotional exhaustion, Eva got into the car, locked the door from the inside, and cried her eyes out until a text message caught her attention.

"I love you; the night seems so long without you; I'm counting the hours until I can see you again.".

So Valentin was awake too... Without thinking twice, she called him back with a sigh.

"Amor, what's wrong? Answer me, please," he shouted at the other end of the line.

"I'm in the car," she sighed.

"What car?" he asked worriedly.

"In my car," she sighed again.

"Are you alone? What are you doing in the car at this time of night? Has something happened?" he asked with growing concern.

But she continued to sigh without saying a word.

"Fuck it, I'll be right there. Text me where you are and stay in touch!"

Eva texted him the address while he spoke reassuring words into the receiver. A short time later, he drove into the car park and pulled up to her car. What he saw was a woman at the end of her rope. A love affair that had been kept secret for months, a husband who was still going through puberty, pregnancy, and uncertainty about paternity. She was on the verge of a nervous breakdown. Caring and loving, he took her hand, gently pulled her out of the car, and silently led her to his car, then drove off while she quietly put her head on his shoulder and held his hand. A few minutes later, they arrived at Valentin's apartment. Hand in hand, they entered the lift and reached the warm penthouse.

"I'm afraid I won't be able to handle the final steps of our separation emotionally," she sighed, clinging to him as he lovingly held her close and stroked her hair.

"I know. We'll get through this together. Your family will be here in eight days," he reassured her.

"I'm so exhausted, I can't take any more. You can't imagine what happened tonight," she said through her tears.

"I'll listen if you want to tell me."

"I don't want to rob you of your sleep," she sighed.

"You're taking nothing away from me. It breaks my heart to see you like this, and if it helps to talk about it, I'm happy to listen. Besides, we have an appointment at the lab in a few hours; I can't sleep anyway."

"David is becoming more and more like his mother, I mean the character traits in certain situations. I don't know how to deal with him anymore," she said desperately.

"What did you do in A&E? Was it for you or for him?" he asked firmly.

"It was for him, but luckily nothing serious happened."

"What upset you then?"

"His reaction when he was discharged. I realised today that I would have ended my marriage with David if I hadn't met you. I look at him, and I see his mother and her toxic behaviour, her shallow choice of words, and her attitude toward life; it's all been so obvious since we've been living in Canada.".

"Try to calm down and, most importantly, get some sleep; it will help you see the situation from a different perspective."

"Why are you awake?" she asked curiously.

"It's the desire for you that keeps me awake. This happens very often. But tonight I felt the need to write to you."

"The message came just as I was wondering if I should call you. Isn't that funny?" she asked in surprise.

"No, it's not funny; it's magical. Our souls always seem to know when the time is right."

"What do you think our souls would do now?" she asked, snuggling up to him.

"I think they would slip into the still warm bed, wrap themselves tightly around each other, and enjoy the closeness," he whispers.

"And then?"

"Then they would make love, slowly and intensely."

And that's exactly what they did. They touched each other gently, kissed intimately, and made love until their bodies came to rest and they fell asleep.

The next morning, Eva and Valentin went separately to the laboratory for blood tests. Once there, Valentin sat visibly nervous in the empty waiting room, holding a few letters in his hand, while Eva spoke to the lab technician.

"The Leblanc family!" the doctor shouted.

In the lab, Valentin immediately put the letters with the negative results and the new invitation on the table to avoid any possible mistakes.

"How could this happen?" he asked in an unpleasant tone, pointing to the letters.

"We're terribly sorry; we don't know how this could have happened. It seems that two samples with similar names were delivered at the same time, and we suspect that they were mixed up," said the doctor.

"There is no excuse for such a mistake. What if it was a matter of life and death? What if a healthy person got a wrong lab result that confirmed a fatal disease?" Valentin replied.

"I can understand your anger, but we're all humans, and mistakes can happen. How about I arrange a blood test to determine the gender of the children as compensation and as an apology on behalf of this laboratory? Could I make it up to them that way?"

Valentin likes the idea, so he looks to Eva for confirmation. After all, the babies are in the womb, and only the mother can provide the blood for a gender test.

"I'd say that would be great," Eva confirms.

Outside, in the car park, Eva is about to get into her car when she is suddenly stopped.

"Hey Eva, I'm here!" Marta shouts.

"Marta? What are you doing here?" asks Eva, surprised and frightened at the same time.

"Yes, I was wondering the same thing. First I see you at the gynaecologist and then here in a genetics lab. Is something wrong?" She asked curiously.

"And what are you doing here?" asked Eva.

"You tell me first," she replied stubbornly.

Not having much time to improvise, Eva came up with the first plausible hypothesis: "Well, this lab isn't just a genetics lab; it's a special testing lab, and my doctor sent me in to check some values.".

"Oh my God! That's terrible!" said Martha.

"Yes, it is. But I'm sure it's nothing to worry about because my family only has adult-onset diabetes. And what are you doing here?" asked Eva curiously.

"Well, I'm keeping my fingers crossed, of course. Well, the reason I'm here is... You remember Moira's asthma attack, don't you?"

"Yes, I'll remember that night for a long time," Eva replied.

"The lung doctor sent us for a special test to rule out genetic lung diseases... and... why don't you look behind you, the lady walking towards us and gesticulating animatedly? Do you recognise her?" asked Martha.

At that moment, Eva turned and looked in panic at the familiar face.

"Mrs Leblanc? Your husband left his wallet at the doctor's."

Chapter 15 The Confession

"Our flight has been cancelled due to heavy snowfall," Eva's mother shouted on the other end of the phone. "You're not serious, are you? It never snows in Barcelona," she said in amazement.

"This isn't about Barcelona! They're predicting heavy snow in Canada; don't you watch the news?"

"I'll call you right back; David is trying to call in the background; it sounds very urgent."

The sight of David's phone number on the screen was enough to trigger an inner turmoil that made Eva's body react immediately with stomach cramps, even before she had answered the call.

"Did something happen?" she asked worriedly.

"Did you panic immediately? Something can't have happened every time the phone rings when I'm not at home," he replied, a little annoyed.

"Why the tone of voice? You're the one who rang three times in a row when I wanted to speak to my mother. It's understandable that I'm worried."

"You don't have a better tone towards me either, in case you hadn't noticed, and yes, there is a problem, but nothing dramatic," he said carefully.

"So there is!" she countered.

"I can't get away today because of the heavy snowfall, and the weather forecast for the next few days looks bad," he tried to explain gently.

"So that's what my mom meant," she replied desperately.

"Why? What did your mom mean?"

"The flights to Canada have been cancelled because of the expected heavy snowfall! They should be here in three days, but they can't leave from Barcelona. It's a disaster.".

"Well, we're all stuck now. Luckily, my mom arrived at Ottawa airport an hour ago," he laughed.

"What do you mean your mom's here? Why am I just finding out now, and what's so funny about it?" She asked him angrily.

"I just think it's funny, and you probably would have laughed about it before. It looks like we're going to have a great Christmas this year; I can feel it already," he said jokingly.

"Oh yes, it will, believe me! .... A few years ago, I wouldn't have thought an unexpected visit from your mother was funny. And who's looking after her now?" She asked sourly.

"I'm stuck here now, so you'll have to pick her up as soon as possible. I'll do everything I can to get out of here as soon as possible."

"I told you it sucks when you go on holiday on sick leave. And you know your mother; you know how impatient she is. What do you mean she needs to be picked up as soon as possible? That I have to leave right away?"

"Well, the holiday was necessary for me and full of new discoveries," he replied calmly.

Why did David suddenly seem so calm, and what insights could he have gained during his holiday? These were questions that were on Eva's mind, but she didn't need answers because her plans for the future were already set and David wasn't part of them.

After the phone call with David, Eva returned to her mother and told her matter-of-factly, "I think I know what you wanted to tell me now, but the weather disaster is not the only impending disaster today."

"What do you mean?" asked Marion, confused.

"Well, David seems to have the same problem... He's stuck in Whistler, and to make matters worse, his mother has just arrived at Ottawa airport."

"What's he doing in Whistler? I thought he was ill. And how did Leonor end up in Canada all of a sudden if she can't do anything in her everyday life?" Marion asked in amazement.

"It's a long story, and this visit has come at a bad time," she sighed.

"Oh dear. Leonor seems to have a knack of choosing the most inconvenient times to visit. But maybe David wanted it that way, or do you think he would have booked the plane ticket unannounced?"

"There's never a good time to have a woman like Leonor as a guest for ten days. It's a real nightmare. Christmas is in five days, and it looks like I'll be spending the holidays alone with her!" she sobbed.

"It's driving me crazy! Your father should have booked earlier, that stubborn bloke; then we wouldn't have this problem now!" Marion grumbled.

"It is not his fault, you know that. We can only hope for a miracle, because my plans can't be postponed and I can't hide my belly for much longer."

"I'm still angry!" she replied disappointedly.

"We have to pull ourselves together. Let's take our time and come up with a plan B," Eva suggested.

"You are talking to the wrong person; you know that your father is the one responsible for such things," Marion made it clear.

On the last Friday afternoon before Christmas, the urgent tasks piled up quickly, but Eva's mind was racing. With great effort, she tried to concentrate until her efforts were interrupted by another call from David.

"I can't work between your calls and my parents' calls, and your mom has to be picked up from the airport too!" she said angrily.

"I just got off the phone with Steven. What were you doing in the genetics lab a couple of days ago?"

Eva remained silent for a few moments, her phone in her hand. The last working day before the Christmas holidays seemed to be turning more and more into a day of annoyance.

"Hello, are you still there?" he asked.

"Yes, I'm still here. Where did Steven get this information?" she asked, irritated.

"It's a long story. After all that online dating over the past few weeks, Steven seems to have realised what he has in his still-wife, so the two of them have been meeting to talk about a lot of things, and yes, she happened to mention meeting you in the lab."

"Steven wants to go back to Martha?" she asked in surprise.

"Yes, who else? You see, Steven doesn't really seem to have found what he needs. In his opinion, most of the women who look for relationships on online dating sites are problematic or disturbed. At least with Martha, he knows what he has. He wants to work on himself and try to save the marriage.".

"I feel sick when I hear this nonsense. And Martha just takes him back?" She blurted out angrily.

"She has no income as a housewife, and he is the father of her children, and they probably still love each other, so why shouldn't she take him back?"

"Say, are you listening to yourself? Having no income is no reason to bring an arsehole like that back into the house!"

"Fuck her, I'm in no mood to argue! Everyone is allowed to make mistakes and work on themselves, don't you think? I also asked you a question, and I expect an answer. Why were you in the genetics lab?" He asked loudly.

"You can't talk to me in that tone. Call me back when you can talk to me normally," she said angrily, ending the call.

Now he persisted, letting her phone ring and ring until she picked it up.

"You have diabetes, don't you?" he asked.

But she remained silent.

"Damn it, Eva! Just answer!" He shouted as loudly as he could.

"No, I don't," she blurted out in a low voice.

"Are you sure? I mean, do you have it in writing?"

"Yes, I'm sure, it was just a check, that's all," she assured him.

"Good, I'll be back as soon as I can; the conversation will continue later," he said, hanging up.

Fortunately, Martha hadn't mentioned how the lab assistant had caught up with her in the car park with Valentin's wallet and called her Mrs. Leblanc. Only at the last second had she managed to avert disaster.

An hour later, she had done most of her work; her desk looked a little emptier, and Valentin had returned from his meeting. With all the chaos in her family life, she had stopped thinking about Valentin's parents, who were due back from holiday for Christmas. So the program of Christmas chaos had successfully begun... was it complete?

"Kiss me," she commanded as Valentin approached her.

"I can finally do something today that doesn't involve stress," he said, his lips glued to hers.

"I feel like I've been in the wrong film all day... if that's any consolation," she replied, falling into his arms.

"Oh, that sounds like stress. Do you want to talk about it?"

"That depends on which disaster you want to hear about first, because it looks like we'll be spending Christmas apart, you with your parents and me with David's mom."

"How did you come to this decision?"

"Well, it seems you haven't been watching the weather either," she said regretfully.

"Television is not one of my favourite pastimes," he remarked.

"My parents can't come here because of the expected snowfall in Canada, and David is stuck in Whistler because of a heavy snowfall. To make matters worse, his mother arrived at Ottawa airport a few hours ago and is waiting to be picked up. Do you know what this means?"

"We're not going to let this spoil Christmas. Didn't David tell you that his mother is coming to visit him?" He asked in surprise.

But Eva remained thoughtful and lowered her eyes when Valentin put a letter on the table.

"What's this? Oh no... I don't think I can handle anything else today. Please don't open it," she said excitedly when she realised it was the letter from the lab and quickly left the room.

Plagued by a thousand thoughts about their impending separation, Eva made her way to the airport. How could David keep Leonor's visit a secret from her? What had made him take such a decision?

"Hello? Over here!" Leonor called as she saw Eva from a distance.

Not exactly pleased, but still very polite, Eva greeted her mother-in-law at the airport.

"What took you so long? I thought I had to sleep here tonight."

"I had to work; today is the last working day before the Christmas holidays, and I couldn't even finish my work. But I'm here now," she replied kindly.

"It can't be that work is more important to you than your family. When the husband is indisposed, the wife must be able to take care of certain things," she scolded cheekily.

Apparently Leonor had not been told the reasons for David's absence, so Eva quietly took Leonor's luggage and left the airport with her. After all, it wasn't her job to tell her that David was going on holiday despite being off sick.

When she got home, Eva made Leonor's bed and ran out of the house. But as soon as she got into the car, David called her.

"The fridge is almost empty," David said.

"Then you'll have to contact the local hotel staff; I can't help you from here. We're almost five hours away by plane," she said, not understanding the meaning of David's statement.

"I don't mean my fridge here, but the one in the apartment," he said more clearly.

"Oh, I see. Your mom never misses an opportunity to badmouth me; even at the airport, she started pointing out what a bad wife I am. Besides, I'm on my way to the supermarket now, but I explained that to her two minutes ago when I left the flat. By the way, I couldn't say anything today, but I have a problem with not being asked if your mother wants to stay with us for ten days in a row," she replied angrily.

"There's a reason for everything, and I'll take care of her when I get back," he replied briefly, ending the call.

Somehow David's behaviour worried Eva. First the discovery during the holidays, then the visit from his mother. Perhaps he had already found out about her relationship with Valentin or her pregnancy, and did he need reinforcement to deal with it?

Outside the supermarket, she quickly checked her phone to make sure she hadn't missed anything that could cause new problems, then noticed an unread message from Valentin and called him back immediately.

"I wish you were here right now," she said sadly.

"I wish that too. I want nothing more than to be with you. You were very upset when you left the office. You can see that the barrel is about to overflow; all the events point to that. But today, at the end of this exhausting day, there is something positive," he said sympathetically.

"Did you open the letter from the lab?" she asked hopefully.

"Yes, I did," he confirmed cheerfully.

"I had no doubt that you were the father of our baby," she said happily.

"But I don't have the paternity results yet."

"But what does the lab report say?" she asked, confused.

"Just the gender of our two babies. The other one is still pending. Apparently the samples were processed separately and sent in by two different people. The paternity results will follow," he said enthusiastically, despite the incomplete results.

"The gender results? And what do they say?" she asked excitedly.

"They say the babies are two different genders," he said, his voice choked with tears.

The day that had begun with problems ended with good news. An unexpected burst of energy accompanied them on their way home as the first snowflakes fell softly on the street.

The next morning, when Leonor looked out of the window, she panicked. There was at least fifty centimetres of snow on the street outside, and she ran around the flat at increasing speed in search of her calming drops. Leonor's nervous breakdown just before Christmas, while David was away, would be the last thing Eva needed, as the weather was threatening her plans more and more by the hour.

"We need an up-to-date weather report!" she shouted through the flat.

On the brink of emotional collapse, Eva tried to find a news program that would report on the weather conditions before and during the upcoming Christmas holidays. But after a few minutes of searching, she realised that there was no change in sight. And now? The image of her and Leonor alone on Christmas Eve became more and more vivid in her mind, while a feeling of helplessness spread through her body.

"Damn!" muttered Leonor.

"Yes, you could say that," replied Eva.

In a rage, Leonor ran into the kitchen, grabbed her mobile phone, and started typing frantically.

"This is shit!" she shouted again, running to Eva.

"We have to stay calm," Eva said promptly.

"My son can't be reached; something must have happened."

"Don't worry so much. His mobile probably has no reception; that's the only possibility. You shouldn't think the worst," Eva said optimistically.

"It's easy to say that; he's not your son," she replied rudely.

A statement like that needed no comment. Even as a child, her father had taught her that not everything required a reaction, and so she preferred to be peaceful, who knew how long she would have to live under the same roof as the enemy.

"If you don't mind, I'm going to the bakery around the corner; we need some bread to freeze for the weekend," Eva announced as she left the house.

In the hallway, she tried to call David again, but the situation remained the same: the mobile phone had no reception. So she took the opportunity to call Valentin.

"You can't imagine how much I miss you three. Lying next to you and stroking your belly was the most beautiful thing I've felt in the last few days and the thing I'm most grateful for," Valentin said wistfully.

"We miss you too, and I'm afraid it will be a while before we can see each other again, because nothing we had planned is going according to plan," she said sadly.

"Everything seems to be turning against us again. Maybe the solution will come in another way, as it sometimes does in life."

"Maybe, but this time we don't have all the time in the world; my belly can't be hidden for long, and we still have a problem, Leonor.".

"I don't know David's mother, but I have to admit that her visit is very inappropriate," he said in a critical tone.

"David invited his mother; apparently he realised during the holidays that spending time with his family is important to him after all. He hasn't been in touch all day, and Leonor is in a panic."

"Why doesn't he have a signal? Maybe there are problems with the mobile networks because of the weather. Have you tried calling the hotel?"

"It could be the weather, of course, but we haven't called the hotel yet; that would really be the last resort if we can't get through to him by tonight. Christmas is still four days away; I'm going crazy at the thought of spending Christmas Eve alone with Leonor," she sighed.

"How about my dad picking you up in the tractor the day after tomorrow, Monday morning, so we can have breakfast in the conservatory?"

"I'd be delighted. But... how will your parents react to the pregnancy if we're still in the dark about the paternity?" She asked worriedly.

"I don't need a confirmation on a piece of paper to acknowledge paternity; I've made my decision and informed my parents about the pregnancy."

"Did you tell your parents that we don't know if you are the biological father?"

"No, I told my parents that they would be grandparents."

"How did they react?"

"They are beside themselves with joy! Yesterday they even went to a baby shop in Gatineau to look for clothes," he said, overjoyed.

Eva was moved to tears by the joy of the family's happiness and the guilt of the ambiguity of their situation. In this love triangle, there were at least two people who had found each other and wanted to stay together for the rest of their lives.

When Eva got home, she was shocked to see Leonor lying on the floor with her legs drawn up.

"Oh my God! What's happened?" she asked.

"I still can't reach my child. I'm afraid my blood pressure has gone up and I'm going to collapse," she said in a frightened voice.

"Oh no, please don't...! Did you bring your blood pressure monitor?"

"I came to your house to celebrate, not to get angry. So the machine is at home."

"Then we'll probably have to find an emergency doctor who makes house calls; otherwise, we'll just have to go to the hospital."

"No, not a hospital. Maybe we can increase the dosage of the drops; I've had that before; check the packaging.".

"I'll call a doctor first; they're always on call here at the weekend, whatever the weather," she replied quietly.

After a few calls, Eva had found a doctor who made house calls. Satisfied, Leonor tried to get back on her feet and took a few steps into the flat.

"Call my son again," she ordered.

"As soon as the doctor has examined you, and if he's still not available, I'll contact the hotel."

Leonor crossed her arms defiantly like a child and snorted. She didn't say another word until the doctor arrived.

A short time later, the doorbell rang.

"Rodriguez, right? We can talk in Spanish if you like. I had just finished with a patient when you called me, so I could come earlier. Besides, most people are busy with Christmas shopping, so you don't need a doctor that much these days," he said.

"At least there are still people who are busy with Christmas, not like my daughter-in-law. There's still no Christmas tree here four days before Christmas. What a disgrace!"

"I see, the Christmas tree is missing. Is that the reason for the excitement?" the doctor asked amusedly.

"There's a lot more missing here than a Christmas tree!" replied Leonor bitterly.

Exhausted by Leonor's behaviour, Eva stood wordlessly in the corner. It was a good thing the doctor spoke Spanish, because whatever she said was wrong or completely inappropriate from Leonor's point of view. For the sake of her own health and that of her babies, she had to remain calm and avoid any provocation from Leonor. Now her silence seemed to be an affront to Leonor, who kept coming up with new barbs.

"We've finished," the doctor said after a thorough examination.

"Tell me, Doctor, how serious is the situation?" Leonor asked excitedly.

"Oh, nothing dramatic, just excitement. A few more drops, and we'll have solved the problem," he said cheerfully.

"That can't be; I've got a burning sensation in my chest, a tingling sensation in my arms, and dizziness. The drops don't help with any of these symptoms," Leonor said firmly.

"You have been overwhelmed by nervousness, all of which are psychosomatic symptoms; nothing that will remain unresolved by taking the miracle drops. I wish you a Merry Christmas," he said and left.

Unwilling to listen to what the doctor had to say, Leonor continued to puff and puff around the flat, but Eva wasn't about to be put off by her behaviour and tried to contact David again. Finally, after several attempts, she gave up and contacted the hotel.

"We are sorry, Mrs. Rodriguez, but your husband left very early last night. That's all I can tell you," the friendly lady said, ending the call.

They hadn't heard from David in 24 hours. If the lady's statement was true, something bad must have happened to David before he was able to contact her.

"Why are you so quiet all of a sudden?" asked Leonor.

"It seems that David is no longer at the hotel..." she replied in a low voice.

"I knew it! I had a bad feeling all the time, so I tried to contact him several times, but no, you wanted to wait, and now we've lost time. This is all your fault!" cried Leonor, breathing heavily.

It was impossible for Eva to face this situation alone. Her husband had disappeared without a trace, and her mother-in-law was standing inconsolably in the middle of the living room, on the verge of a nervous breakdown. The only way out seemed to be to call the police. What had happened over the past two days? Like a whirlwind, one problem after another had hit her, and her life was a mess.

"Why are the police taking so long?" Leonor kept asking, an hour after the call.

But Eva couldn't find the right answer for her. She felt sad and exhausted. Luckily, the excited Leonor didn't speak the language, but she still wouldn't let the others talk in peace.

"Here are the travel and hotel details; he was supposed to go home yesterday, but then his stay was extended by two days because of the weather," said Eva.

The policeman took the ticket and looked at it carefully.

"But according to the hotel, he checked out last night at 17.16. Why would he extend his stay in the morning and leave the hotel in the evening? It doesn't make sense, does it?" the policeman asked.

"Exactly, that's why I contacted you, because I'm afraid something might have happened to him," she said worriedly.

"We can't rule anything out, so we'll ask our colleagues in Whistler for help. When was the last time you spoke to him on the phone?" the policeman asked.

"Yesterday afternoon, I think around 4pm."

"What was the call about? Did you notice anything during the call? Was he in a different mood in any way?"

"It was about his mother. The usual stories; maybe you know them too," she said with some embarrassment in her voice.

"Were they arguing?" the policeman asked.

"My mother-in-law is a very demanding and impatient woman, and yesterday I hadn't managed to do the shopping quickly enough, so she called her son while I was still on my way to the supermarket."

"What were you talking about then?" he asked again.

"About the empty fridge. It was a very short conversation, no discussion. What does yesterday's phone call have to do with his disappearance?" asked Eva.

"Well, it wouldn't be the first time a couple argued about their in-laws. You said your mother-in-law was a handful. Could there be other reasons why your husband would extend his trip or continue it with someone else?" asked the policeman.

"What do you mean, he could have continued his journey with someone else?" she asked, a little confused.

"Your husband is not entirely unknown to us. You remember the story about the golf club, don't you? It involved two other women and a colleague of your husband's."

"The misunderstanding was cleared up long ago; my husband is not the type for such nonsense, and although he found his colleague's behaviour amusing, it had nothing to do with the events of that embarrassing evening. Do you have any questions?"

The policemen looked at each other indecisively and then asked firmly, "Why did your husband go on holiday alone, and how long has your mother-in-law been in the country?"

"Well, he had to recover from an accident and took some time off, but I must admit that his mother's arrival yesterday came as a surprise to me."

The policeman turned to his colleague and asked him firmly, "Would you invite your mother to your home without informing your wife first?"

"No," he replied.

"That's all for today. We'll be in touch if we have any more questions. In the meantime, I'd ask you to contact friends and acquaintances; your husband may have told someone else where he is.".

After a short conversation, the police officers said goodbye. The day was almost over, and there was no sign of David.

"What have they been asking all this time? Why aren't they doing anything to find my son?" Leonor asked through her tears.

"They just wanted to know what we talked about on the phone yesterday and why he went on holiday alone," Eva replied worriedly.

"Instead of asking such stupid questions, they should be looking for my son," she sighed.

Caught up in a thousand thoughts, Eva sat down on the sofa in the living room and rested her head in her hands, her heart refusing to think of anything bad.

"I'm going to call our friends and see if anyone has heard from him; is that all right?" Eva asked politely.

"But why would he contact friends and not his own family? It doesn't make sense," Leonor said.

"I'll leave no stone unturned," she replied, calling Martha first, who answered in a good mood, with the children's happy voices in the background.

"My dear, you don't sound well. What's troubling you so close to Christmas? Is it the lab results for your suspected diabetes?" asked Martha.

"No, it's not the blood results; it's David," she sighed.

"What has he done? Now that Steven has come to his senses, is yours starting to go mad?"

"He's been missing since yesterday; the police were here."

"Are you making pre-Christmas jokes?" asked Martha.

"Do you think I'm funny? David's disappeared; we haven't heard from him for 24 hours. His mother is here too."

"Oh, that doesn't sound good. Didn't you have problems with each other, and that's why he's missing? Give me a moment to talk to Steven about it, and we'll also contact Robin and Sila; maybe Robin has heard from him."

"We are Latinos; with us, you either look for a solution with reason or by shouting, or you end the relationship; there is no middle way; we don't know about ghosting.".

After the phone call with Martha, Eva doubted that Steven or Robin had any information about David's fate. Leonor grew more nervous with each passing hour; the drops didn't seem to be having any effect. The long wait sapped her strength, and her eyes closed. But in the middle of the night, she was awakened by her empty stomach. Still half asleep, she looked for Leonor and found her in the dining room, sitting with her head on the table. Next to her was a half-empty bottle of sedatives.

Had she misused the dose? Had she fallen asleep or fainted? There was only one way to find out.

"Leonor, can you hear me?" she whispered. But Leonor was still asleep. She carefully switched on the light and gently rocked her back and forth until she moved slightly and snored loudly.

"Leonor, wake up!" she called.

"Let me sleep," she slurred.

Startled, she took the note from its wrapper and unfolded it as she heard noises in the corridor. Her pulse quickened with fear. Slowly, she reached into the drawer, grabbed the rolling pin, and ran forward, trembling.

"What the hell are you doing up at this hour?" David asked her.
"You bloody bastard! Where have you been all this time?" she shouted.

Totally relaxed, he put down his bags and ran into the dining room to his mother, then picked up the half-empty bottle of sedatives and asked Eva, "What are you doing?"

"Nervously, Eva took a deep breath and asked, "Is she still alive?
"Of course she's alive? Do you know how often she drank half a bottle? It's all right, she'll sleep like a baby," he said simply.

There he was again, after 24 hours of silence, in good spirits and seemingly carefree.

"I need to talk to you; I feel this is the right time; I've never been so sure," she said in one sentence.

"Please, let me start," he begged.

"No, today I'll start talking while your mother is asleep."

"Please let me start and listen to what I have to say until the end. Yesterday I looked for every opportunity to arrive on time. I was taken from one airport to another, and my mobile phone died before I could reach you. I can imagine what you were going through, and I apologize. Look, here's my ticket with all the changes; everything is traceable," he said calmly, putting the ticket on the table.
"I'm not angry with you for that, but please listen to me now," she said, until he interrupted her again.
"No, it's my turn. I've been too cowardly for far too long, but it's over now. You're a wonderful, reliable woman, and you don't deserve to

be stuck in a relationship based on duty alone. That was one of my biggest realisations during my time in Whistler," he said sympathetically.

"Even if you have realised some things, please listen to me now... I..."

"I'm not finished yet. Do you remember when your boss had the riding accident? At the time, Steven, Robin, and I were sent to Montreal for a two-day seminar. During the seminar, I met a young woman called Sophia."

"You met a woman? Sophia?"

"It wasn't my intention to hurt you, and you didn't deserve it. In the past few months I've been too irritable, and sometimes I haven't behaved like a responsible husband. When I walked into the room at the seminar, all I saw was her staring at me with an indescribable look. We talked about this and that, and it turned out she was also from Ottawa, so we started seeing each other regularly. I'm sorry," he said.

"Do you love her?" she asked softly.

"Yes, we love each other... and that love has borne fruit," he said, handing her a photograph.

"A little girl," she whispered.

"Yes, Emilia Leonor-Mary Morando Rodriguez," he replied.

"So those were the baby shoes you threw out of the window a few months ago? I always thought you didn't like children."

"I thought that too, but I love being a father. I've discovered some very deep values in myself that I never realized. With Sophia, I experienced a kind of emotion I hadn't known before, and it scared me a lot at first."

"Moved, Eva looked at him and simply asked, "Does your mother know the truth?"

"Yes. I'm so sorry."

"Thank you," she said and left the apartment.

Epilogue

"Happy birthday to you, happy birthday to you..." they all sang together.

In the festively decorated garden of Villa Leblanc, twins Sebastian and Isabella clapped their hands in front of their first birthday cake. Grandma Ella and Grandpa Ricardo proudly held them on their laps as Valentin recorded the video.

"Look at this picture," Marion said to Eva, handing her a picture of Valentin at the same age.

"My goodness, he and Sebastian are identical!" she said.

"Yes, I said that when I visited you in the hospital, remember?" Ella said to Eva.

"Yes, but what you didn't tell her is that Isabella looks exactly like her grandmother Ella at her age," Marion said, waving an old photo from the Leblanc album in the air.

"The Bonelli/Leblanc genes have taken full effect; luckily they got their blood type from their mother," Ricardo said with amusement.

As everyone laughed, Valentin ran to the fence. A man ran past the gate and tried to look inside the property.

"Are you lost?" asked Valentin from behind the metal gate.

"I'm a postman, and I'm looking for the Rodriguez family; can you help me? This registered letter had apparently been sent to several addresses and kept coming back until a court ordered it to be delivered. It came from abroad, and this address was chosen. See?" the postman pointed.

"Indeed," said Valentin, taking the letter.

"Valentin, where are you? We want to cut the cake!" shouted his father as he ran towards the group with the letter in his hand.

"What have you got there?" asked Eva.

"I don't know; it seems to be from Spain. The postman said the delivery failed several times until the court ordered it," replied Valentin.

"Por Dios Eva! What have you done?" asked Marion, taking the letter from Valentin's hand.

"Dad, please look at what's in the letter," Eva said to her father. But it was too late; Marion had already started reading and scolding: "Here it is, the reason for Christiano's death."

"Marion, what nonsense is this?" asked Frederico.

Irritated, Eva ran to her mother, took the letter from her hand, read it silently to the end, and then handed it to her father.

"What's going on?" asked Valentin.

"The letter isn't for us; it's for David," Eva replied.

"Then why are we getting his mail?" asked Valentin, confused.

"Because he changed his name to Sophia's at the wedding and is therefore untraceable. Apparently I'm the only traceable Rodriguez with any connection to him."

"What does the letter say?" asked Valentin.

"David fathered a boy in 2005; the child's mother has apparently demanded child support several times, the last time just before David's father died. It's a lot of money," she said, handing him the letter.

"I thought he wasn't ready to be a father," Valentin replied after reading the letter.

"Getting married was not even...," said Federico.